MURDER IN THE COTTAGE

An addictive crime mystery full of twists

ROY LEWIS

Arnold Landon Mysteries Book 12

Originally published as
Suddenly as a Shadow

Revised edition 2022
Joffe Books, London
www.joffebooks.com

First published in Great Britain in 1997
as *Suddenly as a Shadow*

© Roy Lewis 1997, 2022

ISBN: 978-1-80405-088-0

NOTE TO THE READER

Please note this book is set in the 1990s in England, a time before mobile phones and ubiquitous CCTV, and when social attitudes were very different.

The end of all is death and man's
life passeth away suddenly as a shadow.

—Thomas à Kempis, *The Imitation of Christ.*

PROLOGUE

Prague, 1992

There was time to kill.

Havel grimaced wryly at the thought, its irony not escaping him as the cold wind bit at his cheek. He stood on the broad steps of the museum, staring down into Wenceslas Square, beyond the arrogant, mounted figure of the king himself, to where the thin, scattered groups of tourists and entertainment lovers wandered along the central boulevard, hesitating at the student shrine, before moving on to the night clubs and the discos and the strip shows that scarred the square in its neon-lit modernity.

He hesitated, waiting until the hour grew close and then finally he slipped into the museum, pulling back the heavy hangings that screened the warm interior and paying for a ticket to the concert on the stairs.

The Englishman had had a choice of seven concerts this Sunday evening, scattered among the churches, the Old Town Square and the baroque cathedral of St Vitus, perched on its hill overlooking the city. Beethoven, Sibelius, Dvorak had been available . . . the Englishman had chosen light arias on the staircase of the museum. Havel sniffed contemptuously

1

and hawked. The woman checking the tickets shot a sharp, mean-eyed glance in his direction and he shuffled past her, to climb the broad sweep of the museum staircase.

He turned left, head down and eyes averted from those who had already taken their cushions and were sitting on the stairs above him. He walked slowly up to the second level, a broad-shouldered, whipcord-lean man in a black, long-skirted leather overcoat, thinning hair tousled from the cold wind, until he was able to take up a position leaning against a pillar, to the right and behind the staircase itself, where the music lovers sat, awaiting the entrance of the artists.

There had always been music in Prague, even under the iron fingers of communism, so that much at least had not changed. But for him life had changed. Men like Havel had held status, had respect, they were feared. But now it was all gone: discharge and disgrace, and for what? Merely for serving the state to the best of his ability. There was a sour, bitter taste in his mouth.

A ripple of applause broke out below him. A woman in a long blue evening dress walked out to the piano below and acknowledged the applause. She was beautiful, and when she inclined her head something moved in the pit of Havel's stomach, for she reminded him of summer afternoons long since gone, and the scent of woodlands and bracken in his nostrils.

He thrust the thought away and concentrated on the man he sought.

He had removed his hat, the Englishman. He was bald, with tufts of black hair thick above the ears. He was younger than Havel had expected, but that did not worry Havel. He was confident of his own strength and the quickness of his hands. He had kept in trim in spite of the tribulations of recent years for the money had been good. He had lost respect and status, but he had acknowledged professional skills and he was paid well for what he was good at.

Killing.

A second woman had appeared; heavily bosomed, with a wide red mouth, she began to sing something Viennese, to be joined in a little while by a flabby man in evening dress who sang of love and kisses in German.

The Englishman seemed rapt, his attention concentrated on the singers, but there were certain slight movements of the head from time to time that persuaded Havel that the man was not concentrating on the programme of song. He was nervous, tensely wound, a coiled spring. Though Havel's position left him completely out of the Englishman's line of sight, he leaned back against the pillar more closely, nevertheless. He checked his watch. An hour, maybe ninety minutes, and then they would both face the sharp winter wind in the street again.

The programme limped by. The woman had a large, open mouth. The man's chest heaved with mock passion. The voices rang through the hallway, winging their way to the upper floors of the museum, and the audience was moved to regular applause, but it was all beyond Havel. He was concentrating, eyes fixed on the back of the Englishman's head, the bulge in the cranium, noting, remembering . . .

It was ten o'clock before the programme ended, and the audience filtered out down the stairs, leaving their cushions behind, stepping out past the heavy curtains that kept in the warmth, out on to the broad steps of the museum, drifting down uncertainly into Wenceslas Square. Havel moved some twenty metres behind the Englishman, watching, making certain there were people between him and his quarry as they moved out into the darkness.

The Englishman paused on the steps, hunched his shoulders into his topcoat as the wind gusted against him, checked his watch, and then moved off down the steps into Wenceslas Square. Havel watched him from the balcony for a while, until he could be certain of the direction in which he moved, and then he followed him at a safe distance.

They walked along the thinning boulevard, down through the square, pausing for the clanging trolley cars that crossed from the side streets, past the pavement cafes shuttered against the winter cold and down towards the Old

Town Square. Havel knew the route the Englishman would now take, along the narrow twisting streets towards the rendezvous, past the Jewish Quarter with its synagogues and old Jewish Cemetery. He would be using Charles Bridge, the broad mediaeval thoroughfare that crossed the Vltava River to the promontory on which sat the Karlstejn Castle, built by the Emperor Charles IV to protect the crown jewels behind twenty feet thick walls, brooding over what romanticists insisted on calling the city of a hundred spires.

For Havel it was a cold place, a place of business.

He did not know the reason for his commission, he never asked. It was better in a sense that he did not know, for there were no personalities involved, merely business. A commission, a job, successful completion of the task led to a payment through a bank account. Simple, unrevealing, untraceable.

The Englishman was heading for the Charles Bridge, as Havel had known. His shoes tapped on the uneven pavement as he walked past the tourist shops full of T-shirts, mugs, flags of old Prague, miniatures of ancient buildings, models of the mediaeval clock in Old Town Square. Havel moved silently on rubber-soled shoes. There were few people about, for the night was bitterly cold and few restaurants were open on the other side of the bridge.

The water glistened blackly below the two men as they walked across the mediaeval bridge, Havel some thirty metres behind his quarry. The Englishman walked slowly, almost reluctantly, his head down as though he had a presentiment of the future. Havel smiled grimly and curled his fingers around the knife in his pocket.

He quickened his stride, and halfway across the bridge drew alongside the Englishman. He did not look at him, but kept his head down, moving purposefully towards the ornate gateway at the far end of the bridge. Some twenty metres short of the gateway he turned left, walking down the steps to the waterside, and the landing where tourists picked up rides on the cruise boats.

The landing was dark and deserted. Havel glanced back and fancied that he saw the face of the Englishman, peering palely down from the bridge. Then he stepped to one side of the landing into the dark shadows and picked up the heavy stone he had placed there earlier in the day. He waited.

It was several minutes before the Englishman came down the steps. He was nervous, his head held on one side, his hat now screening his head from the cold wind that gusted along the river. He stood at a little distance from Havel, saying nothing, and then came forward, slowly, with a nervous reluctance, to step on to the wooden platform of the landing.

'Havel?'

'I am Havel.'

'You have a message for me?'

Havel raised his left hand as though in greeting and the Englishman came forward almost eagerly. He was careless, this one, easy. Havel grasped his coat with his left hand and swung the rock in his right. The swift, violent blow took the Englishman on the temple and he staggered, lurching backward. Havel struck him again, kicking out at the same time and sweeping the man's legs from under him. The Englishman crashed down on the boards of the landing, his body shuddering. Havel dropped the rock and plunged his hand into his coat pocket, bringing out the knife.

As the Englishman quivered with shock under him, half stunned, moaning slightly, Havel dragged open the collar of the man's topcoat and with the skill of a practised expert, slit his throat.

Little of the gushing blood touched him as he turned the dying man's head away. The leather would wash easily in the river water anyway. Havel waited a little while, eyes searching the bridge for movement, but no one passed, thirty metres above his head, as the gurgling life spouted from the Englishman at his feet.

At last, when the throbbing, splashing sounds began to diminish, Havel heaved at the body of the Englishman, dragging him to the side of the landing. Almost gently, he eased the dead man into the waters of the Vltava.

It had all been even easier than he had expected.

He knelt down on the landing, watching the dark waters as the Englishman's body drifted away from the bank, out under the bridge. It would be found in due course, after the river fishes had played with it, of that he had no doubt. But there was nothing to connect him to this killing. His glance flickered up to the bridge again. He thought he discerned a movement, but it was probably only his imagination, sharpened by the sudden violence of the last few minutes.

He bent low, scooping up water to wash the blood from the arm of his leather coat. He would clean it properly later, but it was sensible to get the worst off here. Briefly, he wondered who the dead man was and then he shrugged mentally.

It was none of his business.

CHAPTER ONE

1

'Things simply can't go on like this!'

Sunlight slanted in through the window and gilded the edge of the desk behind which the Director of Museums and Antiquities sat, hands placed flat on the file in front of him, moustaches almost bristling with the anger that stained his tone. He tapped his flowered tie with impatient fingers, and his patterned waistcoat heaved unhappily under the pressure of his annoyance.

To his left, Karen Stannard sat with watchful, yet lazy, eyes.

Catlike, she seemed coiled in her seat, the sunlight picking up russet and gold streaks in her hair, her elegant, perfectly formed features in repose, her wide, red mouth half smiling, touched by a certain contempt. She seemed unaffected by Brent-Ellis's anger, possibly because she doubted its depth and commitment, but then, Arnold thought to himself, it was never easy to work out exactly what was going through Karen Stannard's mind.

The short silence grew in weight and intensity as no one spoke. From the anteroom came the angry sound of Miss Sansom's word processor printing the letters she had been typing when Arnold and Ms Stannard had entered the director's office. Arnold could visualize Miss Sansom, standing imperiously beside the printer, one hand on broad hip, glaring darkly at the door that barred her from Brent-Ellis's office. Everything she did was tinged with anger. Today, perhaps some of it had rubbed off on her beloved director, the man she attempted to protect from the outside world and its pressures. The same man who had employed as his deputy the impossibly beautiful Karen Stannard who now formed a barrier in terms of access between the director, Simon Brent-Ellis, and his devoted slave Miss Sansom.

Brent-Ellis must have realized Arnold was daydreaming.

'Well?' he barked, uncharacteristically. He was a man who disliked meeting people and making decisions. As far as possible he avoided confrontations, was uncomfortable when there was a hint of aggression in the air, longed to escape from office confines to the open spaces of the golf course — in working hours as far as possible — and desired to run his office and department with the lightness of touch he displayed on the greens.

'I'm not sure what it is you're referring to, Director,' Arnold replied mildly.

Karen Stannard stirred in her seat, her skirt whispering sibilantly as she uncrossed her long, tanned legs. She smiled. It lit up her face but the pleasure was founded in the discomfiture Arnold was feeling. 'It's as I was saying, Mr Brent-Ellis . . .'

'Quite!' The director bared his teeth, white under his dark moustache, and fingered a jawline that was beginning to display signs of pudginess. The evidence under his fingers made him even angrier.

'It's time this department got itself sorted out,' he snapped. 'If it wasn't for the effort that Ms Stannard and I put in, the place would be a shambles . . . an absolute shambles! And why should it be I who has to sort things out all the time?' He blinked, glanced uncertainly at his deputy, as though he felt momentarily that he had gone too far, but she merely smiled at him.

Reassured, Brent-Ellis went on. 'I came in yesterday and there was this pile of memoranda on my desk. I called Ms Stannard, and she told me they were reminders that I'd sent out over the last three months, not ten per cent of which had been acted upon! And when I called for you to get in here and explain yourself, you weren't even in the building!'

'I was at Derwentside, at the conference, attending in your place,' Arnold protested. 'You'll remember — you couldn't make it, and asked me to stand in for you, so—'

'We were talking about the memoranda,' Karen Stannard interrupted.

'I'm not aware the memos were directed to me,' Arnold replied.

'Your name isn't on them, certainly,' Brent-Ellis sneered, 'but you're one of the most senior men in the department and it should be your duty to see to it that these memoranda are not ignored.'

'Even if I haven't seen them personally?' Arnold asked, leaning forward and picking up the top sheet. 'This one, for instance, is directed to Records . . . Fred Alson. It's the first time I've seen it. Fred's been off sick for two months, so he could hardly be expected to respond.'

'You made no replacement?' the director asked, raising his heavy eyebrows.

'Not my responsibility,' Arnold demurred. 'Miss Stannard—'

She was quick to defend her position. 'I think you'll find,' she interrupted smoothly, 'a replacement was put into post within two days. But the routing of the memos was changed. However, Director, I don't know that we need continue with detail like this. After all, I'm here to lighten your own load, and it's something I can deal with in private with Mr Landon. Rather, we should here be concentrating, perhaps, on the wider issues.' She smiled, encouraging him. 'Policy matters, not implementation. That's *my* job.'

'Policy, of course . . . The wider issues?' Simon Brent-Ellis wrinkled his nose in doubt, and his forehead in uncertainty. 'They would be . . .'

'Scheduling, Director,' Karen Stannard said in a firm tone.

'Scheduling . . . ah, yes.' Brent-Ellis swivelled in his chair, staring out of the window towards the blue-hazed fells, and the promise of fast greens and long fairways. 'We're concerned, Landon, about the scheduling. Er . . . there's just too damn much going on, and there's no one keeping tabs on things.'

'I'm not certain what you mean, sir.'

'Ms Stannard?' Brent-Ellis sought guidance.

She smiled, her eyes of an indeterminate colour but steely in intent. 'We were just saying, Mr Landon, before you condescended to join us, that there are at least five different operations being carried on under our . . . ah . . . jurisdiction at this point in time.'

She means now, Arnold thought sourly.

'Five . . . and it may be there are more. There may be some you haven't told us about, since your . . . promotion.'

A glimmer of light at last appeared in Arnold's mind. Promotion. Karen Stannard had not exactly opposed it, not in so many words, because she habitually moved in subtle, discreet ways to reach her own personal objectives. She had not opposed Arnold's upgrading, but she had murmured faint praise, raised half-stated reservations, promoted a close questioning in committee, and shrugged off odd, doubting comments, to prevent the promotion going through two months ago. It had not even been exactly a promotion, merely an upgrading that had been long overdue, in the general view of the department as a whole. But she had used her wiles to fight it — and had failed.

Karen Stannard did not enjoy failure, except in other people. The thought of her own failure discountenanced her, though she usually hid her annoyance well. She was known to bear grudges and work them off later. This, Arnold guessed, was what was happening now.

'Your promotion,' Karen Stannard said in almost gentle admonition, for the benefit of Brent-Ellis, 'as was made

11

clear by me at the time, was inevitably going to mean greater responsibility . . . and a greater *sense* of responsibility.' She inspected her immaculately manicured nails. 'You've drawn around yourself of recent years a certain . . . reputation in your involvement with archaeological digs in the county, and there is no doubt you have done good work. We've all *heard* about it, regularly.'

She glanced archly at Brent-Ellis, confident he would pick up the hint. He was not averse to self-publicity, and he bridled now, resenting the fact that there had been times in the recent past when Arnold Landon seemed to have received more press notices than had the director himself, where the work of the department was concerned.

'So, when these unactivated memoranda came to light, we felt it was time for a . . . chat,' Karen Stannard continued. 'Time to clear the air . . . to make sure *everyone* knows what their obligations might be.'

Mine in particular, Arnold thought.

'Yours in particular,' Brent-Ellis said. He shuffled uncomfortably in his chair, smoothing his waistcoat and glowering at unpleasant memories. 'The whole thing was brought home to me . . . it sort of came up at a dinner I attended the other night. Chief Constable was there . . . Lord Lieutenant and the High Sheriff. Leader of the Council, Chief Executive . . . I was embarrassed, Landon.'

'Sir?'

'Mention was made of the Cossman activity, up at Ravenstone Fell. They started talking about the old railway, and the cutting above Digby Thore, and how the Cossman people were going to do great things up there . . . and then the chief executive asked me about it.'

'And unfortunately, Mr Brent-Ellis knew nothing about the scheme,' Karen Stannard said gravely.

Simon Brent-Ellis frowned and glanced at her. She held his glance for a long moment. He was uncertain whether there was a hint of mockery in her tone, and it puzzled him. He thought she was on his side in this.

'You knew nothing about it, Director?' Arnold asked. 'But I sent a file through to you for information some two months ago. I have to admit that I don't know a great deal about it myself, since I wasn't present at the relevant committee — you were — but when the file came to me, I dealt with it, sent it up to you, and when it did not come back, I assumed, as is normally the case, that it was assigned by you to someone else. To the deputy director, perhaps. That's the normal situation.'

'It didn't come to me,' Karen Stannard announced.

'It didn't go to anyone,' Brent-Ellis flushed, suddenly cornered. 'It got ploughed under here in this room, on my desk, under a pile of other papers, the kind that are always snowballing in here and rendering it impossible for me to . . .' His words died away, as though he had lost the drift, but Arnold guessed that an image of a fairway had again crossed his mind, the thought of lost opportunities . . . 'But that's exactly the point I'm trying to make. There's no damned organization in this department anymore. Why didn't you call back that file, Landon?'

'I had no reason to call it back,' Arnold protested.

'So you just let it sit on my desk,' Brent-Ellis fumed impotently. 'And I was left to look like a fool at dinner with the Lord Lieutenant and the others.'

Not exactly a new experience, Arnold thought. He glanced at Karen Stannard. Her eyes were sharp and he knew she guessed what he was thinking.

'It's just not good enough, Landon,' Brent-Ellis was complaining, in a tone that had become whining. 'Not good enough.' He took a deep breath, flapping at his tie, and glared at Karen Stannard. 'And I don't see the point of keeping dogs and barking myself,' he added.

'Succinctly put,' Karen Stannard replied in a honeyed tone. 'You are quite right, Director . . . you can leave it all to me to get sorted out. We need waste no more of your time. Mr Landon . . . my office, if you please.'

Brent-Ellis sighed and swivelled his chair to face the window.

His fingers were drumming on the desk as Arnold left the room. They'd be itching to get on the leather grip of his Number Two wood within the hour.

* * *

'Well then, Mr Landon,' Karen Stannard purred as she gestured him towards a seat in her room. 'High office suiting you?'

Arnold sat down. She seemed to be in a good mood. Normally he was not offered a seat in her office. 'I'm not sure what you mean by high office. My job seems to be much as it was before the upgrading.'

'Ah, well, we're just about to change that, aren't we . . . ? That was the whole point about the meeting we just had with Mr Brent-Ellis. A redesignation of responsibilities.'

Arnold leaned back in his chair and eyed the deputy director. 'I've always had the impression you were unwilling to see me with too much responsibility.'

She smiled a crocodile smile, gleaming, but untrustworthy. 'Oh, come now, Mr Landon, I think you're under a misapprehension. I don't mind you undertaking responsibility for areas of work — it's merely that I feel you need watching . . . Indeed, you're one of the departmental members who needs *constant* supervision. That's why I was against your promotion . . . you did know I was not in favour of it, didn't you?'

'The fact hadn't escaped me,' Arnold replied drily.

She extended a slim hand to the file in front of her and opened it. 'Well, never mind, it's a fact now, isn't it? We must just make sure that you undertake the appropriate range of duties for such a *senior* position.' She was silent for a few moments, glancing at the details in the file in front of her. 'Now then, what we have here is a list of the digs that are current in our jurisdiction. Some of them you'll already be familiar with . . . Rena Williams, for instance, an old friend of both of us, she's still active at the Romano-Celtic site at Garrigill. Have you been up there recently?'

'Time—'

'Hasn't permitted,' she purred. 'Well, you'd better get up there soon and let me have a report. And then there's the following: the Iron Age pottery finds at Chelmer Bridge, the seventeenth-century lime kilns at Friary Fell, and the Saxon cemetery at Evison Church—'

'I thought work had stopped there, because of problems with the Church Commissioners—'

'Sorted out,' she interrupted briskly. 'And then we have the mediaeval pit that's being excavated at Hawksbury, the Roman bridge foundations at Aylestone Hall . . . the list goes on, doesn't it?' She raised her eyes to his and smiled. 'And no coordinating hand, no reports coming in, no departmental *presence* . . .'

Arnold had the feeling that was about to change. He waited as she closed the file carefully, smoothed it with her left hand and then pushed it across the desk towards him. 'Over to you, Mr Landon.'

'What exactly is it you want me to do, Ms Stannard?' Arnold asked.

'A little overtime, I would think. Unpaid, of course . . . we are all aware of how much you love your job. In a nutshell, Mr Landon, it's now your responsibility to produce a report on the status of these digs and investigations. It's been six months since the committee has had a status report, so it's time you prepared one. I shall present it to the committee, of course . . .'

As your own, Arnold thought sourly.

'. . . but I can't be expected to undertake the fieldwork. I'm *much* too busy with other matters here at the office. Policy matters. Ah, yes, and that reminds me . . . the matter which particularly upset the director. The Cossman business . . .'

'I know very little about it.'

'Quite. But you'll inform yourself. I'll make sure the file gets to you today. But I'll want an early report from you. After that, it's likely I'll take it over myself. It's a big project and will need careful handling. There are complications to do with external funding and techniques . . .' She smiled mysteriously to herself. 'But you can get started on it. Then we'll have a discussion.'

Arnold rose to his feet. 'Is that all, Ms Stannard?'

'All for now, Mr Landon . . .'

* * *

The Cossman file landed on Arnold's desk within the hour. It was accompanied by a hefty envelope from which he drew a hundred-page project design report. He skimmed through it, noting that it was very detailed: it covered lighting systems, an air-purification design for the archaeologists who would be working on the site, arrangements for submersible pumps. He was engrossed in it when he suddenly became aware that he was not alone.

He glanced up to the open doorway and saw Jerry Picton standing there.

Arnold did not like Picton. He didn't care for his appearance — the man had a mean mouth and bad skin. More importantly, Arnold cared even less for his manner and his attitudes. Picton was a gossip and he seemed able to root out all the indiscretions current in Northumberland generally and of Morpeth in particular. He displayed prejudices that Arnold found offensive. he was untrustworthy, and most of his conversations were tinged with malice. Arnold tried to discourage him with coldness, but the man had a thick skin. Now, he bared stained teeth at Arnold as he looked up.

'Another dressing down, Arnold?'

'I don't know what you're talking about.'

'On the carpet again with Brent-Ellis and the delectable, desirable but ultimately untouchable Ms Stannard.'

Arnold made no reply, but turned back to the file in front of him, and the design report.

Picton shuffled his feet in the doorway. 'Still, you got your upgrading and that'll have pleased you, because it will have miffed her. So she's putting the boot in, I hear, kicking you where it hurts. That's her style, though, isn't it? Emasculation, I mean. Her being of the other persuasion, if you know what I mean.'

'Picton—' Arnold began wearily.

'Still, there's always the possibility she might layoff a bit now, I hear. Maybe she was nicer to you than you expected today, hey?' When Arnold made no reply, Picton went on with a maliciously philosophical air. 'Who knows, now her love life's getting sorted out to her satisfaction, maybe she'll be less inclined to twist our genitals merely because we're males — and *normal*.'

'There's more than one definition of normality,' Arnold replied coldly.

'Not in my book,' Picton snickered. 'I like my sex straight . . . and with the opposite sex.'

Arnold glanced at his weaselly face, doubtful that any woman would ever find Jerry Picton attractive. 'I've got work to do.'

'Ain't we all?' Picton shrugged. 'I just stopped by for a chat . . . since you've been shut up with her and the big boss, I wondered whether you'd seen any change for the better in her attitude and demeanour. Whether she's softened up, like.'

Unwisely, Arnold asked, 'Why should I?'

'Because as I told you, life's turned out better for her. I thought maybe she'd be more relaxed. But you clearly haven't heard!'

Arnold sighed and shook his head. He knew he was going to hear.

'She's got a new girlfriend, man! It's the recent appointment up at the university. You know they've founded a new chair up there. Something to do with pathology, but I hear the appointment was a funny one. Caused a bit of a rift among the old dodderers who make up the selection committees. Haven't got the details yet, but it seems the new professor is a bit . . . odd, shall we say,' He snickered again, unpleasantly. 'In more ways than one, if you know what I mean.'

'I don't.'

'Oh, come on, Landon! Don't pussyfoot around with me. You've been working with Karen Stannard long enough — and close enough, I hear — to know where her inclinations lie! So it can't be a great surprise to you to know that she's got a new girlfriend. A new *bosom* pal.' He giggled. 'I wonder what the atmosphere is like when they get together . . . A *queer* combination, I would guess! Brimstone and formaldehyde, you reckon?'

He giggled again as he made his way down the corridor. 'Brimstone from the wicked witch of Morpeth and formaldehyde from the Newcastle pathologist . . .'

2

'One of these days I'm going to break his malicious, weaselly neck,' Arnold growled.

'I don't know why you even listen to him,' Jane Wilson replied. 'Why give him the time of day?'

Arnold sighed. 'It's not easy. He sort of wanders around the department, dispensing gossip. Never stops long enough to be kicked . . .'

He leaned over to the table in front of the settee and freshened Jane's gin and tonic from the two bottles thoughtfully placed within reach. He handed her the glass, then settled back on the settee, slipping one arm casually around her shoulders. 'Anyway, it's good to see you. It's been a while.'

'Deadlines,' she said and sipped her gin and tonic. She had called unexpectedly this evening. She had been working up at Kelso during the last few weeks, getting some local background for her next book, which was going to be a new experience for her. She had over the years attained some success as a writer of historical fiction, but her publishers had now suggested she turn her talents to a history of the Border Reivers.

Arnold watched her for a little while, contemplatively. Her absence, trailing around the Border towns, had served another function. They had met through his old bookseller acquaintance Ben Gibson. They had been uneasy friends thereafter for some time, but recently the relationship had warmed, changed, and they had become lovers. But in each of them there was still a reserve, a certain holding back, a refusal of commitment. He guessed it was because they were too alike, and had both been alone too long. But he had meant it when he said he was glad to see her again. Working on her new book had given them breathing space and a time for evaluation of the relationship. Not that they would talk about it. Not for a while.

'So how's it going?' Arnold asked.

'The research? Fascinating,' she murmured. 'It gets me into the Border towns . . . Jedburgh, Kelso, Coldstream . . . and there's so many side-tracks I'm tempted to follow. But things are coming along. I need to get some photography done, though the publishers may well want some more professional shots once I've found the locations. But the peles, and the ruined castles . . .'

'You feel some fiction stirring?' he suggested.

She laughed.

He liked to hear her laugh. She was not a beautiful woman, quite unlike Karen Stannard, but when she laughed she could turn heads, and her personality softened. There were occasions when she could be brutally direct, but her laughter was always soft and pleasant. He kissed the tip of her nose.

'Keep looking at me like that, and there'll be other things stirring,' she said.

'An objective to be desired.'

'When you've things like *that* on your mind?' she questioned, pointing to the thick project report on the table. He'd been reading it when she called, and had not put it aside. 'What is it, anyway?'

'You trying to change the subject?'

'The evening is early yet,' she replied, stroking his thigh. 'I asked you — what is it?'

Arnold scowled at the report. 'It's a project design commissioned by Cossman International. You heard of them?' Jane wrinkled her nose.

'Contractors . . . development company, aren't they? I heard they were about to start work up near the North Tyne somewhere.'

'That's them.'

'That's *they*, you mean.'

'Something like that. Novelists! Pedants, rather. Anyway, yes, they're trying to establish a building development at the Ravenstone burial site. It's an interesting situation, really. A twelfth-century church had been built on a much older burial site . . . at Buckler's Gate, that is, near Digby Thore — but the church was burned down around about 1700. It was never rebuilt, and the fact that it had been located on an earlier cemetery site was not even suspected until, in the 1850s, the railway company extended its line up to Digby Thore and they slashed a cutting through the area where the church had been. The Victorians did carry out some excavations at the church and they discovered that the lower part of the church was built of Roman ragstone except for the quoins. Limestone blocks had been used to form long and short work in the Saxon style. Moreover, they found pottery in the primary floors which dated from 1050 or thereabouts, so the church was probably built after the Conquest but in the tradition of the Anglo-Saxon—'

'Arnold . . .' she warned.

He laughed, conscious that he was being carried away by his own enthusiasms, yet again. 'Sorry . . . Anyway, after the excavations, the railway company came cutting further through, — an ill-fated line, of course, like most of the country lines closed by Beeching. That exposed over fifty post-fire burials, which were reburied — but they also found evidence of the older cemetery.'

'I've never heard of an ancient burial ground at Ravenstone Fell,' Jane doubted.

Arnold shrugged. 'The site was never worked to any extent.'

'Why ever not? I thought the Victorians were heavily into seeking out the past.'

'They were,' Arnold agreed. 'But they were also great pragmatists. Commercial interests came first, above all — and when the railway navigators exposed the old cemetery the railway company had a clear choice: get on with the work and make money, or allow archaeologists on to the site. Commerce won.'

'Philistines.' She gestured towards the file. 'Is the Cossman development plan going to cause further problems?'

Arnold shook his head. 'No, as a matter of fact it seems to be a particularly responsible attitude that they're showing. From what I've read of their proposals, there should be a good opportunity to open up the ancient site in a manner that was never allowed in the 1850s.'

'So the Victorians just built the line, then, and ignored the old cemetery?'

'That's right. They allowed no access to antiquarians. And when the line became operative I suppose the old site was largely forgotten. But the company never flourished, and when the line was dosed in the 1950s, Digby Thore became a ghost village in effect, young people moved away, the pubs closed, some of the hill farms became derelict and the whole area was left sad, and abandoned, used only by walkers—'

'Until Cossman International came along?'

'Something like that, but not quite so simple.' Arnold gestured towards the project report. 'It wasn't an idea they came up with, really, rather it was a proposal that was put out to tender. A large tract of land in the area of Ravenstone Fell is owned by the Farston Trust — a substantial bequest from Lord Farston, who died some twenty years ago. The trustees finally came up with a proposal that a country park should be constructed, with a completely enclosed leisure complex, craft centre, a model village, sawmill, country heritage site—'

'Sounds environmentally interesting and politically correct.'

'Which is why a lot of government money will go into it. Rehabilitation of the North. Pre-election periods always seem to produce such grand ideas.'

'Don't be cynical, Arnold.'

'Anyway, it's Cossman International who've come up with the best tender. But don't be fooled by the company name. They're not the biggest of outfits, going by their history. But they've come up with a good scheme, which allows access to the ancient burial site. They've ploughed a lot of money into it already. Like the project design, for instance.'

Jane put down her drink and snuggled closer to him on the settee. 'So what's to be your involvement?'

'Karen Stannard,' he groaned. 'She's just finding work for me. Wants me to report on the project — before she takes it over when it gets interesting. This project and about five others. Chelmer Bridge, Friary Fell, Evison Church, Hawksbury, Aylestone Hall, Garrigill—'

He felt her body tense slightly. He was amused. Their relationship had begun partly because of Garrigill, and a perceived threat on her part, in the person of Dr Rena Williams, who was supervising the Garrigill dig. He waited.

'So you're going to be travelling?' she asked finally, in a deliberately casual tone.

'All over the county.'

'That's something you never object to.' She raised her head, glanced at him quizzically. 'Of course, it's better when you're not alone.'

'I don't mind being alone on the fells.'

'I didn't say you minded. I just said it can be better when you . . . have company.'

'Well, I'll know some of the people at the sites.'

'Like Rena Williams, I suppose.'

'Not just her.'

'Anyway,' she grumbled, 'I could do with some time off from my own research. I wouldn't mind a trundle for a few days, through the Northumberland hills. Does the thought of a congenial companion to while away your lonely, country-hotel-bound nights strike you as an attractive proposition?'

'Depends on what incentives you're prepared to offer me this evening.'

She took the glass from his hand, placed it firmly on the table and turned to face him, a wicked glint in her eyes. 'Well, let's see how *this* grabs you, for a start . . .'

Arnold was easily persuaded.

* * *

He enjoyed that part of his duties that took him out over the fells. It was his father who had instilled in him a love for the wide curve of the hills and the windswept, heather-strewn beauty of the high country of Yorkshire and Northumberland. Together they had tramped the dales, and his father had pointed out to him the signs of a long-since lost industry: deserted, crumbling lime kilns, rusting winding gear, ancient slag heaps that had greened over with time.

And the seasons played their part also. On quiet summer days the pair of them had walked the riverbanks, winding through head-high fern and catching occasional glimpses of roe deer, startled in the woodlands. In winter, when the frost lay hard on the ground, icicles played patterns with the pure air lichens, grey and green on the three-hundred-year-old drystone walls, and the fells were white and glistening under the winter sun.

And things had not changed, not significantly, since those young days. There was still fluorspar to be found among the gravel beds of the rivers that tumbled down from the high fells — purple and mauve pebbles thrown away as waste material from the old lead mines — and rounded as they were tumbled down by the winter-swollen streams into the valleys. There were old drovers' roads to walk, green bog mosses to cross, stumps of ancient Caledonian pine trees to note among the eroded blanket peat on the slopes above the brown burns that gurgled through gnarled and knotted scrub, lining the scars in the hillside.

It was an added pleasure now, to drive and walk the hills with Jane as a companion. He had taken the week, leaving the office under instructions from Karen Stannard, and had spilled it over into the weekend, combining duty with pleasure. He had picked Jane up at her home in Framwellgate and together they had visited Chelmer Bridge and Friary Fell, talking with the field teams, checking on the progress of the digs. He had shown Jane some of the Bronze Age artefacts that had been discovered at Aylestone Fell: a bronze brooch with a distinctive rosette of red garnets, disc brooches and bracteates, a long, Kempston-type cone beaker. At the ruins of Evison Church he had explained to her the traditional way in which the character of an Anglo-Saxon cemetery could be determined — looking for graves containing swords, the status symbols of the Anglo-Saxon world. She provided him with a good audience and she had listened, entranced, while he explained how the iron blades had been pattern welded, and the scabbards mineralized, showing they had been made of wood covered with leather, but lined with sheepskin, still preserved in the iron corrosion.

'I'm surprised you don't get bored,' he suggested, as they took dinner on the Saturday evening, at the Lord Crewe Arms, in Blanchland.

'How do you mean?' She seemed genuinely puzzled. Arnold smiled.

'Well, I trail you around the fells and these archaeological digs, and you have to listen to erudite discussions about buttons and flint knives and burial cists, and then when we find a hotel for the night — like this one — I can't resist traipsing you around the sculpted tombstones of a chapel, showing you a pelican window here, a mediaeval gatehouse there—'

'And you've told me that the cellar bar and the lounge in this hotel were once storerooms for the abbey, and you've pointed out the remains of an old priest's hole in the chimney,' she added, waving an admonitory fork and grinning at him. 'Yes, I suppose at times you can be a bit much — let your enthusiasms run away with you. But I wouldn't be here with you, listening, if I didn't find it fascinating. It's an old truism — an expert in any subject can be interesting, if he's also enthusiastic.'

'I wouldn't exactly describe myself as an expert in anything,' Arnold demurred.

'So how would you describe yourself?'

'Jack of a few trades? A scattering of superficial knowledge, gleaned from here, there and everywhere? I'm not sure, Jane, not really — when I talk to real experts, like the people we've been meeting at these digs, I realize just how shallow my knowledge really is.'

'Rubbish! You know stone and wood, construction systems and mediaeval history. And, rumour has it, you're lucky! Things *happen* when you're around.'

Arnold smiled. 'Lucky having you here to flatter me?'

'Flattery is not my strong suit! I'm better known for my plain speaking and my cynicism.' She eyed him sardonically. 'But I get the feeling you're enjoying my summation of your skills too much. We'd better stop right now.'

'Well, tomorrow you can measure me up against a real expert. We're calling in at Garrigill.'

She grimaced. 'To see the formidable Dr Williams.'

Rena Williams. Arnold was silent for a little while. Jane still thought the professor from York had a soft spot for Arnold. He himself was less certain. There had been the odd moment, months ago, when they had been working together at the Garrigill site and the ancient pit, when he had felt she was somewhat vulnerable, was perhaps on the edge of saying something, but it had in his view been due to pressures weighing upon her, and the moment had passed. On the other hand, it had pushed Jane and himself together.

Tomorrow could be a slightly awkward situation, nevertheless. It depended on how Jane felt — and behaved.

In the event, she behaved impeccably.

Rena Williams was clearly glad to see him. A tall, handsome woman, she had been with him when they had discovered the *Kvernbitr*, the two-edged Viking sword which was now on display in York, and she had later sought his assistance at the Garrigill site, somewhat to Karen Stannard's annoyance. Now she expressed a degree of disappointment that he had been unable to continue working with her at Garrigill.

'It must be very boring being stuck in the office at Morpeth,' she suggested.

Arnold grinned. 'I'm not so sure. There's always office politics to liven things up from time to time. But how is the site developing?'

'Slowly.' She gestured towards the pit. 'It's all but cleaned out now, I think. We've managed to raise the bones and the artefacts and I reckon we've just about hit the lowest level now. And the cave temple, too . . . No, I think we'll be reducing the size of the team over the next few weeks. And then it'll be back to the university for me, cataloguing, writing up—'

'And lecturing?' Jane asked mischievously.

Rena Williams laughed. 'A bit of that too, I guess.' Her glance lingered on Jane for a few moments, then turned to Arnold, reflectively. He guessed she'd be wondering about their relationship. Rena and Jane had met several times, but it had been a surprise to the Garrigill site director to see Arnold bringing Jane with him on an official visit to the site. 'Anyway . . . I hear there's interesting developments up at Ravenstone Fell.'

'The Digby Thore dig?' Arnold nodded. 'We'll be heading up there later this afternoon.'

'They seem to have achieved an enviable level of financial support,' Rena Williams suggested. 'You know these Cossman International people?'

'I don't. But from what I've seen in the file they've put in some money — but not a great deal. They have connections, clearly . . . it'll be government money that provides the major funding in due course.'

'At least they've been able to pluck the right political chords.'

Rena Williams sniffed. She glanced around her at the field site. 'They'll have been able to move faster than we could, because of the earlier excavations made by the railway navigators last century. Not the ideal way of starting a dig, but it does get some of the back-breaking stuff out of the way. And they've already uncovered bones, I understand from the grapevine. An ancient cemetery . . . have they dated it yet?'

Arnold shook his head. 'I don't know. Let you have more information when I've checked it out. You wishing you were up there?'

Rena Williams sighed. 'A tempting prospect. But there's still a lot of work to be done on what we've found here. Still, it's been nice to see you again, Arnold. We must get together for a drink, or a meal, sometime.' Her glance drifted reluctantly towards Jane. 'And you too, Miss Wilson.'

'Huh!' Jane snorted, as they walked back to Arnold's car. They drove on from Garrigill, making their way back north along the black tarmac road that wound and dipped past high scars and isolated farmhouses, crossing the amphitheatre of Upper Teesdale and heading for the rock bastions of Falcon Clints. Thereafter, the landscape opened out along unfenced moorland, far from the old galleried lead mines, crossing brown becks and silent fells, towards the great, dark-green tattered arc of the forested hillside where sparrowhawks hovered, and the wind brought a tang of the distant sea to their senses.

It was three in the afternoon before they dropped down into the valley below Ravenstone Fell. They had already caught glimpses of the decayed railway line that had been built in the 1850s, driving up to Digby Thore. The road ran over and under the track, passing ruined bridge heads, slaty embankments browsed by sheep, deep cuttings still black-earthed after more than a hundred years. The line had never been a commercial success. In the railway boom years money had been ploughed into it recklessly, but it had managed to struggle on for only four decades before rust and decay and collapsing buildings had demonstrated the lack of ongoing investment. It had been closed, finally, fifty years ago.

'It was about that time that an excavation was carried out on the edge of the railway cutting below Ravenstone Fell Halt,' Arnold explained to Jane. 'It was largely exploratory, according to the file, but they did discover that there was an old cemetery there. The earliest graves had been inadvertently destroyed by the railway excavators, but there was some evidence to suggest that the cemetery was quite an extensive one.'

'And they are now extending the dig?'

'Seems so. But that's what I'm here to find out, at the behest of Ms Stannard herself.'

They drove along a narrow lane, between high hedges, until the road opened out into a field where a car park had been laid out with gravel and cinders. To their right the field dropped away, and they could see in the hollow below them the grey-roofed village of Digby Thore nestling in the afternoon sunlight. To their left the hillside rose steeply, scarred by a cutting driven through a hundred years ago, where the old line lanced down from its ascent of the fell to the village below. It had been designed to serve a location expected to expand. The dream had never been realized.

'Maybe it will all happen now, as it was intended to happen long ago,' Jane suggested.

'A romantic thought.'

They parked the car and Arnold led the way to a small huddle of single-storey, stone-and-timber constructions, that served as offices and facilities for the workers on site. Beyond the buildings were earth-shifting equipment, lorries and hard-hatted men. The office sign bore the name of the controllers in large letters: COSSMAN INTERNATIONAL LTD.

As they approached the office, the door opened and a man stepped out. He was above medium height, well-built, and about forty years of age. His features were craggy, eyes dark under heavily ridged brows, and there was a strength about his mouth that suggested he was used to getting his own way in most things. His hair was unfashionably short-cropped, tinged with grey at the temples and he wore a well-cut tweed jacket, twill trousers and gumboots.

'Can I help you?'

His voice was deep, his tone wary.

Arnold explained who he was and introduced Jane, without mentioning that she was not there in an official capacity.

The big man extended his hand. 'Ah, yes, I got a call earlier in the week. We've been expecting you, but weren't certain which day . . . I'm Paul Stillwater. I work for Cossman as a sort of trouble-shooter . . . PR, all that sort of thing. I'll be able to take you around the site, make the necessary introductions and all that. But you've not picked the best of days.'

'Oh? Why is that?'

Stillwater smiled. 'Well, in one sense it's a good day, since it'll give you the chance to meet Thor Cameron, the chairman of our company. On the other hand, he's fairly busy . . . you know Jim Rawson?'

'The MP?' Arnold shook his head. 'I've heard of him, of course, but we've not exactly met.'

Stillwater grimaced. 'He's called in to see Thor Cameron . . . get up to date on the project. They're up at the cutting right now, but I'm laying on tea for them, so maybe you'd like to join us here and get to meet them both.'

He gestured them towards the office and ushered them both inside. There were two girls working at word processors in the anteroom. Beyond there was a comfortably furnished sitting area with low chairs and a coffee table. At the far end of the room was an office which displayed Stillwater's name as site director.

'You an archaeologist?' Arnold asked, surprised.

'No, no. I leave that to the experts. The site director title, that's really just for the heavy work stuff, the development of the site as a whole. The archaeology . . . well, I'll be able to explain it to you later. I think Thor and Mr Rawson are just arriving . . .'

He waved them to seats and left the room. Arnold heard voices in the other room and a few moments later a tall man in a grey suit came in. 'Mr Landon? I'm pleased to meet you. I'm Thor Cameron.'

Arnold could only guess that when Cameron had been born his mother must have had the presentiment that he would turn out like a Viking warrior. The man's hair was red-gold, curling, cut short and his eyes were a piercing blue, sharp, quick and intense. His skin was smooth and tanned, with the hint of a reddish stubble on his cheek. His mouth was wide and firm and his manner friendly. He was well over six feet in height and though powerfully built he moved with ease, lightly, and confidently. He smiled as he took Jane's hand, and Arnold could see from the expression on her face that she was more than a little smitten by the handsome magnetism of the man.

'I'm sorry it's something of a busy time,' Cameron was saying smoothly, 'but Jim Rawson found time to drop in.' He was turning, waving the politician in behind him. 'Jim, Mr Landon's from the county department, checking on our progress.'

Rawson shook hands. He was a little above medium height, with thinning hair and the insincere smile of a politician, with grey eyes that never seemed to stay still, always seeking escape. 'Nice to meet you. But can't join you for tea, as it happens. I can't be stopping long now . . . We'll be in touch again soon about the funding, Thor . . . and I found the little tour most interesting. You've sent for my car?'

'It's waiting outside, Mr Rawson,' Stillwater replied from the doorway.

'Then I'll be off. A swift meeting, Mr Landon, but . . . the House calls!'

Cameron walked out to the car with him. In the interval Stillwater offered Arnold and Jane a cup of tea. Cameron returned after a few minutes and joined them, smiling easily.

31

'Sorry about that, but one has to smooth the way, you know? Jim Rawson's an important contact. You might even say he's our voice in the Treasury.'

'So he's supporting your company on the funding for this project?' Arnold asked.

'That's right. It's a fact of life these days,' Cameron said ruefully, 'if you don't get political support, you don't get funding, no matter how praiseworthy the work might be. And at the cost of a small consultancy . . . well, it has to be done, you know what I mean?'

Arnold could guess.

'Anyway,' Cameron said, settling back in his chair and smiling at Jane. 'What exactly are you wanting to find out about the project?'

'It's really a formality, I guess,' Arnold replied. 'Strictly speaking, the department has no formal role in the work going on here. I mean, you got planning-committee approval for the leisure centre and other development—'

'After a lot of hassle,' Cameron interrupted, grinning.

'That's par for the course, surely,' Jane said, responding to his smile. 'Local authority bureaucracy.'

Arnold glanced at her, suspecting the gibe was aimed in his direction, then went on, 'But although my department has no formal involvement, we do need to keep tabs on any archaeological investigations that are being carried on in the county. What I find interesting from the file we have in the office, is the fact that the dig seems to have been supported by you right from the beginning. That's fairly unusual among business enterprises, if you don't mind me saying so.'

Cameron flashed a smile at Jane and ducked his head a little ruefully. 'I wouldn't want you to run away with the idea that we're all philanthropists around here! The reality is, it's a good business venture for Cossman.'

He paused as Stillwater came back into the room, and pushed a cup in his direction. 'As Paul will be able to tell you, Lord Farston owned a lot of land in this area. After his death, a trust was established — since there were no surviving heirs to the old man. He'd used the land for shooting, in the main — it had quite a good reputation in the Victorian period, but went into decline in the 1920s. Anyway, of recent years the Farston Trust was keen to redevelop its holdings in the area — an attempt to renew the place, bring some life back to Digby Thore. The village — indeed, the whole of the area — virtually died once the railway was closed fifty years ago. So the main impetus was from the trustees of Lord Farston's estate — they asked for tenders for redevelopment. That's where my friend Paul came in — with his local knowledge.' Cameron smiled. 'He's been around a bit, has Paul — troubleshooting for companies in eastern Europe and the States, but he was only too pleased to get back to his roots, as a good Geordie.'

Stillwater poured himself a cup of tea, nodding. 'There are some similarities between Newcastle and the cities of eastern Europe — prodigious drinkers in both, even if the tipple is different. But yes, it's good to be working back here . . . Still, there were a few small problems . . . not least, the fact that the project wouldn't have been viable without the addition of some extra land, on the outskirts of Digby Thore, for access and other purposes. It was held by yet another trust — the Adler Foundation — and they were never on the best of terms with the Farston family. However, I managed to persuade them it would be a good thing for the area if they were to relinquish some of their holdings—'

'And that, in its turn, put us in a good light with the government,' Cameron added. 'It also gave our tender some teeth that were lacking among the competition.'

'But how did the commitment to the excavation come about?' Arnold asked.

Cameron hesitated, glancing at Stillwater, then said, 'Well, let's just say it was a . . . considered decision on our part. You have to remember, Mr Landon, we had a number of hurdles to get over: planning permission, environmental groups, local interests, political pressures . . . it was Paul who came up with the idea that if we were prepared to write in a commitment to the archaeology of the site, it might put us in a good light, and provide the little bit extra that would shoot us ahead of our rivals.'

'You wrote it in the tender?'

'Right slap bang in the middle.' Cameron waved a confident hand. 'We guaranteed we'd put in a system that would enable a team of archaeologists to investigate the site of the old burial ground, even as we were working on construction above and around them. In other words, the construction would not be delayed, but the dig would not be interfered with. It was an imaginative concept, and it persuaded a number of difficult people to back us.'

'How will you manage that?' Jane asked, puzzled. 'Surely, building and digging are mutually incompatible, as activities.'

'Let's just say it's going to cost us a lot of money,' Cameron laughed. 'At least, it's going to cost the *government* a lot of money. Rawson's impressed, as he's told me before today. He'll be giving us strong backing, and his recommendations carry weight. But rather than tell you how we're going to do it, why not take a look at the site first? I can't take you around myself, but I'm sure Paul will be happy to do so.' He hesitated, thinking for a moment, eyeing Arnold reflectively. 'And as for an explanation . . . Paul, the planning committee meets next week, when we'll be displaying our systems. I see no reason why Mr Landon shouldn't be invited along, so he can see at first-hand what we'll be about.'

'I agree.' Paul Stillwater stood up. 'I'll fix it, Thor. Meanwhile, Mr Landon, if you've finished your tea, maybe we could take a walk along the site.'

Thor Cameron shook hands, told them he looked forward to seeing them at the planning committee, and left them. As Arnold and Jane made their way out of the offices, Jane whispered, 'I *like* him.'

Paul Stillwater led the way up the slope of the field towards the cutting in the hillside. The afternoon light was fading now, dark clouds had gathered on the distant hills beyond Digby Thore and deep shadows lay under the rock face. It was not easy to imagine how it had been here before the railway arrived, but Arnold could guess that if it had been a site for burial it would have been a holy place, a high hill site where the dead could look out over the hazy fells where they had lived out their lives.

The railway navigators of old had dug their way through the rock and earth here; swarming like ants over the area, armed with pick and shovel, and the cutting and embankment would have been a black scar above Digby Thore. Now, the passing years had covered the embankment with trees and banks of fern and bracken, shrubs, alder, ash, a few stubby oaks, and the line itself had long since disappeared, leaving only the flat, level run of the track itself.

Stillwater raised a hand, pointing. 'You see where they came driving through the rock face up there, and then curved their way gradually around the shoulder of the hill before creating the gradient that took the engines down into Digby Thore? Well, it's just there, on the northern edge of the cutting that we'll be concentrating the efforts. The construction plans envisage a leisure centre just above there, leaning into the hill, a five-storey building that will merge into the hillside, with hotel rooms in a banked design so that all windows will be opening out to the vista across Digby Thore and to the far hills. And just there, at the beginning of the roadway, that's where the old cutting disturbed the ancient burial ground.'

He led the way, scrambling over loose shale and rock, disturbed by the excavating equipment that was still working away noisily some three hundred yards from them, at the top edge of the field. As they grew closer to the edge of the cutting, Arnold could see that the rock face itself curved above them in a vast overhang, at the base of which the earth had been piled up by the navigators to form a protective embankment.

'That's where they found the first signs of the old burial ground,' Stillwater explained, waving his arms theatrically.

'When they dug out the first bones, I gather from the old newspaper records that there was a bit of a panic.'

'They didn't know what they'd found?'

Stillwater grinned. 'Superstitious Irish navvies. Thought the place was cursed, downed tools and fled! But once the company realized what it was they'd found, they did allow an investigation of sorts . . . but the drive of commercialism soon decreed that the place had to be buried again. The original burial ground seems to have extended the length of the overhang . . .'

An important area then. A site protected by the overhang from the wilder elements of wind and storm, Arnold thought, a holy place where ancestors could lie for millennia, under the shadowing overhang of the rock, undisturbed in hallowed ground.

'. . . but the railway company had shareholders to satisfy and they were always in financial trouble anyway. So they took out what bones they felt they should — I believe they're stored at the university now — reinterred the rest, and then built the embankment above the burial ground. And now we're here to disturb the place once more.'

'Are you saying,' Jane asked, 'that this embankment will be dismantled again?'

Stillwater shook his head. 'No, that's not part of the plan. There's no way we can look to expose the whole site now. If we hit anything interesting, of course, we'll investigate, but this whole area will have to be levelled for the construction work. No, we've got to accept that most of the burial ground is now irrecoverable. We'll expose just a small part of it . . . the archaeological dig will take place over there.'

He pointed ahead of them. Some fifty metres distant the embankment came to an abrupt end. Clearly there had been some geological problem there in the old days, a fault in the rock that had created a gully, because there were the remains of a bridge to be seen, crossing a small beck. Beyond the beck the embankment levelled off and began to drop in height as it moved into the slope of the gradient down into the village of Digby Thore, two miles away.

'That's where we'll be working side by side with the archaeologists,' Stillwater explained. 'Those are their huts along there. The skeleton team has already started working and I understand there'll be another group coming up at the weekend. They've already hit the eastern edge of the burial ground and unearthed several skeletons. We have photographs down at the site office. But the major project will begin in about three weeks' time, when our own engineers will be on site and the construction work will begin.'

'Side by side with the archaeologists?' Arnold asked.

'That's the idea.' Stillwater grinned. 'But all will be revealed at the planning meeting next week.'

3

On the way back from their travels around the archaeological sites, Arnold and Jane had struck a deal. She was of an independent turn of mind and had stressed her unwillingness to freely accept his hospitality in driving her around for days, at his expense.

'But we're friends!' Arnold had expostulated.

'All the more reason,' she'd asserted illogically. 'Anyway, the deal is that since you've given me an interesting and expensive time, I intend to respond by raising your cultural levels somewhat. I'm taking you to a concert.'

'I'm not sure—'

'I am,' she interrupted firmly. 'I'll be meeting you at the Quayside on Wednesday evening. I'll be at the bookshop all day, so you can park nearby and pick me up there. I would suggest we walk up into Grey Street from there. It'll save fighting for the few car-parking spaces near the theatre.'

'The concert's at the Theatre Royal in Grey Street?'

'Where else? And I'm treating you. Concert, followed by dinner at Matcham's. Let's not have an argument about it. It's all fixed.'

Arnold decided not to argue.

On the Wednesday evening, he drove down from Morpeth in good time to meet her at the Quayside Bookshop. She spent very little time there these days. She had found a dependable middle-aged lady to work in the shop which meant that Jane was able to avoid the drudgery of work at the bookshop her uncle, Ben Gibson, had left to her. She hated the packing, and invoicing, though she would never have dreamed of closing the bookshop down.

Arnold had been aware Jane had begun to look upon the bookshop as something of a millstone, since she had other things she wanted to do. Like write historical fiction and, latterly, local history. On the other hand, he understood the sentimental attraction it held for her. It had been developed as a business by Arnold's friend Ben Gibson, and both she and Arnold enjoyed the opportunity for research her uncle's collection in the bookshop gave them, idiosyncratic though its stockholding might be.

As Jane had anticipated, Grey Street was already full of parked cars, so Arnold drove on down past the castle and made his way to the Quayside itself, near Dog Leap Stairs. There were several light frigates moored on the Tyne but he doubted that the personnel on shore leave would be attending the concert. The floating restaurant and night club on the Gateshead bank was all lit up as though there were some special celebrations to be held there that evening, and he had no doubt it would prove a greater attraction than the Theatre Royal.

Arnold locked his car and walked towards the Quayside Bookshop. He had dressed carefully, but nervously, in a dark-blue suit and white shirt. He wasn't sure of the form for a concert at the Theatre Royal.

When he rang the bell at the bookshop Jane opened the door in her dressing gown and looked him over critically. She said nothing about his attire, so he supposed he passed muster. 'Come on in,' she said. 'You're a little early. I'm not quite ready. I'll just be a few minutes. Perhaps you'd like to go into the back room and wait a while? There's some brandy in the cupboard there, as well as some gin and mixers. Help your-self. And on the table there's a pile of Victorian volumes on art history. You see, I'm determined to improve your mind!'

'Befuddle it, more like!' Nevertheless, Arnold did as she suggested and poured a brandy and soda for himself and a gin and tonic for Jane, while she went upstairs to finish dressing. It looked as though she had been working in the bookshop earlier. She tended to be somewhat untidy, and there were signs of her untidiness on the desk — a discarded pair of glasses she sometimes used for reading, a half-finished mug of coffee and a packet of chocolate biscuits, and an incomplete inventory of stock bought in during the last year.

There was a television set against the far wall. Idly, drink in hand, Arnold walked over and switched it on. He moved between channels: game shows, a quiz . . . he settled for what seemed to be a discussion programme. He had not seen it before. It was hosted by a woman he did not recognize, neatly dressed in an oddly formal, dark-grey suit. She was interview-ing another woman. He sipped at his brandy, and as the talk went on behind him, he flipped his way casually through the Victorian histories, prowling through their contents with a desultory air.

He was not terribly interested in the articles on art his-tory, as seen through Victorian eyes, and he became vaguely aware of the discussion that was going on in the television studio.

'. . . I must suggest that the view you're expressing, Professor, is to say the least, a little unusual. The programmes you've commented upon have developed a certain . . . cult following, I think is the best way to describe them. But you seem to be arguing they're—'

'Facile, and unworthy of the subject matter or the man. I leave aside the homoerotic undertones of the script. I've no idea who is responsible for that bias.'

Arnold glanced at the set. The interviewer, smiling tensely, was good-looking, with short, curling dark hair and an amused raised eyebrow. She was briefly identified by a caption on the screen: Angie Rothwell. Then the camera switched to the other person in the studio, as Angie Rothwell asked, 'Homoeroticism. That's a challenging statement, Professor, but I'm not sure we have time to pursue that argument — perhaps we'll leave it for another time — but leaving that aside, is it really ethical of you to criticize a person who works in your own department?'

The woman being interviewed smiled and waved a deprecating hand. She sat at ease, her features in half-profile, confident, in control and entirely certain of herself. She would be about forty years of age, Arnold guessed. Her dark hair was cut rather severely in a way that emphasized to advantage the bone structure of her face. She had striking eyes — the kind that Arnold would describe as piercingly direct, and an amused mouth suggesting an arrogant belief in herself that would brook no argument with her views. Her voice was like those views, positive and vibrant, deep in tone and sharp in comment.

'The question of ethics hardly arises in the context we're talking about. Joe Pitcher has had the . . . perhaps *induced* courage to put himself and his views on the line through the medium of television. He is a man of *some* learning and *some* discernment; he has been regarded in the past as having a sound reputation in his field. But what we are talking about here is not the fact that he works in my department at the university — effectively or otherwise — for his situation at the university is a matter of record. It is however completely irrelevant to this discussion. He's chosen, quite independently of his university role, to air some theories through a television programme. I choose to suggest at this moment that his arguments are weak, ill-founded and of the kind that, when he has had time for reflection, he might regret having expounded.'

Angie Rothwell smiled and leaned forward, smoothly catlike. She was enjoying the discussion, and she clearly felt it was good television. Her tone was tinged with the eagerness of a vicarious blood hunger. 'Reflection, you say. But his theories are not new, so to speak. I should perhaps point out that he has already gone into print on the theories—'

'Equally ill-judged. And it is a *minor* publishing house, after all.'

'But his reputation at the university—'

'Is in danger.'

'You surely would not argue that his interpretations—'

'Angie,' the interviewee interrupted almost gently, in a tone Arnold thought patronizing, 'rather than have you put words in my mouth, perhaps it would be better if I explained myself more clearly. I am aware Joe Pitcher is regarded in some . . . ill-informed, and perhaps . . . juvenile quarters as an historian of some . . . quality. I am aware also that he has worked for a very long time at the university . . . without the promotion some would say was due to him. On that, of course, as a new member of the university I cannot pass comment. But he has chosen to use the medium of television to expound some of his wilder theories, theories that the more sober among us have regarded with amused tolerance but significant misgivings for some years. It really is time that Mr Pitcher pulled in his horns and stopped giving the university, and his academic discipline, a bad name through ill-researched, ill-judged performances on television.'

'But as a popularizer of academic—'

'Please!' The interviewee raised a hand, as though warding off satanic suggestions. 'To popularize is one thing, to raise the public interest in the eternal academic truths is splendid. I'm certainly not against that! But to peddle half-truths and unfounded theories and pander to a gullible public used to soundbites instead of reasoned argument — that is quite another. And that is certainly how I see Mr Pitcher's last series—'

'Have you discussed this with Joe Pitcher?'

'Let's say we have agreed to disagree . . .'

Arnold heard Jane entering the room. He turned to look at her. She was wearing a long, dark-blue dress with a neckline somewhat lower than he was used to seeing on her. She wore a Victorian necklet that set off her skin to perfection, but she appeared slightly nervous. Her hair was carefully dressed, and seemed to glow with a warm sheen. Her eyes were doubtful, nevertheless. 'Do I look all right?'

'Gorgeous!'

She stared at him in distrust. 'That's a word that would never apply to me. And I prefer understatement to insincerity. But never mind, you're a man.' That seemed to dispose of the argument as far as she was concerned. 'What are you watching?'

'Half watching,' he corrected her. 'Some woman slagging off that programme you've mentioned to me a few times. Joe Pitcher on "The Rise of European Man".'

'Oh, yes? I always thought he was quite interesting. Occasionally a bit over the top in his theories . . . a bit difficult to swallow. Little, sharp, bearded guy. Works at the university.'

'Not for much longer if this lady gets her way, I'd guess,' Arnold suggested. 'She's really torn a strip off him in a civilized but underhand sort of way . . . you know, using loaded words like "sober" and "some" quality . . . and she also put in a few digs about his length of tenure and failure to get promotion . . . Does Pitcher have a drink problem?'

'I don't know. I seem to remember there was something in the newspapers once, in the gossip columns . . . not that I read them, of course.'

'Of course.'

'He'd been picked up having a row in some bar or other. Talking of which . . .' Jane sniffed, and walked across to take the gin and tonic Arnold had poured for her. She glanced at the television set. The credit titles were rolling for the end of the programme. 'Who was the woman being interviewed?'

'I didn't catch her name,' Arnold replied, as he sipped his drink. 'But the interviewer — Angie Rothwell — she seemed to be enjoying spurring her on. It was a hatchet job on the unfortunate Mr Pitcher. I'd shiver at the thought of that pair getting their teeth into me!'

Jane laughed. 'You're not famous enough! Though I seem to detect some envy in your tone. Sounds to me you'd like to be punditized yourself.'

'The good Lord forbid. My only experience on the box, some years ago, was more than enough for me . . . Anyway, I wasn't being insincere.'

'About what?'

'You look great.'

Uncertainly, Jane stared at him over the rim of her glass. 'Then I'd better accept the compliment. Given in drink though it might be.' She finished her gin and tonic quickly and set down the glass. 'Come on, time we were walking up the road to the theatre.'

* * *

Arnold enjoyed the programme.

Jane hadn't given him details of the entertainment, but it turned out to include Beethoven's Ninth Symphony and Schiller's Ode to Joy. The theatre was packed for the visit of the London-based orchestra and Jane had booked good seats for them, but the bar at the interval proved an impossibility and Arnold guessed it would be as well that Jane had booked a table in Matcham's later, because there was likely to be quite a stampede towards the tables when the concert was over.

He was proved right. At ten-thirty they made their way to the restaurant, and it was already well-patronized. They passed some disgruntled faces on the stairs, people turned away at the door. The table had been booked in Jane's name, since she was treating him, and when they were ushered to their seats Arnold noted she had also taken the trouble to arrange for an expensive Mouton Cadet to be waiting for them.

'Splashing out,' Arnold suggested.

'Why should I let you make all the running in this relationship we've developed? I'm a woman of independent means and determined character. Maybe tonight it's my turn to do the seduction bit.'

Arnold grinned. 'If that's the reason for the fine wine I look forward to what follows.'

The meal was splendid. He was allowed no choice. Jane had ordered on their behalf and he approved of her selections: smoked salmon, Beef Wellington. But then, she well knew his tastes by now, he concluded. They had almost become a couple.

'A shadow in your eyes,' she accused him.

'Just thinking about our relationship,' he replied.

'Good things or nasty things?'

'Haven't struck any nasty things so far.'

'There's time yet,' she warned.

The time passed quickly. They chattered inconsequentially, about the programme, the restaurant, the previous week on the fells, and they paid little attention to any of the other diners in the restaurant. It was when Jane called for the bill, and was signing it with her credit card, however, that Arnold was suddenly aware of someone standing at his elbow. He looked up.

It was Karen Stannard.

She wore a stunning, low-cut dress and a light wrap. The dress emphasized her figure to perfection. Arnold was aware as he struggled to his feet how eyes had turned towards her in the restaurant as she stood at his table. She raised an immaculate eyebrow to him, and glanced to where Jane was signing the bill.

'Good evening, Arnold. A kept man, I see,' she said, smiling.

It wasn't the kind of smile that was warm enough to remove the sting from the comment.

'They don't pay me enough at the department to allow me to eat out,' Arnold replied coolly. 'You've met Miss Wilson.'

'Of course. She's turned up in all sorts of places,' Karen Stannard said dismissively. She half turned to the woman standing beside her. 'I don't think you'll have met Cate Nicholas, though, I imagine?'

'Oh, I think so . . .' Arnold began, nodding his head in recognition, then his words died away. Briefly, he thought he had met her, but then he realized he was looking at the woman he had seen earlier, being interviewed on television. 'Oh, no, I'm sorry . . . it's just that I saw you tonight, on a programme about Joe Pitcher . . .'

'A repeat,' Cate Nicholas said. 'It caused some tremors a month ago, so they repeated it.' She paused, weighing him up carefully, and clearly unimpressed. 'It's now been treated as a pilot for a series.'

Arnold did not envy the subjects she would be tearing apart.

He held her glance. The studio lights had not flattered her. She was a mature, striking-looking woman. Her figure was good and she knew how to dress well, to advantage. Her features were strong, with an aquiline nose that added power to her face and her green eyes were sharp and intelligent, if marred by a certain mocking light, as though she viewed the world with a degree of amused contempt. There was a network of fine lines around her mouth that betrayed the fact that she was in her forties. She was taller than she had appeared on television, almost as tall as Karen Stannard.

'This is a colleague of mine,' Karen Stannard said, a hint of contempt in her voice. 'Arnold Landon.'

'And this is Jane Wilson,' Arnold added, slightly nettled by the air of subdued hostility that had already sprung up between them.

'Ahhh,' Cate Nicholas intoned sagely, as though all had been revealed to her. Her glance flickered away from Jane. 'Mr Landon . . . Karen was telling me a little about you earlier . . .' She observed him with some care, and the mockery in her eyes grew. 'You're addicted to ancient things, and the faded past, I understand.'

Arnold disliked the way in which her eyes slid past him again to Jane, the woman had a sharp tongue. He glanced at Karen Stannard. The deputy director was standing back slightly, amused, waiting for knife blades to be exposed.

'Did you enjoy the programme?' Cate Nicholas asked.

'Very much.'

'Yes, I suppose you would . . .' Cate Nicholas mused. 'For myself, I have reservations. I'm of the view that classical-music lovers suffer delusions if they think they are immersing themselves, when they listen to Schiller, in the values of rationality, unity, universality and truth. I tend to believe they are really sinking in the mire of projections of complex relationships of domination and desire — bourgeois obsessions tied in with the rise of consumer society—'

Arnold was bewildered. He felt he was in some way under attack, but did not know how to respond. To his surprise, Jane took up the cudgels immediately.

'Ah, I see,' Jane interrupted spiritedly. 'I imagine you'll regard Schiller as a phallocentric archetype. I do understand that some of the hottest subjects in musicology these days — among the intellectually purblind, at least — are feminism, homosexuality, race and class.'

Arnold realized Jane hadn't much liked the look Cate Nicholas had given her earlier, either. She received another now, a slow, withering, contemplative glance seeking to sum up, and dismiss. 'You've been *reading*, Miss Wilson.'

'I pick up the odd book.'

'And what is your view of the other piece we heard tonight . . . the Ninth Symphony?'

'Triumphant.'

'Hitler thought so, too. He played it on his birthday, to celebrate Aryan Supremacy.'

'And when the Bayreuth festival reopened after the war, the Ninth was chosen to purge the event of Nazi associations.'

Cate Nicholas's eyes were cool. 'The fact is, Miss Wilson, we cannot divorce music from its reception.'

'Which accounts for Schoenberg receiving ridiculous feminist readings, and Ravel's life being explored for

47

homosexual tendencies?' Jane countered swiftly. 'I think such attitudes are nonsensical.'

'And I,' Cate Nicholas commented with a dismissive, though edgy air, 'consider it is equally mistaken to view music in the language of poetry and angelic visitations . . . But there, this is idle chatter. We must talk further. Miss Wilson, some other time, when we are both seeking fresh stimulations.'

Jane Wilson's chin came up defiantly. 'I'm sure *I* would enjoy that, Ms Nicholas.'

Arnold was sure he wouldn't. His palms were damp. Karen Stannard gave him an enigmatic smile and walked towards the door, linking arms with her companion. Arnold looked at Jane. Her lips were white with suppressed anger.

'Supercilious cow!' she snapped.

Arnold smiled. 'I don't think she was expecting your riposte.'

'I hate arrogance and rudeness. Did you see the way she looked at me?' Jane called for her coat. Arnold helped her into it without further comment, but patted her approvingly on the arm. She flashed him a look still scarred with anger. 'Don't you dare patronize me, Arnold!'

'Hey!' he exclaimed, half mocking, '*I'm* not the enemy!'

'Well, *she* sure as hell is!'

They left Matcham's and began to walk down Grey Street towards the Quayside. There were a few stragglers coming out of the bars and restaurants, debouching from Pilgrim Street and the Bigg Market, but as they descended to the riverside past Amen Corner, the street became deserted. They walked down Dog Leap Stairs. Ahead of them they could see a couple walking arm in arm, and Jane squeezed Arnold's hand.

'It's that pair,' she muttered. 'Slow down.'

They slowed, and Karen Stannard and Cate Nicholas vanished around the bend ahead of them, heading for the Quayside car park. 'I wonder how they met?' Arnold said.

'Didn't you tell me that that office gossip of yours . . . Picton . . . had said Karen Stannard had a new friend at the university? That must be her.'

They walked around the bend and the Tyne Bridge loomed above them to their right. Cars and the occasional lorry rumbled over the bridge, and the lights from the Gateshead bank danced in the dark waters of the Tyne.

Ahead of them there came a muffled scream, and then some loud imprecations. Tugging at Jane's hand, Arnold started forward. The two women who had been walking ahead of them were now standing at the edge of the quay. As they drew closer, Arnold could hear Cate Nicholas swearing. Her language was furious, liberal, and wide ranging in its obscenities.

'What's happened?' Arnold called out. 'Can I help at all?' Cate Nicholas swung around to stare at him as he came forward, half running, Jane just behind him. Her face was shadowed, but he could guess at the fury that would be displayed there.

'What's happened? Some bastard's just pushed my car into the Tyne, that's all!'

'If I can help—'

'Help? Why should I seek help from a useless bloody man!'

CHAPTER TWO

1

Detective Chief Inspector Culpeper sighed as the meeting broke up for coffee. He walked across to the window and stretched. His reflection showed a big, broad, thick-waisted man in his late forties, sober-suited, grey-haired, with a discontented mouth. He peered past the reflection, unhappy with the image of a man who was going nowhere, except to retirement in due course.

There was a seagull perched on one of the chimneys outside, white and grey against a cold blue sky, and he watched it idly for a little while as the room cleared of police officers. His mind was far away, thinking of a summer beach.

For years he had taken his holidays on the Northumberland coast, in a cottage at Seahouses. It had become a second home for him, a place where he could relax for a couple of weeks and avoid the thought of policing; where he could get out his fishing tackle and take a boat out near the Farne Islands, where he could spend quiet evenings with taciturn locals in the Jolly Fisherman.

But his wife Margaret had changed all that. She was a Durham lass, straight-talking, direct, simple in her approach to life and generally placid in her acceptance of her lot. But just recently she had started to put her foot down in an uncharacteristic manner, had folded her arms across her ample bosom and looked him straight in the eye.

'You buggered up the trip to Majorca,' she'd accused, 'by traipsing up to the fells on that Ridgeway case. Well, I'm not havin' it any longer, John Culpeper. It's just not good enough, man! So I've gone and booked and you'd better not tell me they can't let you loose from headquarters at Ponteland, because I'm telling yez, hinny, we're off to Greece come June!'

He'd never been to Greece, neither had she, but their neighbours had. Culpeper sighed. No doubt it would be a good break, and certainly warmer than the north-east coast. Only frozen-skinned Scots really enjoyed June at Whitley Bay. Meanwhile, he had these long-winded conferences to get through.

They seemed to be arising with monotonous regularity. If it wasn't on drugs, it was on prostitution; sandwiched between probation officers' talks, knife amnesties, gun trawls, a sociologist discussing the causes of juvenile crime, and a seminar to consider whether it was in any way productive in street policing to clip a young villain across the ear. The psychiatrists thought not.

Culpeper expelled his breath sourly. He blamed the Chief Constable. New to his post, he'd allowed himself to be seduced by siren songs from sociologists, psychiatrists and psychologists and instead of toughing things up on the beat he had convinced himself that more training was needed — at all levels.

Young Farnsby was in his element, of course, Culpeper knew, a product of the accelerated promotion programme for young graduates, the conference programme was milk and honey for him. Indeed, he had proved so bright, eager and bushy-tailed in the seminars that he had now been identified as a suitable person to lead discussion groups. Culpeper groaned mentally. He just hoped he'd never have to sit in on one of those groups chaired by Detective Inspector Farnsby. The triumphalism would be too much to stand. At least, he humphed to himself, Farnsby wasn't at this session, called in Newcastle as a joint venture between two forces.

He followed the others into the crowded tea room where coffee and tea and biscuits were being served.

He had collected a coffee and a chocolate biscuit and was turning away, seeking a quiet corner in the hubbub of the room, when a big, grey-haired detective sergeant from the Newcastle force tapped him on his spreading belly. 'Chocolate biscuits, Culpeper? Don't know if you can afford such indulgences with a gut like that!' Culpeper grinned sourly at the detective sergeant. He'd known Fred Poulter for twenty years or more. They'd worked out at Wallsend together in the early days. Hadn't been a bad patch, that: sea winds blowing, clean, fresh air, salty tang and not too many local villains, if you discounted those who'd come out of Newcastle and bought houses on the Victorian front.

'Glass houses, Fred. You've sunk a few too many pints yourself, to be able to point the finger of scorn.'

'What do ye mean, man? Sylph-like, me! But talking of pints, I could do with one now, and that's the truth.' Poulter squinted around the gathering. 'Don't know why the hell they put me on this programme. It's meant for keen young men, and neither you nor I fill that description. Looking to retirement, more like.'

Or Greece, Culpeper thought.

'Anyway, how're things going?' Fred Poulter asked. Then, typically, without waiting for an answer, he went on, 'Saw a friend of yours last night.'

'Is that so?'

'Came into the local nick with a bevy of birds. One of them was a real stunner, but they was all mad as hell and didn't even seem to be getting on too well with each other, either.' Culpeper frowned, and shook his head. 'Who are you talking about?'

'That chap called Landon.' Arnold Landon. Culpeper sipped at his coffee. It tasted bitter. Everything this morning seemed to be unpleasant to his tongue. 'Arnold Landon . .

. in your nick. Nice to know he spreads his talents around the north east. What's he been up to now? What was the problem?'

Fred Poulter grunted. 'Oh, there was all hell on. There was this woman from the university . . . what the hell's her name. She's been on telly, it seems . . .'

'Can't help you.'

'Nicholas, that's it. Bloody hoity toity Nicholas. Full of herself, and real snooty, you know what I mean. Like what are we doing about crime rates in Newcastle, and can't we control the tearaways. You know the kind?'

'I've met them. So what was she on about?'

'What was she on about? She'd just been to the Theatre Royal, that's all, man, came out to collect her car, and found someone had shoved the bloody thing into the Tyne. Now you know the bother that causes. It was the last thing we wanted to get involved with. So it was always going to be morning before we got the tackle out, and hauled the damn thing out of the water. She seemed to feel it was her right to get it out there and then. In the bloody dark!'

Culpeper shook his head. 'But how come it got shoved in? The bollards . . .'

'Oh, believe me, this was pretty deliberate. Not a case of pinching the vehicle. The side window had been smashed. The guy had got in, hot-wired the car, smashed through the rail fence, and then trundled the car forward, jumping out at the last moment before it took the dive.' Poulter sipped his tea noisily, then considered. 'Bonny car, too. Toyota Celica.'

'Sounds malicious,' Culpeper suggested.

'Bet on it. But can't say I'm surprised, bonny lad. She's the kind who'd make enemies. Now the other one . . . she's the kind to make your toes curl.'

'How do you mean?'

Fred Poulter rolled his eyes and blew out his cheeks. 'Let's just say she's the kind I wouldn't throw out of my bed . . . in fact, I'd make every effort to drag her in. She was a cracker, her.'

'And Landon was there as well?' Culpeper mused. 'I wonder . . .'

'She said her name was Karen Stannard. Now that's a name I would not forget.'

'I've met her,' Culpeper said briskly. 'Her personality doesn't match her looks. She's tough. So what was she doing there with Landon? She's Landon's boss and they don't get on, and if Landon was with the Nicholas woman—'

'I don't think that was the way of it,' Poulter interrupted. 'There was a sort of tension crackling about them all. Nicholas and Stannard were together. It seems Landon was around when they discovered the car had been pushed or driven into the Tyne. He'd offered to help — drive them to the nick to report it. My guess is they didn't want his help . . . but Karen Stannard didn't have her car, so they had little choice.'

'So Stannard was with the Nicholas woman,' Culpeper reflected. 'Interesting . . .'

'Why?'

'No matter.'

'Anyway, Landon hovered around a bit, looking unhappy . . . in fact, it was an unhappy bunch altogether. Landon went off, we bundled the other pair into a taxi in the end. Still, we got the car out for her next morning, and the press was there, and that seemed to cheer her up a bit, Miss Stuck-Up-Bloody Nicholas, but she had some choice words to say about the policing of Tyneside.'

'She wasn't favourably impressed.'

'That,' Poulter replied heavily, 'is an understatement. She waltzed in to see the Deputy Chief to give him a piece of her mind.'

'He agreed to see her?' Culpeper said, surprised.

'Power of television, Culpeper, power of television. Seems she's been given a chat series on the local network, and in situations like that the top brass jump.'

'Did she come up with any ideas about who shoved her car in? I mean, it doesn't sound much like young tearaways. They're more likely to nick the vehicle for joyriding.'

'Oh, she was pretty vociferous about the likely villain. Said she was convinced she knew who it was. A guy from her own department, she reckoned. Wanted us to pull him in there and then. But it all sounded a bit of an overreaction to me. One thing though — I wouldn't like to cross her. Looks to me like she could be a real harpy, when she's roused. Scimitar-swinging stuff around the goolies, you know? So whether she nails this guy at the university or not, he's going to get a torrid time of it.' Poulter glanced around at the departing group. 'Come on old son, time to drink up. They're calling us back into the breach . . . Do you really *believe* all this guff we're getting . . . ?'

* * *

Jerry Picton had heard about the car in the river, of course. He was quick to call into Arnold's office to pick up any extra gossip that he might add to the general account.

'What exactly were *you* doing there, Arnold?' he pressed.

'A mere bystander,' Arnold grunted. If an annoyed one, he thought to himself. Cate Nicholas had been extremely distressed when he spoke to her on the Quayside, but the distress had manifested itself in a blazing anger against men in general. She had refused his offer of assistance and he had been about to walk away when Karen Stannard stopped him. Arnold had heard her pointing out to Cate Nicholas that the pair of them had come in one car, and that was now in the river, they needed transport both to get to the police station and afterwards, home — unless they were to start hunting for taxis.

Reluctantly, Cate Nicholas had accepted the logic of the argument and Arnold, now equally reluctant to extend the acquaintance, had driven them to the police station after seeing Jane back to the Quayside Bookshop, where her own car was parked.

Surprisingly, Karen Stannard had asked him to come into the station with them. Consequently, he had heard the tirade that Cate Nicholas had launched against the inefficiencies of the Tyneside police force. But he was also surprised to hear her rail against the person she was convinced had consigned her vehicle to the dark waters of the Tyne.

'Of course it was Joe Pitcher,' she insisted snappishly. 'He saw that television programme the first time it was shown, and he had an argument with me about it later. But I'm entitled to describe things as I see them and the rubbish he's been putting out, masquerading as academic theories, is exactly what I say it is! But he took it all so *personally* — a typical man, suffering from wounded pride and bruised ego instead of having the guts to stand up in a proper academic debate. And it's equally typical to get his malicious revenge by pushing my car into the river!'

There was no proof available, of course, but that did not deter Cate Nicholas in her accusations. The desk sergeant had rolled his eyes in Arnold's direction. Cate Nicholas had seen it and at that point had stated icily that she saw no further reason to detain him.

Arnold had not seen Karen Stannard since. It was now time to remedy that, since he had prepared the reports she had requested on the archaeological sites he had visited.

Miss Sansom cracked her whip-like tongue when he appeared, announcing his presence in contemptuous tones to the deputy director. Typically, Karen Stannard kept him waiting in the silent, glowering Miss Sansom's office for some twenty minutes before she deigned to grant him an audience.

When he was finally summoned to the presence she was standing near the window, her arms folded, looking impossibly beautiful, as always.

'You can put the reports on my desk,' she suggested. 'I'll read them later. Meanwhile, you might like to summarize them for me, orally.'

Arnold remained standing, since she had not offered him a seat. Carefully he went through his findings — Garrigill, under Rena Williams's capable control, was well-advanced and would probably soon come to an end. Karen Stannard sniffed — she had once held Rena Williams in some awe but now seemed slightly dismissive of her because of tension that had arisen up at Garrigill. Friary Fell, Chelmer Bridge and Hawksbury were progressing well, Arnold reported. Evison Church had exposed additional artefacts over which negotiations might have to be conducted if they were to be retained within the county archival collection, and the dig at Aylestone Fell was proceeding satisfactorily.

'The reports may all now go to committee whenever you wish,' Arnold suggested.

Karen Stannard smoothed a finger along one perfect eyebrow. 'That brings us to the Ravenstone dig, near Digby Thore.' Her eyes seemed to be green this morning, Arnold thought, and yet there were other colours, darker, deeper, swirling there also.

'Ravenstone, yes,' he said, collecting his thoughts. 'An interesting situation. I've not done a full report concerning the dig because I thought I should talk to you about it first.'

'Problems you can't handle?' she asked coolly.

'Not that. No, it's interesting because of the plans that Cossman International seem to have for the site. As you'll be aware, the area was first exposed by Victorian railway excavation. Now there's a real attempt by Cossman — the chairman's called Thor Cameron, by the way, and he was up at the site when I called — to undertake a proper investigation of the site of the old burial ground.'

'I gather they've managed to get financial backing.'

'That's right, but not only from Northern Heritage. It looks as though there'll be Whitehall money coming in as well.'

'Indeed . . . He's got someone's political ear? I see.' Karen Stannard's glance grew thoughtful and she moved away from the window to take a seat behind her desk. She linked her slim fingers together, placed her elbows on the desk and rested her chin on her knuckles. She looked sinisterly innocent to Arnold. 'Who's the politician involved?'

'Rawson. I gather he's got a line into the Treasury, or so Cameron says. Cameron seems confident of getting the financial support — provided his presentation goes over well.'

'Presentation?' Karen Stannard pricked up her ears.

'There's a planning meeting later this week. The press will be there, so will Rawson and a couple of civil servants. Cameron and Stillwater — that's his PR guy — will be talking about the system they intend using to implement the building programme at the same time as the archaeological investigation is carried forward. It sounds an exciting concept — and I gather it's one of the reasons why the government is prepared to put in financial backing. Concern for the environment. Good story in the face of an election.'

'You're cynical, Mr Landon,' Karen Stannard purred, smiling to herself. 'But possibly right. So . . . it looks like a full-blown operation, hey?' She was silent for a little while. 'The dig . . . it's going to be investigating a burial site, isn't it?'

'Saxon, probably.'

'And they've already located some bones?'

'They have. Complete skeletons in a number of cases.'

'Including feet?'

Arnold was nonplussed. He shrugged. 'Well, since they're complete, I assume they'll include foot bones, yes. But why do you ask?'

Karen Stannard unlinked her fingers and with her left hand tapped contemplatively on her desk. 'Hmmm . . . Am I to understand you're wanting to be there at this . . . presentation?'

'I've been invited. I thought it . . . best to clear it with you, first.'

She flashed him a brilliant smile. 'Oh, I've no objection to you being there, Mr Landon. But I'm thinking, since it's going to be such a . . . high-profile presentation, maybe the department should be represented additionally, at a higher level.' She dragged forward her diary, inspected it for a few moments. 'Unfortunately, the director will be at a committee meeting. What a shame . . . But I should be able to free myself. And since it is high profile, it might be the opportunity to . . . add a little spice of our own.'

'I don't understand,' Arnold said distrustfully.

'You don't have to, Mr Landon, you don't have to. But I'll be making my own way up there for the meeting.' She picked up a pencil and tapped it thoughtfully against her gleaming white teeth. 'Yes . . . we'll see you there — at the dig itself, I would suggest, perhaps before the presentation begins?'

We? thought Arnold, puzzled. Who the hell was we?

2

Arnold left Morpeth early to drive to Digby Thore. Although Paul Stillwater had taken him and Jane around the site, it had been a cursory inspection, bedevilled by the need to avoid the heavy earth-moving equipment and building-site workers, so he was keen to take a good look at the site again now, before the presentation took place. There was to be a brief planning meeting, it seemed, followed by the presentation to which Arnold and others had been invited. It was planned for midday, in the only remaining inn still active in the village: the Mason's Arms.

He stopped off at the hotel on his way to the site since he had taken no breakfast before he left home, and managed to get a cup of coffee there. He noted that the room set out for the presentation was not a large one. Thor Cameron was expecting press and politicians but clearly he was keeping numbers to a manageable size.

When Arnold finally arrived at the site he found a number of cars parked there already, but no heavy vehicles. He guessed that the excavation and building workers had been laid off for the day. The contractors would be kept away so that anyone who wished to visit the dig would be able to do so in relative peace before or after the presentation.

A small group of people had already assembled at the dig. They were standing around sipping coffee from mugs, and from their clothing — anoraks, windcheaters, warm sweaters, gumboots — Arnold guessed they were all members of the archaeological team. Several of the group were quite young, possibly students.

Arnold selected one of the older men to ask who was in charge. He was then pointed in the direction of a middle-aged man of medium height, with a grey stubble on his chin and flyaway eyebrows. Arnold introduced himself.

'I gather you're the site director. My name's Landon . . . from the Department of Museums and Antiquities.'

The man scratched at the grey stubble and smiled a welcome. 'Ah, yes, heard you'd be coming around. My name's Loxton — Sam to me friends. Taking a look at the dig before Thor Cameron does his bit, is that it?'

'I thought it might be useful. Help me get my bearings with the presentation later. I had a quick look around the other day, with Paul Stillwater.'

'Oh, yes, you know him then?'

'Not really.'

'Hmmm. Stillwater it was who brought in the extra access land from the Adler Foundation — and that's caused a bit of a rumpus.'

'Really, how do you mean?'

Loxton hesitated. 'Not for me to say.'

After a few moments' awkward silence Arnold glanced around the site. 'At least it's clearer today. When I was last here there was a lot of heavy work going on.'

'Aye, they've been putting in some of the initial piling. Pity, really, because it'll destroy part of the burial site, but beggars can't be choosers. We're fortunate in that we're going to be given the chance to work alongside — or rather under — the builders, once the piles are in. Here, grab a cup of coffee, and I'll walk you around the site.'

Arnold took a mug, accepted coffee from the proffered flask and then walked along with Sam Loxton while the site director explained the layout of the burial site. 'You'll already have seen where the cutting curves away under the overhang . . . that's where the Victorian excavations were undertaken. The railway destroyed the next section, so that's completely lost to us, though there are some of the artefacts in York Museum, of course, in the Channing Collection.' Loxton paused and waved his mug vaguely to take in the whole area of the site. 'Our initial task, of course, was to plot the outline of the whole burial ground, taking in both sides of the railway excavation, but in the short term, with the building work about to be started, we have to make use of what areas we can. As far as we can gather the whole cemetery would have covered maybe three hectares in the first instance, but of course much of it is lost to us now.'

'Paul Stillwater was telling me that you've already found some burials,' Arnold said. 'And I saw some photographs in his office.'

'That's right.' Loxton gestured towards a roped-off area that had been covered by tarpaulin tenting. 'We found a high-status burial just over there. It was a warrior — we found a spearhead alongside him, a badly corroded sword, or large knife, and an axe head. Good find, really, because it emphasizes that the site could have had important religious significance as well as being used in a community sense.'

They paced along the area of excavation, inspecting the ditch that had been opened up under the overhang by Loxton's archaeological team. 'Have you managed to date the cemetery yet, from the finds you've made in the graves themselves?' Arnold asked.

Loxton shook his head doubtfully. 'We don't think it's one of the very earliest Saxon cemeteries. That is, unless the railway cutting destroyed the earliest graves and left us just those sections that came into use in later centuries. The Victorian dig report suggested it was a seventh-century cemetery. Our early indications would seem to point to a rather wider range of usage.'

'It wouldn't be uncommon, would it? I mean, it's often the case that a burial ground was used and reused during several periods,' Arnold suggested.

'That's right. Particularly if the location came to be held in some religious awe, or to be regarded as the burial place of famous leaders, or kings.' Loxton nodded towards the tarpaulin tent. 'The warrior, we think, was sixth century, but as you say, it was quite common for cemeteries like this to be reused over long periods, and we feel that could be the case here, from some of the pottery we've found in the graves. We could even be looking at periods ranging from maybe 450 to 750 BC. Nothing to clinch that yet, but it's a possibility we're working on.'

Arnold glanced around the site area. 'I see you've split your team.'

Loxton nodded. 'We found the warrior over there. Now if this — or part of it — was a military cemetery, we'd expect to find the sword carriers buried close to the area where we found the warrior. The spearmen would be buried elsewhere — and we have found some iron shield bosses in that trench over there — bosses, grips and the disc-headed rivets are all that have survived of the shields, of course. But I suspect the total number of weapon graves will in fact be small.'

'Why do you suggest that?'

Loxton shrugged. 'Evidence of community. We've found several female graves. Quite interesting, too — considerable number of bracteate brooches, amber necklace, an ivory ring which looks like the mouth of a purse, and a rock-crystal ball.'

Arnold glanced at the site director with raised eyebrows. 'Magical properties?'

'Looks like,' Loxton replied, smiling. 'Could well be we have a witch buried here, or a shaman. Whoever she was, she wasn't powerful enough to resist the railway. Or maybe it was her ancient curse that caused the shareholders to lose their investments.'

Arnold laughed. 'I suspect the reasons were rather more mundane —like shortage of passenger traffic. Where have you placed the skeletons you've exhumed?'

'We've got them in an inspection and research building, at the far end of the site. I'll take you down there right now. Some interesting stuff — even a finger bone with a silver spiral ring still intact on it.'

'So you've really got quite a rich—'

'Mr Landon!'

Arnold stopped. He looked back down the slope towards the site offices. Two people were walking up towards them. He recognized the one who had called immediately — he had after all been expecting her to visit this morning. 'It's the deputy director at Morpeth,' he said to Loxton. 'Karen Stannard.'

But he was surprised to see her companion. It was the woman he'd last seen in a furious temper at the police station in Newcastle: Professor Cate Nicholas.

He waited while they made their way along to join him and Loxton, wondering why Karen Stannard would have brought the university professor with her.

Arnold carried out the first introductions. Karen Stannard added to them by informing Sam Loxton that Cate Nicholas was a head of department at Newcastle University.

'I also hold a chair,' Cate Nicholas added loftily. 'A new one, funded by the Northern Heritage.'

'In archaeology?' Loxton asked, surprised. 'I hadn't heard.'

'No, rather more specialized in field. Forensic pathology — but concentrating on long-dead, rather than modern, police finds. That kind of work has never appealed to me.'

She hesitated, glanced at Arnold. 'You might say I specialize in old bones. In fact, I'm conducting research into skeleton malformations, diseases of the bone, that sort of thing. My main periods are tenth century, and I've undertaken work at a number of sites, but I have a subset of interest, which I suppose you might describe as Anglo-Saxon and earlier historical bone deformation.'

'Hmmm.' Sam Loxton looked doubtful. 'We're just about to go take a look at the skeletons we've exhumed, so I've no doubt you'll be interested in inspecting them with us.'

'That's really why Cate has come along today,' Karen Stannard announced. 'She's not here in an official capacity — she came at my invitation, because I thought she might find it interesting. I've already seen some of her work, at the cottage. It's really incredible!'

'Cottage?' Loxton queried.

Cate Nicholas nodded. 'I have a small place on the fell about six miles from here. I invited Karen across — now I've managed to put the place to rights after early disasters, I've been keeping some of my own photographic collections there. It's more pleasurable working in isolation on the fells, rather than in the university all the time.' She eyed Arnold thoughtfully. 'I gather you spend rather a lot of time walking the fells.'

'As much as I can.'

He fell in behind Loxton as they made their way towards the research office. Cate Nicholas looked different this morning. She seemed younger, more attractive; her skin being freshened by the fellside air. She was clearly well used to attending archaeological digs, for the sensible clothes she wore were certainly not new, and were somewhat work-stained. Karen Stannard of course managed to combine old clothes with elegance, as always. She and her friend made a striking-looking couple.

Walking beside Cate Nicholas, in an attempt to make light conversation, Arnold asked, 'Your cottage — where exactly is it located?'

'Bickley Moorside.'

'Pleasant area. I know it quite well,' Arnold said. 'There's some quite interesting stone circles up there. Have you had the place long?'

'Not long. I've only been in the North about six months. Since I took up my appointment at the university.'

'You were lucky to get hold of a cottage up there, then. In fact, I can't say I ever saw one recently advertised for sale at Bickley,' Arnold puzzled. 'Are you renting it, then?'

After a short silence, Cate Nicholas turned her head and regarded him with cool eyes, as though she felt he was prying. 'The cottage was left to me by a friend.'

Her tone suggested she wanted to speak no more about it. They reached the inspection building and Loxton led the way inside. It was a long, tin-roofed structure, laid out internally with a series of broad tables, and the walls were lined with shelves on which various artefacts, recovered from the graves, had been laid out for tagging and identification. On the wall, a large map of the dig had been pinned up, marking the presumed extent of the burial ground, and showing how the railway cutting had driven through the south side of the cemetery, leaving a large area in the north to be excavated.

'So that's the extent of the archaeological dig,' Cate Nicholas mused. She inspected it carefully for a while. 'Where exactly is the section handed over by the Adler Foundation? Colleagues at the university have told me about it — some were more than a little incensed over the whole thing.'

'Green Party, were they? It's just here.' Loxton showed her, pointing his finger at the area abutting on the main access road towards Digby Thore. 'It was critical to the whole development, really, because without the access the leisure complex just wouldn't have been feasible. And without the complex, we couldn't have gained the funding to do this wide-ranging exploration.'

'So everyone benefits?' Cate Nicholas said. There was a cynical smile on her face that puzzled Arnold.

'We do, certainly,' Loxton agreed. 'But the problem is going to be to get enough investigative work done in the south area. The new buildings will be going up against the rock overhang, so that part of the site will soon be lost to us. It's on the north side we'll do most of our work, that's where Cossman are going to install their piles — in fact, they've started doing it now — to allow us to continue while they carry on building above us. The jargon, I understand, is that we'll be working "below slab".'

He glanced sideways to the two women. While Karen Stannard was still looking at the map, Cate Nicholas was now moving away to inspect some of the complete skeletons that had been laid out on the tables. She was looking at the tags and location finders, and was leaning over one of the skeletons, peering at it closely.

'That one's from a south-side burial,' Loxton informed her. 'Female inhumation. What's already clear to us is that the burial ground was probably for a complete community, with men, women and children present. We've found warrior graves, and several female graves with pottery — claw beakers, cone beakers, shallow bowls. There's also some graves with no bones at all. From their size we'd guess they were for children. The warrior we exhumed, that one over there — we can tell the cause of death with him, because there's a weapon injury to the skull. We've also got one that looks like a case of bone cancer. But—'

'I should be able to come up with some other suggestions in due course,' Cate Nicholas interrupted. 'But that's if the university is prepared to fund some research for me here. I take it you'd have no objection? I think, for example, I could help you date the remains by looking at bone samples.'

'The more the merrier,' Loxton replied easily. 'If you know what you're doing, we're glad to have you.'

Coldly, she replied, 'I know what I'm doing, Mr Loxton. Indeed, I might be able to give your dig some rather interesting information about the kind of people these were — and where they came from.'

'How would you go about doing that?' Loxton asked, raising his flyaway eyebrows in interest.

'By looking at their feet,' Cate Nicholas announced calmly. There was a short silence. Loxton stood stunned, a half-smile on his face, uncertain whether she was joking or not. Behind him Arnold caught sight of Karen Stannard. She had an oddly triumphant look in her eye, as though she felt she had achieved some kind of *tour de force* by bringing the university professor to the site.

'Are you serious?' Sam Loxton asked, furrowing his brow.

'Let me demonstrate,' Cate Nicholas said coldly.

Arnold did not care for Cate Nicholas. He had found her rude, sharp-tongued and waspish in her attitudes. A fine match for Karen Stannard, in fact. He could understand how they would become friends: they had outlooks in common. Nevertheless, he found the next couple of hours fascinating, as Cate Nicholas leaned over the skeletons that had been laid out in the inspection shed and made comments about each, coming up with interpretations that surprised him but which rang true, were entirely logical and seemed to be borne out by the evidence to which she was directing their attention.

'The key to an understanding of my work,' she said, 'is a recognition that, first, anomalies in the bone structure of a foot are carried on through generations, and secondly, that repeated intermarriages in an isolated area can result in slight deformities of bone structure being converted into a recognizably typical and strongly hereditary shape of foot.'

'I've never heard that theory before,' Loxton muttered.

'That doesn't mean it isn't soundly based,' Cate Nicholas remarked sardonically. 'Rather, it suggests to me you're not up with the literature in the field. My own researches have already proved that such deformities can prevail over a long period of time, centuries at least, not only in the direct family line but even in a wider circle — such as cousins twice removed . . .'

Arnold listened carefully as she expounded her thesis. It seemed she had started her examination of foot bones when she had been living in Gloucestershire, and had been involved in a study of bones recovered from a pre-Saxon burial site. It had been rare to find completely excavated feet, but since the larger of the bones were the more diagnostic — and they were more frequently present in exhumations — she had been able to discern significant distinctions.

'The question that exercised my mind was — did the inhabitants of Britain before the incursion of the Saxons have an established shape of foot? That might seem a trivial field of study, but it could lead to important implications. In a study one could ignore the apparent splaying of the metatarsals—'

'Why is that?' asked Loxton.

She sighed impatiently. 'Because they are no longer bound together, as they are in life, by ligaments and tendons.' Cate Nicholas shook her head dismissively. 'But ankle and heel bones certainly have recognizable variations — and if you look at the cuboid bone . . . here, see this one?'

She indicated the bone on the outside of the skeletal foot on the table before her. She spoke as though she were addressing a group of callow students in a lecture theatre. 'This one, between the heel bone and the fifth—' She glanced at Arnold, her mouth twisting contemptuously. 'That's the little toe, in other words.'

'So I see.'

'In the pre-Saxon foot I very quickly noted that the cuboid bone was indeed cuboid. In all *Saxon* feet that I studied, however, the cuboid bone is more quadrilateral, with a very short outer border. Of course, differing shapes are a formative factor in the outer border of the foot — other bones have characteristic shapes. But the cuboid is always the first I look for, and hope to find.'

'What about this skeleton?' Karen Stannard asked.

Cate Nicholas shrugged. 'I believe Mr Loxton has already concluded from pottery finds that the burials are Saxon in time. There are certainly signs from the skeletal remains that they are Saxon . . . but I should stress my work is comparative in nature, and localized.' She leaned forward, inspecting the foot of the skeleton in front of her closely. She nodded.

'What I'll be able to tell is the extent to which a typical foot structure from this burial site has significant differences, for instance, from others found, say, in Durham. If one gains a knowledge of the foot structure of people from one early settlement, it's relatively easy to differentiate between the ethnic origins of people buried at various stages within a cemetery that has been used and reused over generations.'

'Or,' Arnold suggested, 'to distinguish between those buried here in, say, the sixth century, and those buried later?'

'Or earlier,' Cate Nicholas suggested. 'I've been able to identify, elsewhere, the characteristics apparent in a Romano-British foot, and those from a Saxon era or a Bronze Age foot.'

'It's not a study I've come across previously,' Loxton admitted.

'It got me my chair at Newcastle,' Cate Nicholas said off-handedly. 'I intend to demonstrate that it is as useful a method of determining the age of skeletal remains as, for instance, dating from ornaments or pottery found beside human remains in a burial place.' She moved forward to the next table. 'Now then, let's take a look at this one, for comparative purposes . . .'

She was able to demonstrate in the next hour that there were extensive similarities in the shape of the skeletal feet held in the inspection area. She claimed she could see an overall tribal shape of foot, and Arnold was disinclined to disagree. What he found equally interesting, however, was her pointing out how the bones were worn, indicating that the women had in life been very hard-working — by comparison with the foot bones of the warrior, where the signs of wear were less intense, there were indications of greater weight and more robust texture.

'In this warrior culture,' she said with a hint of asperity, 'women were clearly regarded as little more than beasts of burden. We've moved some little distance from that idea, at least, in modern times.'

'If not far enough,' Karen Stannard added meaningfully, to be rewarded by a warm glance of approbation from Cate Nicholas.

It was clear that Sam Loxton did not exactly know what to make of his guests. He was as fascinated as Arnold by the expertise demonstrated by Cate Nicholas, even if he disapproved of her manner, and he was more than half convinced that the work she did could prove to be a useful addition as a method of determining the age of burials on the site.

'I can see it would be a useful cross-reference, when used alongside pottery remains,' he suggested.

'I would prefer to regard it as a primary dating source,' Cate Nicholas commented freezingly.

But then, Arnold thought, all experts liked to regard their expertise as primary. He glanced at his watch; time had passed quickly since Cate Nicholas had started her exposition. 'I think we'd better be moving on down the site to the presentation. It'll be starting in about ten minutes or so.'

'Hell, is that the time?' Loxton gasped. He seemed to be relieved. Arnold got the impression he would be pleased to get away from the forceful Ms Nicholas. 'Yes, we'd better move.'

'If it's all the same with you,' Cate Nicholas said, 'I'll stay on here for a while. I want to take a look at those other skeletons. Karen and I will join you later at the presentation.'

As they walked away, leaving the women, Sam Loxton glanced at Arnold uncertainly, and then looked back to the door of the inspection room.

'Bloody jumped-up chiropodist,' he muttered.

3

A group of about twenty people had already assembled at the Mason's Arms when Arnold arrived. There were a few faces he half recognized, but could not put a name to. Thor Cameron and Paul Stillwater were present, of course, but in deep discussion with a group of dark-suited men who looked like typical civil servants and probably were. Arnold took the coffee offered and stationed himself near the door.

A few minutes after Loxton came in, nodding to Arnold, there was a flurry of activity. The politician Jim Rawson strode into the room, flanked by two other men who looked like minders: burly, sharp-suited. Rawson walked straight up to Cameron to join his group and there was much nodding and hand shaking. 'Looks as though we'll be starting soon now.'

Arnold turned his head to look at the speaker, standing just behind him. He was a youngish man, perhaps in his late twenties, slim, narrow-shouldered in his pin-striped suit, he had a long-chinned, lugubrious face and unruly dark hair. His eyes seemed sad, and his mouth unhappy, his general air one of uneasiness and lack of self-confidence.

'Now the bigwigs have arrived, you mean?' Arnold smiled. 'I guess so. We've not met. I'm Arnold Landon.'

'Nick Towers.'

They shook hands. Arnold gestured towards the platform party, who were mounting the dais — Thor Cameron, Paul Stillwater, two men Arnold did not know, and Jim Rawson. 'You know very much about this projected development?'

Towers shook his head. 'Not really. I'm just a simple country solicitor. I'm here because of my involvement with the Adler Foundation. I've been acting as their legal adviser.'

'The Adler Foundation. That's the people who granted the access area, I believe.'

The solicitor nodded. 'That's right. It's made this whole thing possible. And you?'

The room was settling down. 'We'd better grab a seat at the back there . . . Me? I'm here from County Hall, you might say . . .'

They took seats in the back row of the room. There were a few vacant chairs to Arnold's left. They, at least, would be available for Karen Stannard and Cate Nicholas when they finally deigned to turn up. Thor Cameron was standing forward on the dais. Behind him, to his right, was a large white board, on which a flip chart had been mounted. Cameron cleared his throat.

'I'd like to give you all a welcome here this morning — or afternoon, I should say, since it's almost lunchtime. And don't worry — you won't miss your lunch — we have a buffet laid on for you here at the Mason's Arms. Wine included, no extra charge!' He waited until the appreciative laughter died down. 'We're all here, of course, so that Cossman International can tell you about the project which is starting at Ravenstone Fell — one which we know will result in a rejuvenation of the whole area and put Digby Thore itself on the map again . . .'

He began to introduce the platform party to the audience: Jim Rawson MP, Paul Stillwater, and two engineers called Peterson and Caine.

'It's these two gentlemen who will be taking us through the details of the project — I'll shut up from this point on,

75

except to say that please feel free to question our experts here when they describe to you what we believe is an exciting and innovative project, and one which will be of great benefit to the area as a whole.'

The burly, sandy-haired man introduced as Peterson stood up and moved towards the flip chart. He turned over the cover sheet to display a map of the site.

'I'll begin by explaining the site itself to you — the configuration of the hillside, the rock outcrop, the railway cutting that was driven through by the Victorians, and then I'll take you through the plans we have for the leisure complex, the heritage site, the entertainment areas, and the administrative block. Now, if we could begin with the natural configuration . . .'

Nick Towers shuffled uncomfortably beside Arnold; the seats were hard and the exposition from Peterson rather technical. Arnold glanced back over his shoulder towards the door. There was no sign of the two women yet. He only half listened to Peterson's droning voice. He had already seen the site, and Paul Stillwater had earlier described the extent of the buildings that were to be erected, so, as far as Arnold was concerned, the talk was tautological. Moreover, he had had the advantage of seeing the planning applications in the first instance, when they had been sent down to him by Simon Brent-Ellis.

'So that's what we intend doing,' Peterson was finishing, 'and now I'll be happy to take any questions you might wish to raise about the project as a whole.'

There were a few brief questions, mainly from journalists, Arnold guessed, about the financial support for the scheme from Northern Heritage, and the likelihood of damage to the environment — firmly denied by an intervention from Thor Cameron and vigorous nodding from Jim Rawson MP. There were also a few questions about likely job opportunities for the local labour force. Paul Stillwater fielded the non-technical questions; Thor Cameron played his part and Jim Rawson made a few enthusiastic comments about the benefits to the area. It was what Arnold would have expected of them — it was their project — they were bound to be enthusiastic. There would be a great deal of money tied up in the scheme. Finally, as questions dried up, Thor Cameron called upon Mr Caine to speak.

'I'm not the kind of engineer that Jack Peterson is,' Caine explained, smoothing a hand over the bald patch at the back of his head. 'I'm more interested in systems, and that's my function here today — to explain the system we've devised to take on a real challenge. What is the challenge?' He paused for effect. 'It's the fact that we have here at Ravenstone Fell an important archaeological site which could disappear for ever if the building of the leisure complex goes ahead in its entirety. Now that's something that Cossman International were aware of and consequently they asked me to come up with a scheme that would enable both the building to be carried on, and the investigation and preservation of the site for the archaeologists to be undertaken, as far as possible. Some of the site will inevitably be lost, of course, but we are convinced we've come up with a system which will enable us to achieve the best of both worlds.'

He flipped over the chart with a flourish. 'This is how we're going to do it.'

Displayed on the flip chart was a cutaway architectural drawing lightly shaded in orange, blue and green. 'You'll see here.' Caine pointed out, 'coloured in blue, the basic concrete framework — a concourse slab which will have two large entry holes. Rising above the concourse we have in orange these two cranes . . . to demonstrate how we'll be putting in the block-work for the floors above the concourse — you see the whole programme outlined here in longitudinal section.' He paused. 'Everyone can make it out?'

There was a murmur of assent. 'OK,' Caine continued, 'I've put in here a line to show the external wall, stone cladding, rising to the first-floor level, just to demonstrate how it will look. These four levels above I've just drawn in outline, to demonstrate the block-work that will be put in as each floor is constructed.'

He turned away from the flip chart to face his audience. 'We have photographs of the designs in folders that you'll be able to pick up after lunch. But as you'll have realized, the work has already been started. Currently, we've begun to put in perimeter piling — we expect to insert about sixty internal piles which are up to a metre and a half in diameter and fifty metres deep. These piles will support the new building. It's inevitable that some archaeological opportunity will be damaged or destroyed by the piling work, but at least the archaeological team already assembling at the site will be able to investigate the site without the need for massive temporary works to support the area—'

'Like the system they had to put in for the Underground in London?' one of the journalists asked.

'That's right — a good point. The dig at Number One Poultry in the City of London needed support systems for the Central Line, and the travelator for the drain to the south. We've removed the need for that by arranging for the dig to be carried out at the same time as the construction, and in a sense protected by it.'

'So how are you going to achieve that?' another question came.

Caine smiled triumphantly. 'By making the whole excavation *below slab*. I pointed out to you the concrete concourse with the two entry holes. Well, what we've arranged is to have the archaeologists digging — underneath the concourse slab — at the same time as the erection work is going on above their heads. The two activities will take place simultaneously. That's an immense saving in cost — the erection work need not be delayed while the dig is carried on. Indeed, time constraints on the dig are no longer relevant, unlike most construction situations. We can permit an excavation to a level of eight feet below the concourse — that's the suggestion from the field team, by the way, not a constraint placed upon them by us.'

One of the journalists in the room stood up, pointing to the flip-chart illustration. 'But how will they be able to work down there, under that solid concrete floor? It'd be worse than a pit level.'

'Not so.' Caine flipped over the chart again. 'This will demonstrate how they will work. You'll see here the details of the air-purification system we'll be putting in for them — it'll amount to at least six changes of air per hour. We've commissioned a lighting system — interestingly enough, from a Newcastle firm of theatrical-lighting contractors — and we've also made arrangements, as you'll see here, for dealing with the water table, if it rises. The dig team have already pointed out to us that there could be a problem — they've discovered some "wet" archaeology with well-preserved wood, for instance — but we can deal with that. We're installing six wells and submersible pumps at strategic points right along the dig. In addition, we've made provision for a chainsaw work area so that samples can be taken for dendro-dating . . .'

'Impressive,' Arnold murmured. He glanced at Nick Towers. 'I'm sure the Adler Foundation will be pleased to see that their gift will be making a contribution both to the environment and to archaeological research.'

'Sale, not gift, Mr Landon,' Towers said nervously. He brushed a hand across his eyes. 'But as you say . . . impressive.'

Caine had moved on to the technicalities of the air-purification system, like all enthusiasts he was getting carried away, and Thor Cameron glanced at his watch several times. Arnold was aware of the door opening at the back of the room and saw Karen Stannard and her companion, so he gestured to the seats beside him. She shook her head, and the two women remained standing at the back of the room, leaning against the wall.

Thor Cameron was standing up at last, thanking Caine and Peterson for their presentation. He went on to pay a tribute to Northern Heritage who had supported the archaeological dig, to the finance houses who were backing the leisure-complex scheme and added that he hoped Jim Rawson was sufficiently impressed by the whole project to find it in his heart to press strongly for the government support that had been intimated might be available. 'It's either that,' he added to laughter, 'or we'll have to win the Lottery!' He closed the meeting by inviting everyone to partake of the buffet lunch set out in the main bar of the hotel.

As the chairs scraped back, Thor Cameron put his hand on Paul Stillwater's arm and, turning his back to the room, engaged him in a brief, animated conversation. Arnold gained the impression that something seemed to have upset Cameron. There was a striking of fist in palm, a demonstration of annoyance. Stillwater nodded, and nodded again, and then stepped back, as Cameron turned, smoothing his features and taking Jim Rawson's arm to steer him down from the dais towards the bar entrance. Stillwater also stepped down, to point out to the assembly where the hotel facilities were and which door gave access to the bar — for those who had not already discovered it. 'I would be extremely surprised if our friends from the press,' he joked, 'won't already have sussed it out, as a matter of course.'

Arnold waited for a little while as the throng moved towards the bar door and then he himself began to walk forward, alongside Nick Towers. Stillwater had stationed himself at the doorway, nodding, grinning, speaking to various members of the audience as they walked past him. When Arnold and Nick Towers approached, he smiled in welcome. 'Hello, Mr Landon — you made it, then. And Nick, how are you?'

'Well enough, Paul. An impressive presentation . . .'

'Glad you enjoyed it.' Stillwater's glance lingered on the solicitor's face for a moment. 'Any of the other trustees of the foundation here today?'

Nick Towers blinked. He wet his lips nervously, glanced around him as though for confirmation and shook his head. 'No, I haven't seen anyone — none of them seem to have turned up.'

Stillwater held his glance for a few moments, then nodded smoothly. 'Well, I'll see to it that presentation packs are sent direct to them, for their information. We want to make sure they all know what's going on, and remain convinced of the benefits of the project. You'll be staying to lunch anyway, Nick.'

The solicitor hesitated, then grimaced and shook his head. 'No, I think not. I was just coming forward to say I can't stay. Marjorie . . . she's not too well, and I've got to get back to the office first . . . I don't want to be late home.'

Paul Stillwater's craggy features expressed concern. 'How is she generally?' he asked, leaning forward confidentially, dropping his voice and putting a friendly hand on Towers's shoulder.

Nick Towers bobbed his head, almost apologetically. He glanced at Arnold. 'My wife, she has a heart condition . . . and is asthmatic. I'm afraid she's not too well generally . . . but she remains cheerful, Paul. I'll tell her you were asking after her. Anyway, I'd better get away. Good luck with the project . . . and nice to meet you, Mr Landon . . .' He turned and hurried away, a slight, despondent figure. Paul Stillwater stared after him, chewing at his lip.

Arnold seemed to detect a frown on the man's face: concern about Towers. Then Stillwater clucked his tongue, shook his head in sudden irritation and glanced at Arnold.

'Remains cheerful, did he say? Bloody hypochondriac, if you ask me. She gives Nick a hell of a life, that woman . . . she's a bag of nerves for someone so young — she's only about twenty-five. I'm bloody certain her illnesses are largely psychosomatic. And it's all she can talk about. Yet he runs around after her . . . worries himself sick. He's obsessive about her . . . Anyway,' he said, dismissing Nick Towers and his problems with an irritated wave of the hand, 'what did you think of the presentation? Peterson was a bit over the top — that droning voice! I did warn Thor . . . but Caine was good, I thought. Lucid. You think it'll have impressed Jim Rawson?'

'It impressed *me*,' Arnold said. He hesitated. 'You need to impress Rawson, then? Does that mean you're still not certain about obtaining government money?'

'Oh, I didn't say that,' Stillwater commented easily. 'It's all sewn up bar the shouting . . . Thor's quite confident. But you know these damned politicians . . .'

Arnold nodded in sympathy. 'Anyway, you seem to have got the logistical problems sorted out most interestingly. This whole scheme could be a showpiece operation, I would have thought . . . a model of its kind, from the archaeological point of view, at least.'

'I'm glad you think so. You're taking lunch, I trust?'

'I'll do that, thank you. However . . .' Arnold looked back behind him. 'I'd better wait for my colleague . . .'

Karen Stannard was talking to Cate Nicholas at the back of the room. They had begun to make their way forward, slowly, to the doorway where Arnold was standing with Paul Stillwater. As they approached, Arnold said, 'Paul, this is the deputy director of the department I work in. Karen Stannard . . . Paul Stillwater.'

'We were expecting you,' Stillwater said, and shook hands.

Arnold glanced at him. His tone had cooled.

Karen Stannard turned to her companion. 'And this is—'

'We were expecting to see just the two people from the department,' Stillwater said in a flat tone.

Karen Stannard shot a sharp glance at him. 'No, she's not from the department — this is Cate Nicholas, she's from the university.'

The geniality had drained from Stillwater's features. His mouth was set in a thin line and his eyes were cold. His glance moved from Karen Stannard to stare at Cate Nicholas. His manner was unwelcoming. 'I'm afraid we're somewhat restricted as far as numbers are concerned, for lunch.'

Arnold stared at him in surprise. There was a short silence.

Karen Stannard's eyes had darkened. 'I beg your pardon? You said it was a buffet lunch. I wouldn't have thought an extra person would have made a difference.'

'We've catered for a specific number,' Stillwater replied in an insistent tone, his eyes holding hers stubbornly. 'There's not a lot I can do now, at this stage. We won't be able to accommodate your uninvited friend.'

'But there were empty seats in the room,' Karen Stannard protested. 'Are you really saying you're unable to provide lunch for the three of us?'

'I'm sorry,' Stillwater said stiffly. 'Invited guests only.'

There was a short, awkward silence. Arnold felt warm with embarrassment and was about to say something when Cate Nicholas moved forward. She smiled. It was a frosty smile, hard at the edges but her eyes were lidded lazily. She seemed very much in control, and Arnold suspected she was almost enjoying the confrontation. 'One moment, Karen. I suspect this is a matter of *won't*, rather than can't.' She looked at Stillwater, as though she was weighing him up. Her tone was almost sleepy, yet Arnold felt it was all the more menacing for that. 'When Karen introduced us, I didn't actually catch your name. What is it, again?'

'Stillwater,' he said, holding her glance aggressively, as she continued to stare at him, a half-smile on her lips. The silence around them deepened, almost crackling with the electricity of dislike.

Arnold cleared his throat. 'Look, if it's a matter of numbers, I'm not particularly hungry — Ms Nicholas can take my place. I'd just as soon get on the road back to the office anyway—'

'No, that won't do, will it, Mr Stillwater?' Cate Nicholas interrupted. She continued to stare at him calculatingly, her lips thin with controlled contempt. 'That would remove the whole point of this . . . stance, wouldn't it? Because it's not a question of numbers at all. Now, I wonder what it could be . . . Perhaps Mr Stillwater doesn't like people who work at a university. Would that be it? Were you denied a university education yourself, Mr Stillwater, and have a chip on your shoulder? Surely not . . .'

He made no reply, but his chin was up and he held her contemptuous glance unflinchingly.

'This is disgraceful,' Karen Stannard snapped. 'I don't think I've ever been in such a situation . . .'

Arnold glanced at her. He had never seen her so put out of countenance. She was a strong-minded woman, one who was equal to most awkward situations she had found herself in. She saw herself as a woman fighting against prejudice in a man's world, and she used all her skills, intellect and physical beauty, to get her own way. But she clearly felt at a loss in the present situation.

'I can't believe this,' she stormed. 'The Department of Museums and Antiquities and the council itself has given a great deal of support to this project, and now to find that a guest — someone I myself invited along here — is to be treated in this way . . . Do you *realize* what you're doing, Mr Stillwater?'

Paul Stillwater was like a rock, unmoved, unmoving, quite determined to give no explanation for his behaviour. For once, Karen Stannard found herself helpless.

She glared at Arnold. 'I don't think any of us should accept hospitality in these circumstances. You'll hear more of this, Mr Stillwater. Both the director and I will be making representations!'

She turned away, furious, but Cate Nicholas remained where she was. There was a feline stillness about her as she stood there, observing the unswayed Paul Stillwater, a cold menace that was apparent in her eyes and her mouth. She stood looking at Stillwater for several seconds and his glance locked with hers. 'You're a brave man, Stillwater,' she said at last. 'But a foolish one. I don't take insults . . . or humiliation . . . easily. I'm not quite sure what this is all about, although I can hazard a guess. No matter . . .' She hesitated, thoughtfully, a slight, supercilious smile slowly touching her mouth. 'Although we haven't met before, I have heard your name . . . I believe you work as a PR man for Cossman International. And did I not hear that it was you who were instrumental in persuading the Adler Foundation to grant a piece of land to support this project here?'

When he spoke, Stillwater's voice was formal, but strained. 'No. It was not a grant. Payment was made to the foundation for the land.'

'A *satisfactory* price, I'm sure,' she replied.

'I'm not sure what you mean by that remark,' he said harshly.

'Mean? But nothing. I am constantly surprised by the ethical standards demonstrated by large and small companies in their pursuit of profit,' she said pointedly. Stillwater reddened slightly, but made no reply.

'Well, we shall see . . .' she went on enigmatically. 'These things do have a way of coming out in the wash, don't they? I'm sorry about lunch . . . I'm sure it would have been a pleasant social occasion. But one should always pick one's friends carefully, I suppose. And you seem to have picked yours, Mr Stillwater. Ah, well . . . until the next time, then . . .'

'It won't be up here,' Stillwater barked suddenly.

Cate Nicholas was stopped in her tracks. She had been about to walk away, now she glared at him. 'What on earth is that supposed to mean?'

Paul Stillwater's breathing was ragged. 'It means you're not welcome on the site.'

Walking away, Karen Stannard heard the comment, stopped, turned and came back to re-join them, her eyes blazing. 'Now wait a moment! What was that? Are you aware . . . you can't . . . don't you appreciate that Ms Nicholas is a well-regarded archaeologist, whose credentials for working on this site are more than—'

'Forgive me, Miss Stannard,' Stillwater interrupted crisply. 'Her credentials might be impeccable. I wouldn't know. That's not at issue. This is a private site. We have all the necessary permissions and planning agreements, so it's no good you threatening me by calling in your director or anyone else to bite me, if that's what you have in mind. The fact is, Ravenstone Fell is private land, made over to

Cossman International by the Farston Trust, with additional land obtained from the Adler Foundation by way of appropriate payments and under certain covenants. And as such it remains a site under our complete control in all respects — including the archaeological dig.' His glance flicked briefly to Cate Nicholas, and then came back to Karen Stannard. His voice was firm. 'We did not invite Ms Nicholas here. We do not intend to invite her in future. And without invitation — or permission from Cossman International — Ms Nicholas cannot take part in the dig, or even come on site. I trust that is clear.'

Karen Stannard turned her fury in Arnold's direction. 'Mr Landon — is what this man is saying . . . is that right?'

Arnold shrugged. 'The site *is* a private one, not within our jurisdiction other than for—'

'I can't *believe* this! Mr Landon,' she snapped, as though it was all his fault, 'I want to see you tomorrow morning in my office. This behaviour is . . . insupportable.'

She swept away, linking her arm through that of Cate Nicholas. Arnold glanced at Paul Stillwater before he followed them. The man's features were like granite; his jaw locked, his eyes hard.

It was the first time Arnold had ever seen Karen Stannard beaten and lost for words. He had the feeling he would be the one who would suffer, for witnessing her humiliation.

CHAPTER THREE

1

Next day, the expected summons from Karen Stannard did not come. Somewhat relieved, Arnold got on with his work. He was due for some leave and thought this would be a good time to take it, accordingly, he booked it in the office diary for the following week. He phoned Jane, inviting her to consider going away with him, but she had meetings with her publisher which she felt could not be put off, so she declined.

So Arnold decided he would take the week alone in Scotland. He could do some walking there, and there was also the prospect of taking a look at the crannogs that had been recently investigated at various sites in the North.

He had no idea how Jerry Picton could possibly have heard about the argument at the Ravenstone presentation, but it had obviously come quickly to the man's ears. He was ensconced in Arnold's doorway that first afternoon.

'So what was it really all about, then?' Picton asked. 'I gather Her Highness was absolutely flaming mad.'

Arnold shrugged. 'I've no idea. Who told you about it?'

'Ahah . . . Little birds.' Picton winked and placed a nicotine-stained finger against his nose. 'But I gather being turned away from lunch didn't exactly please Ms Stannard — and as for the insult visited upon her friend—'

'It wasn't Karen Stannard who was turned away,' Arnold responded in irritation. 'It was Cate Nicholas who was refused lunch, and barred from the site, in addition — which I thought was uncalled for.'

He regretted his statement immediately, because Picton's eyebrows shot up. 'I see . . . thrown off the site as well, hey? Now, I wonder what that's all about? Though I did hear a rumour . . .' He stared at Arnold in calculation. 'Maybe our Ms Stannard should pick her bosom friends more carefully, hey, bonny lad? Though, of course, birds of a feather do tend to use the same nests . . .'

'I've got work to do,' Arnold said brusquely.

'Ain't we all,' Picton replied in a cheerful tone. 'Tell you what, though, Arnold — I can't see Ms Stannard taking this lying down, if you'll excuse the expression.' He leered confidentially. 'She'll want to get her long fingernails dug deep in this one . . . she won't be able to let it alone. Not her . . .'

He was proved right the next day.

Arnold had been in the office for only an hour when he was called to Karen Stannard's room. On this occasion he was ushered in immediately, without any of the statutory waiting time in the outer office with the glowering Miss Sansom.

'Sit down, Arnold,' Karen Stannard said briskly, clearly seeing this as an occasion when they would be on the same side. She sat upright behind her desk, the image of efficiency, crisp white blouse, dark-blue suit jacket, a minimum of make-up, hair drawn back discreetly, long, slim fingers placed firmly on the folder in front of her. Her eyes were fixed on him; they seemed a deep, honest colour this morning, marked with departmental concern.

She came straight to the point.

'What did you make of that disgraceful performance at Ravenstone?' she asked bluntly.

Arnold shrugged. 'I found Stillwater's behaviour incredibly rude — and inexplicable. It was an attitude that I found — I don't know — out of character in the circumstances.

I admit the presentation was by invitation, but my guess is that there was some other agenda, some other reason for the exclusion of Miss Nicholas from the lunch.'

'Not just the lunch.'

'That only makes my point.' Arnold furrowed his brow. 'I was extremely interested to hear Miss Nicholas talking about her work . . . she has clearly opened up an exciting field of study which could prove of great assistance to archaeological investigation. Her expertise will be a loss to the dig — assuming she had intended helping out there.'

'I'm sure she'd have wished to do so. And as for your summation of her skills and talents, I quite agree,' Karen Stannard said, preening as though she had been personally responsible for the discovery of those talents.

'So why Stillwater should insist that she be barred from the site is beyond my comprehension. There's clearly bad blood between her and Stillwater—'

'Not so. They hadn't met before, according to Cate.'

'Then Stillwater's been told something about her — and her work maybe — that caused him to impose the ban. Do you know what it might be?'

Karen Stannard was silent for a few moments, staring fixedly at Arnold. Then she said, 'You've booked some leave next week.'

Arnold's heart sank. 'Yes. I'm going to Scotland.'

She considered the matter. He summoned up arguments in his mind to counter any suggestions that he should postpone his leave. Then, to his surprise, Karen Stannard said, 'I hope you get good weather. I trust you'll enjoy the break — you've been working pretty hard lately.'

Astonished, Arnold replied, 'I'm looking forward to it. I'm going to take a look at the crannogs up—'

'You've got a fair amount on at the moment,' she interrupted tensely. 'But most of it can wait, I would think. There's something I want you to do, however, before you go on leave.' She tapped a finger on the file in front of her. 'I've pulled this file — it doesn't say a great deal. I want you to look more carefully into it.'

'What is it?'

'It relates to Ravenstone.' She hesitated. 'There's something funny going on, I feel it in my bones. I've talked at length with Cate about it — the barring from the site seems to me to have some sinister implications. Are you aware that university staff were involved as consultants at one stage, on the feasibility study for the Ravenstone development?'

Arnold shrugged. 'No, but it's common enough practice.'

'Some of them have been talking to Cate. They gave her a copy of the feasibility study. There's something rather interesting about the background . . . involving the Adler Foundation.'

'I don't understand,' Arnold said, frowning.

Karen Stannard leaned back in her chair, placing her fingertips together thoughtfully. She lowered her head, fixing her brilliant eyes on Arnold. 'Had you heard that there was bad blood between the Farston Trust and the Adler Foundation?'

'I'm not sure . . .'

'The background is that Lord Farston held a large tract of land on Ravenstone Fell; he and his ancestors treated it merely as a grouse moor, and didn't handle that too well, in fact. The railway company was floated in the 1840s as a limited company largely owned by the Farstons, but with a substantial shareholding later sold to the Adlers. When the company collapsed in the 1860s it seems the Farstons themselves managed to come out of it fairly well. The Adler family did not. They held a substantial shareholding, and were always, as a family, rather more philanthropically inclined than the Farstons. They didn't take kindly to the collapse — and their losses. They held a grudge for years — they felt that the Farstons had milked the railway company, failed to support it, and were largely responsible for the decline of Digby Thore.'

'That's all rather a long time ago,' Arnold murmured.

'Old wounds can fester,' Karen Stannard snapped. 'Anyway, the battle has been rumbling on for two generations, until the Adlers set up their foundation to hold the neck of land above Digby Thore, when they sold up generally and moved out of the area. This was shortly after the Farston Trust was established, just before Lord Farston died, without issue. Now, the question is, how come the two trusts became chummy enough recently to actually arrange for Adler Foundation land to be transferred into the Ravenstone operation, in support of the use of Farston Trust objectives?'

Puzzled, Arnold shook his head. 'I don't see a problem there — both trusts are probably concerned with the support and development of the area.'

'Maybe . . .' Her tone was distrustful. 'But what about the trustees? From what I hear their attitude towards each other can be described as . . . inimical.' She grimaced, baring her immaculately white, even teeth. 'There's something that just doesn't ring true. It's nothing I can put my finger on, nothing in the file, but . . . I'd like you to look into it.'

'Into what?' Arnold asked in surprise.

'I want you to find out just what persuaded the Adler Foundation to hand over the access land to the Ravenstone project.'

'This is departmental business?' Arnold queried.

'It's an instruction from me,' she replied crisply, 'and as far as I'm concerned it is departmental business. We made recommendations to various committees about the Ravenstone project. The last thing the department will want is to find that there's some skulduggery in the background that could cause us embarrassment.'

'But we've no real reason to believe—'

'Look into it. You can put other matters aside. Look into it, and let me have a report on my desk before you go to Scotland.'

* * *

There was no escape from the commission. Angrily, and with considerable misgivings, Arnold collected all the departmental files relating to the initial submissions for planning approval, and the supporting papers, and began to delve deep into the establishment of the Ravenstone Fell development. He pulled out plans for the area, pored over early railway documents and gleaned what he could from the documentation held by the local authority archives with regard to the original railway. That led him towards the newspaper archives in Newcastle Library. He spent hours in the carrels reading local newspapers that carried details of the building of the railway in 1850, and the disputes that had inevitably arisen out of the work being carried on.

He soon realized that the arguments that had occurred between the Farstons and the Adlers were more serious than he had thought. To that extent at least Karen Stannard was right. There had been much bad blood between the Farston and Adler families.

Some of it went back to the early 1800s. Lord Farston had been a typical landed aristocrat with a large number of acres in the North and a fixed idea about a person's place in the world. His family had inevitably, from time to time, been somewhat impoverished by wastrel sons, but had managed to struggle on with the title and their landholdings. They retained their sense of social status and it was therefore with a sense of dismay that the then Lord Farston saw the arrival of a city entrepreneur, Simon Adler, in the area.

Adler was a merchant banker — in 'trade' as far as Farston was concerned — who had made his millions out of discounted loans to Russia and Chile in the frenetic activity after the Napoleonic Wars. He had linked himself with the great financier Nathan Rothschild and had managed to steer clear of the financial disasters that had struck many in the city during the 1830s. He had retired to Northumberland, purchasing a large tract of land adjacent to Ravenstone. He was seen as an upstart outsider by Lord Farston, who resented his presence and his opulent lifestyle.

Things had changed by the 1850s. The Farston family had promoted the railway line. The Adlers had been persuaded to support it and had done so enthusiastically, expecting to buy a more favourable social position among the neighbours. But it had all turned sour when the railway venture collapsed. The then Lord Farston had got out when the shares were at their peak, and had made a large amount of money. The Adler family had not fared so well — they were left holding virtually worthless shares.

The Adler family protested bitterly when they found their shares worthless — they claimed they had been conned by the Farstons, and had proclaimed the fact. There had been a court action for libel as a consequence. The two parties had finally settled out of court in 1882, after a protracted and bitter legal wrangle — the Farston fortune was being badly bitten into by legal costs and the Adler fortune also was being drained by legal fees. The resultant bitterness had lasted for generations. Then the last of the Farstons had set up the trust to hold Farston land, including Ravenstone Fell, and the Adler Foundation had also been established. Given the bad blood between the families, setting up the trusts was almost a competitive tit for tat, Arnold thought — but it did nothing to support Karen Stannard's thesis, whatever that was, and it took Arnold no further forward.

In the end, he thought the best thing to do was to take advantage of his acquaintance with the solicitor to the Adler Foundation, the man he had met at the Ravenstone presentation: Nick Towers.

The solicitor had an office in Morpeth, a significant enough distance away from the centre of the town to make the address unfashionable in legal terms. It was clearly a small country practice — a one-man operation tucked away in a side street, in a row of town houses that were used as small business offices, interspersed with flats that had seen better days. There was a decayed, depressing dinginess about the road that caused Arnold to wonder why Towers would have chosen to set up practice there. When he climbed the stairs to the first floor, he found that there was a middle-aged secretary sitting in splendid isolation in a small room furnished with threadbare carpeting and scanty office equipment. He got the impression she was the only employee.

'Mr Towers will be able to see you right away,' she said in a soft Scottish burr. 'You can go straight in.'

She led the way down a narrow corridor, introduced him, asked if he would like a cup of coffee and closed the door gently behind him. Nick Towers was standing behind his desk, shirt-sleeved, with a pile of files in front of him. Arnold glanced around. The shelves were clear, and he wondered whether Towers had deliberately taken the files from the shelves to give the appearance of being busy. To Arnold's eye, this one-man practice did not seem to be a flourishing one.

'The life of a country solicitor.' Nick Towers laughed nervously. 'Back streets and overwork. Do you smoke? No? Do you mind if I . . . ?'

Arnold shook his head. 'It's good of you to see me at such short notice.'

'No problem,' Nick Towers exclaimed. He lit a cigarette and drew on it deeply, explaining that Arnold had come at a good time. While he was usually inundated with work, it so happened that apart from the files in front of him he was relatively free at the moment, and he was able to fit Arnold in without too much trouble.

'Well, I don't want to take up too much of your time,' Arnold said, as the door opened and the secretary came in with two cups of coffee.

When she had gone, Towers asked, 'Well, what is it I can do for you? Legal problems?'

'No, not really,' Arnold hastened to say, conscious of the hopeful note in the solicitor's voice. 'It's information and background I'm seeking, really. We've had some queries arise with regard to the Ravenstone development. There are a few outstanding points we need to deal with in the department. I thought maybe you would be able to help. It's largely to do with the Adler Foundation.'

'Anything I can do,' Towers said slowly, inspecting the glowing end of his cigarette. 'What specifically is bothering you?'

Arnold was struggling. He was still not convinced that the Department of Museums and Antiquities should be involved in this investigation. He didn't even know what he was supposed to be looking for. But Karen Stannard expected a report by Friday, so he had to do his best. 'Well, I suppose it's not so much specific points . . . Really, it's a matter of the relationship between the Adler Foundation and the Farston Trust, and how they came together in the Ravenstone development. I understood from you, when we met at the presentation, that you are legal adviser to the Adler Foundation.'

'That's right,' Towers said carefully.

'Are you also a trustee?'

There was a short silence. Smoke wreathed upwards from the cigarette in Towers's fingers. The solicitor's lugubrious features seemed to lengthen. He stroked one thin lip with his finger, pulling at it in a nervous gesture. Finally, he admitted, 'Yes, I'm a trustee. We've . . . my family's had a long legal connection with the Adlers. My father . . . he had an office down near the marketplace . . .'

Somewhat different from this backwater, Arnold thought, as the man's voice died away. 'There's a long history of animosity, I understand, between the Adlers and the Farstons,' Arnold said carefully. 'That would seem to be all over now, since the trusts were established.'

Towers cleared his throat nervously. 'I think it was all a personal thing . . . people got angry with each other way back, it got sort of carried on as a family feud. I remember my father telling me . . .' He drew nervously on his cigarette. 'But things inevitably change when personalities are removed. The setting up of trust arrangements naturally takes a lot of the sting out of problems that were of long standing.'

Arnold nodded. 'That stands to reason. The Adler Foundation was established after the Farston Trust, I believe?'

'That's right. After the last Lord Farston died, and the Adler family — cousins really of the original family — moved away.'

'Was it in any way competitive?'

Towers blinked. 'I don't quite understand.'

Arnold shrugged. 'You know . . . if there was bad blood, there might have been the feeling that if one party was trying to do something, the other might try to stop it, or compete with it, in the setting up of the trusts.'

'Nothing like that.' An edge of strain seemed to have come into Towers's voice. He coughed, and sipped his coffee. Arnold looked at him thoughtfully.

'Is there anything in the objects of the Adler Foundation which is . . . shall we say, inserted as a counter to the objects of the Farston Trust?'

'I'm not over familiar with the Farston Trust,' Towers said quickly. 'But I don't understand the drift of your questions, Mr Landon. What exactly are you after? What is it you want to know?'

Arnold shook his head. 'I'm not certain, really,' he said ruefully. 'I've been given this task, but . . . well, I'm pretty much in the dark. It's really a matter of finding out what led to the Adler Foundation grant—'

'Sale,' Towers interrupted quickly.

'Sorry, *sale* of land to the Ravenstone development, in support of the Farston arrangement with Cossman International. Without the addition of the Adler land, the project could not have gone forward. Who are the other trustees of the Adler Foundation, by the way?'

'Oh, you needn't bother them,' Towers said quickly. 'One is a retired farmer from Felton, then there's Mrs Savage, living up at Berwick — she moved to be near her daughter — and Mr Torrance and his brother, who used to be tenants on the land. For two generations . . . their families, that is. Long-standing arrangement.'

'I see. And you advised them.'

'Of course. That was my function.' Nick Towers hesitated, furrowing his brow and injecting a serious note into his voice. 'I think it's worth saying, Mr Landon, that in all situations where two families fall out and a long-standing argument runs and runs—'

'Even getting to court,' Arnold added, noting Towers's growing nervousness, as he licked his lips and narrowed his eyes against the cigarette smoke.

Towers squinted at Arnold. 'The libel case, you mean. Ah, that was settled. Anyway, the point I'm making is that there must come a time when someone has to stand up and stop the nonsense. After all, as the generations pass even the *reason* for the quarrel gets lost in the mists of time. And what's it all for? As someone said — "The end of all is death, and man's life passeth away suddenly as a shadow"—'

'The quarrel was financial,' Arnold suggested patiently. 'Such quarrels leave scars. The Adlers felt they'd been conned by Lord Farston.'

'Even so. But it was all so long ago. More than a hundred years, for God's sake! And when the Adler trustees looked at what was being proposed for Ravenstone Fell, what it would mean in the long run for Digby Thore, what employment it could bring to the area, it was obvious what my advice should be — and the other trustees agreed with me. We could not in all conscience allow a specific provision in the objects to be used as an argument to deny progress, and we took a vote on it and the decision was—'

'A *specific provision*, Mr Towers?' Arnold asked.

There was a short silence. The sad eyes seemed to grow larger and the thin mouth drooped as Towers realized he had said more than he had perhaps intended. For a moment Arnold thought he detected a swift panic in the solicitor's face, but then the man made a clear effort to pull himself together — the long jaw tightened and the eyes were hooded. 'Do you know much about trusts, Mr Landon?'

'I can't say I do.' He had been involved in trust activity several times, in fact, but was curious to hear what Towers had to say.'

Nick Towers finished his coffee slowly, then stubbed out his cigarette in the saucer. He stared at the stain of wet ash for a little while, thinking. Arnold felt he was trying to give the impression of a keen legal mind at work, explaining things to a layman. But a tell-tale vein beat regularly in his forehead. His skin seemed pale, his demeanour vulnerable.

'When a trust is set up,' he said portentously, 'the objects are stated. They might seem at the time to be good, sensible, clear objects. But time has a way of eroding the meaning, or the rationale for those objects. The initial trustees will certainly be insistent on the completion of those objects . . . but as time goes on, views can change . . .'

'But surely, trustees, whenever they are appointed, are under an obligation to fulfil the objects of the trust. Or they incur personal liability, for breach of trust.'

'It's all a matter of degree,' Towers contended. 'As time goes by some objects become . . . unworkable. Others become, impossible, undesirable, or against the mood of the times. I might cite an example: a trust for the legalization of smack.' He laughed unconvincingly. 'That would go down a bomb, wouldn't it! However . . . the formality in such cases is that if the trustees want to change the objects of the trust they must apply to the Charity Commissioners to . . . vary the terms of the trust imposed upon the trustees. In that manner, with agreement of the Commissioners, the trust can be . . . brought up to date.'

'Is that what was done with the Adler Foundation?'

'Yes.' There was no prevarication in the solicitor's tone.

'What was the object that was changed, then?' Arnold asked gently.

Nick Towers sighed. 'There's no reason why I can't tell you,' he said stiffly. 'I suppose in a sense you were quite right . . . there was an underlying imperative in the Adler Foundation. It was inserted to prevent the Farston Trust attaining the full enjoyment and benefits of its own holdings. It was a continuation of a policy carried out by the Adler family ever since the libel action ended. Ravenstone has good grouse moors, but it's not good farming land — the farms have a problem: access to water. Simon Adler had bought his land with riparian rights that prevented Lord Farston getting access to certain streams. In the early days, that wasn't a problem. But after the railway business, the Adlers withdrew permissions. It remained a bone of contention between the families after the railway share crash. The Adlers refused to allow access and the quarrel continued. Finally, after the last Lord Farston died and the Farston Trust had been set up, the Adler Foundation was established with the same underlying imperative.'

'To block the full use and enjoyment of Farston properties.'

'Precisely.' Nick Towers eyed Arnold with a sideways glance and scratched nervously at his hollow cheek. 'When the Ravenstone project was first mooted by Cossman International and tenders were being put out we were approached to sell some of the Adler holdings, to allow access to the main road at Digby Thore. We . . . we discussed it among the trustees. The view was certainly expressed that the trust deed prevented any such arrangement. It would be against the imperative: no assistance to Farston land. There was also a view that old quarrels should be allowed to die, that the income would be welcome from a sale and that a number of charities would benefit — and I was able to advise them that the permission of the Charity Commissioners should be sought.'

'Normally they would agree to any request they deemed reasonable,' Arnold suggested.

'That's right. And this was reasonable. End of a family feud. And it was for the benefit of the area,' Towers stated with a sudden vehemence. 'The need to sustain the trust objects, to continue an old, long-dead quarrel, should not be seen to be paramount. There . . . there was a great deal at stake . . .'

They were both silent for a while. There was a general air of nervousness in the room which puzzled Arnold. What Towers had told him seemed reasonable enough, given the objectives of the Ravenstone Fell project as he understood them. And in one sense the Adler imperative would not be broken, since the Ravenstone land had passed to Cossman International. But perhaps it was just that Towers was generally a nervous individual. He was clearly not a successful lawyer, and he had problems at home . . .

Abruptly, Arnold rose to his feet. 'I've taken up too much of your time. Er, I trust your wife is feeling better?'

'Marjorie?' Towers seemed startled for a moment, and then he shrugged. 'Thank you for asking, but she's never . . . never very well. Asthma, a heart condition . . . she seems weighed down with illness most of the time. And treatment . . . nursing can be expensive.'

He accompanied Arnold to the secretary's room. When Arnold left the building and turned into the street, he looked back to the first-floor windows. He thought he caught a glimpse of the solicitor staring after him as he made his way back to the town centre.

Arnold finished his report on the Thursday evening. He placed it on Karen Stannard's desk on Friday morning, then went back to his own office to try to clear a few files away, prior to his departure for Scotland. He had decided to start the drive north that evening, and had booked a room in a hotel at Kelso. He was a little later clearing his desk than he had expected, and most of the staff had gone when he made his way down to the car park. But Karen Stannard never left the office early, either. He met her on the stairs.

'Have you had time to read the report?' he asked her.

She looked at him vaguely for a moment, and then her eyes cleared. She gave him a half-smile, slightly secretive, as though they were sharing some hidden knowledge. 'Yes, Mr Landon, I've read it. Food for thought, don't you think?'

In the context in which she'd asked him to carry out the investigation, he couldn't decide what on earth she meant.

2

Arnold left Morpeth about six-thirty and drove to Kelso. It was a pity that he was driving in the dark for the last few miles because he always enjoyed the scenery in this part of the world. He stayed overnight at the hotel in Kelso, taking a walk around the square before dinner, and browsing around the ruins of the abbey. He left early next morning and drove north-west, heading for Galashiels and Peebles. He stopped for a pub lunch north of Glasgow and in the afternoon drove alongside Loch Lomond, under the bulk of Ben Lomond, on to Taynuilt, where he intended basing himself, to take a look at Loch Awe.

Arnold enjoyed the break from the Morpeth office hugely, spending his time walking the hills, climbing Ben Cruachan to take in the far views across Oban towards Mull and the distant island of Skye. He took the ferry from Oban one day, through the Sound of Mull to Ardnamurchan and the air was bright and clear, the sun warm on his back. It was odd, whenever he came to Scotland, the weather turned out fine. It was not the same for many tourists.

But he spent time at Loch Awe also, where he was able to discuss with a local team the underwater excavations they had made, locating a man-made island consisting of a two metre thick layer of vegetable material overlain with stones, silt and gravel and capped by larger boulders. It had been built in the mid-first millennium BC, and was located some fifty metres from the shore, linked to the shoreline by a wooden causeway.

The preservation of wood was excellent and they had found flat wooden dishes, wooden mugs, a paddle and even a whistle, but bone had been poorly preserved in the deposits. The presence of live animals on the crannog, however, was proved by sheep and cattle droppings excavated from the floor of the round house that had been erected on the crannog.

The excavation director was flattered by Arnold's enthusiastic interest and close questioning, and responded by bringing him into their circle when he explained who he was. It all ended up, before he left to go south again, with an extended ceilidh, where a considerable amount of alcohol was consumed, much singing was done, a certain amount of dancing undertaken, and eternal friendship drunkenly sworn to by all present.

Arnold had a hangover when he drove back south.

He rang Jane when he reached Morpeth on the Sunday afternoon, feeling fairly certain she would have little sympathy for his condition, but her answerphone had been switched on, so he merely left a message for her, to say he was back safely. He opened his mail, but there was nothing of interest or significance for him. He made himself a meal; opened a bottle of wine on the hair-of-the-dog theory, and watched a film on television.

He did not feel up to watching the news, national or regional. He felt vaguely unsettled — the result, he guessed, of having enjoyed himself so much in Scotland, and not being particularly happy at the thought of a return to work on Monday morning. By ten he was bored and decided on an early night. He read for a while, but thereafter slept badly. The tunes from the ceilidh kept ringing in his mind.

Nevertheless, he was at his desk at the usual time next day. He had an appointment to visit the Evison Church dig, to finally complete the series of reports Karen Stannard had asked for in the first instance, so by nine-thirty he was on the road again. He felt better now, with the Northumberland air in his lungs, and the morning was bright after overnight rain. The fells were a washed grey-green, with the distant Cheviot a hazy blue against the sky.

He took his time at the dig. The Bronze Age burial was proceeding on schedule within the financial constraints, and he knew the dig leader fairly well, having met him several times at various archaeological sites over the years. They took lunch together in the local pub, and Arnold did not leave to return to the office until after three.

He checked in at five, when most people were preparing to leave. One of the secretaries saw him come in and hurried across.

'Mr Landon, have you spoken to Miss Sansom? She's been looking for you.'

Arnold groaned mentally. He had a presentiment that this meant trouble. He rang through to her office. She advised him he had better join the director in his room immediately; there was a certain pleasure in her tone that boded ill, as far as Arnold was concerned.

He walked along the corridor with a sinking heart. Miss Sansom smiled at him when he entered her room. It was the first time he had ever seen her smile and it was not a pleasant experience — it held hints of satisfied malice. He tapped on the door to Simon Brent-Ellis's room and when he heard the director call out, he entered.

They were sitting around the boardroom table at the far end of the room, staring at him. Karen Stannard was there, eyes blazing with wrath and embarrassment. Simon Brent-Ellis sat beside her, his features pale and tense. In the chair at the head of the table was the chief executive, Powell Frinton, a lean, ascetic-featured lawyer with a mean mouth. He was noted for being completely lacking in a sense of humour and for holding the view that rules were there to be rigidly enforced. He was an unloved man, but an effective chief executive for all that. Arnold didn't like him. He knew no one who did. There were rumours that Powell Frinton's wife felt the same way.

Arnold stared at the group facing him, aware of the grim silence, but puzzled at the fact that the hostility in the room seemed to be directed at him.

'Where have you been?' Karen Stannard snapped nastily, first into the arena. 'I've been trying to contact you all day.' There was an oddly defensive note in her aggression.

'Evison Church,' Arnold explained. 'You'd asked me to—'

'Never mind that,' Powell Frinton interposed briskly. 'You're here now. Sit down.' He waited while Arnold pulled forward a chair, to sit opposite Karen Stannard and Brent-Ellis. Powell Frinton exposed his teeth in an unpleasant grimace. 'I suppose you know why you're here. We want an explanation.'

'Explanation? About what? What's happened?' Arnold asked, completely bewildered.

There was a brief silence. Powell Frinton's mean little eyes bored into Arnold's. Simon Brent-Ellis shuffled nervously, adjusting a gaudy tie which Powell Frinton no doubt disapproved of, and Karen Stannard sat stiff-backed, her glance frosty and her mouth tight, but with an uncharacteristically edgy nervousness apparent in her bearing. Arnold stared at her, but she did not meet his eye. He suddenly had the clear impression that he was not the only one in trouble.

'What's happened?' he asked again.

'You were on leave last week,' Powell Frinton said in measured tones.

'That's right.'

'When did you get back?'

'Yesterday afternoon.'

'You have a television set, I suppose?' asked Powell Frinton, in a sarcastic tone, as he leaned forward slightly and interlaced his fingers.

'Of course. What is this all about?'

'You didn't watch the programme last night?' Simon Brent-Ellis burst out, angrily. 'You didn't watch that damned woman . . . you didn't see what your stupidity has brought about?'

He was blustering, trying to make up lost ground with the chief executive, attempting to demonstrate his authority and control in his department. He was a weak man trying desperately to demonstrate strength. Arnold shook his head. 'I'm afraid I've no idea what you're talking about.' He glanced at Karen Stannard again, but she was sitting rigidly, avoiding his eye.

'Then we'd better bring you up to date,' Powell Frinton suggested in a silkily menacing tone. 'Ms Stannard?'

She rose, her back stiff with resentment but unable to make a protest at his assumption it was she — a mere woman — who should do what was necessary. She walked across the room to the television set against the wall, pressed the power button and switched on the video cassette recorder that was located on the stand underneath it. There was a whirring sound, she paused, wound the tape back and the pictures leapt up on the screen.

She stepped back, stared at it angrily for a few moments, and then returned to her seat.

'Perhaps you'd better watch this rather carefully,' Powell Frinton suggested to Arnold.

It was Cate Nicholas. She was speaking directly to the camera in the television studio. Her features were composed, but there was a hard glint in her eyes that seemed to be accentuated by the studio lights.

'. . . But enough of the problems that we are seeing in the West End of Newcastle. I'm sure we'll all have our own views about how they could be sorted out with relative ease — and who should be held responsible for the moral degeneration, evidence of which we've seen on the screen, in this programme tonight.' She paused, smiling grimly. 'But I promised you controversy in this series, so let's finish with another item, which I think might be of interest to us all.'

Briefly, she consulted a paper in front of her, then her eyes came up to the auto-prompt once more. 'I promised you that this programme will be one that brings to your attention the anomalies, the scandals, the wrongdoings that occur in our midst—'

'You're aware, Mr Landon, that this is the first of a series of new programmes put out by Ms Nicholas?' Powell Frinton rasped.

'I'd heard she might get a series, after her first appearance . . .'

'—and I'd like to sign off with an item that's come to my attention just recently,' Cate Nicholas was continuing. 'It stems from what has been described as an important, innovative scheme for the benefit of the Northumberland hinterland — I always get suspicious when I hear words like that! Its claim includes the regeneration of an almost deserted village; the provision of new jobs and new opportunities in an area of exceptional beauty; environmentally sound, politically correct activity, I'm sure you'll agree — and thrown in with it is the chance for an archaeological investigation that will show us some of the secrets of our ancestors! Do I hear you applaud? Do I hear you raise the roof with your acclamation?'

'I don't care for the woman's style,' Powell Frinton ground out. 'Nor for her sarcastic, somewhat hysterical delivery.'

On the taped programme, Cate Nicholas was smiling in amused contempt, as though she had heard the chief executive's comment. 'Well, I suppose you would be forgiven for believing that such a scheme does deserve acclamation. After all, it's received the blessing of the local authority — and they must be right — the planning committee — all full of well-meaning men — and our very own Department of Museums and Antiquities—'

Simon Brent-Ellis wriggled uncomfortably in his chair and cast a despairing, vindictive glance at Arnold.

'—not to mention Northern Heritage, who are pumping in considerable sums of money to support the archaeological activity. And then there's central government. Can it really be true that in a notoriously tight-belted period they are going to put up several million by way of grant in aid of the building programme envisaged by this development programme? It seems they are . . . but maybe they should be taking a cooler look at the whole thing.'

'Here we go,' Powell Frinton announced, grimacing.

'You see, if you take a look behind the facade of this huge development up on Ravenstone Fell, there are some questions you might like to ask. Some little birds tell me, for instance, that the company developing this programme is not as financially sound as it would like us to believe; that its management is in trouble, and that this development is a last-gasp effort on its part to prop up its failing fortunes.'

She smiled again, confidentially.

'Moreover, one has to ask whether the local authority concerned ever asked the right questions when the planning application came in. Can a near-bankrupt company — and I mean intellectually as well as financially — really expect to complete this project — with government money or not? And is the project merely one to benefit the area as a whole? Or is it lining private pockets? Let's take a particular example . . .'

Arnold was aware of Karen Stannard tensing in her seat across the table from him. He glanced at her. She was staring fixedly at the screen, even though she must have seen the programme several times by now.

'Trust law is pretty hard on trustees. If they act in breach of trust, they can be held personally accountable for their actions. Prison sentences, financial ruin . . . it can happen. So what about this development I'm talking about? Would it be of interest to you to know that there are two trusts involved — two trusts whose trustees don't speak to each other, and who are representative of a long-standing legal battle, a feud that's gone on for almost a hundred years? And here they are suddenly — all lovey-dovey, working in harness. I wonder how that's come about?'

Cate Nicholas raised her chin, staring challengingly at the camera. A jeering note came into her voice. 'They'll tell you it's because it's time to end quarrels, to put the past behind them. But my information is that there's something else behind this agreement of rivals. It's all to do with an approach from an ailing company to one of the trusts. It's about the whiff of corruption, of under-the-counter payments. It's about people who are short of money being paid to support appropriate decisions. It's about tainted legal advice from a lawyer who has a practice on its last legs and who possibly hopes to gain financially from the transaction. It's about planning departments who don't do their job properly, local authority officers who turn their heads away from problems, simplistic clods who look at a development scheme and fail to see the cardboard nature of the company promoting it. It all adds up to failure and perhaps more than failure . . . the sour, sad whiff of corruption . . .'

'That's enough,' Powell Frinton snapped. 'You can turn it off now, Ms Stannard.'

Arnold sensed that the chief executive was enjoying his role, whipping Karen Stannard. He wondered whether she had already received a tongue-lashing, of the kind he suspected he was about to get. Powell Frinton waited dourly until she had resumed her seat, and then he turned to fix Arnold with a stony glare.

'Now you've been . . . put in the picture, as they say, what comment do you have to make?'

Arnold shook his head. 'I'm not sure what to say. This whole thing is a . . . surprise.'

'You've met Ms Nicholas?'

'Of course. She was up at the development a week or so ago, when they held a presentation.'

'Do you believe what she says is accurate?'

'Accurate?' Arnold stared at him in surprise. 'I've no way of knowing exactly what she's driving at! Certainly, what she's saying seems to me to verge on the libellous, but you as a lawyer will know more about that.'

'Truth is a good defence to a charge of libel,' Powell Frinton snapped, 'and a woman like that wouldn't speak out on television unless she had grounds for what she says. Certainly, we're studying the broadcast carefully in the legal department at the moment. I've no doubt other people will be doing the same. But I return to the specific issue. Do you believe it's accurate?'

'I don't understand.'

'You were responsible for the preparation of a report for Ms Stannard. I've read it. I've got it here.' His thin, bony fingers tapped the manila folder in front of him.

'The report provides no basis for what Cate Nicholas said on that tape.'

'Doesn't it?' Powell Frinton's tone became edged with menace. 'It seems from this report that you had a meeting with a certain Mr Towers, solicitor to the Adler Foundation. You state the background to the agreement between Cossman International, the Adler Foundation and the Farston Trust. And you hint at the possibility that the legal advice given to the Adler Foundation might have been in breach of the trust objectives—'

'I didn't actually say that!' Arnold argued. 'I suggested that there *might* be a breach, which would have been agreed to by the Charity Commissioners, and I added that I hoped they'd been given the full facts. That's not the same as saying—'

'Forgive me. To ears willing to hear, it says a great deal' Powell Frinton smiled thinly — 'and perhaps more than you suspect. I have already been in touch with the Charity Commissioners. They have confirmed verbally and unoffi-cially to me — I have an old acquaintance who works there — that Mr Towers did in fact seek their permission, and received it. But your point remains valid — they might not have been given all the facts.'

Arnold took a deep breath. 'You'll excuse me, sir, but I fail to see what this all has to do with my report. The state-ments I made to Ms Stannard in that document were made in confidence, to be used only in the department, and contain no libellous matter, though they do raise certain questions. It seems to me that Cate Nicholas is raising the same questions, but in a more aggressive, public manner, and with access, it seems, to more information that I was able to glean. I mean, the comments about Cossman International, the hints about corruption, I've discovered no such evidence and I don't know where she's got it from.'

'Not from you, then?' Powell Frinton asked, sarcasm marking his tone.

Arnold glared at him, his temper beginning to rise. 'What's that supposed to mean?'

The chief executive observed him for a little while as the atmosphere in the room grew even more tense. He stroked his chin thoughtfully. He glanced at Simon Brent-Ellis. 'Director, you have thoughts about this?'

If he did, Simon Brent-Ellis seemed reluctant to spell them out. He wriggled in his chair, tugging at his flowered waistcoat. 'When I saw the programme last night I was appalled. I read Landon's report this morning, after an interview with Ms Stannard. It seemed to me that maybe Landon was holding information back, that he had spoken to Cate Nicholas, that he had fed her the kind of basic information which should have been confidential to this department, but which allowed her to make these public accusations — which make us look not just fools in County Hall, but even tainted by the allegations of corruption. My wife agreed with my summation.' He coughed, wriggled uncomfortably. Lamely, he added, 'As a councillor, she advised I talk to you, Chief Executive, immediately.'

It was a long speech for the Director of the Department of Museums and Antiquities. On any other occasion, Arnold might have been amused, not least by the thought that Brent-Ellis's political wife might have been making his life hell at home on a Sunday night. Now, he was just angry. 'I submitted that report a week last Friday. I have not kept a private copy. I drove to Scotland on Friday evening. I neither spoke to anyone

— least of all Ms Nicholas, for whom I had conceived a personal dislike, now exacerbated by her performance on television — and I was in contact with no person from Northumberland the whole week I was away.' Arnold lifted his head angrily. 'I leaked no information from that report to anyone.'

'You've covered the situation since you wrote it,' Powell Frinton said with the caution of a lawyer. 'What about before it was submitted?'

'It was confidential to Ms Stannard. I discussed it with no one,' Arnold insisted, his temper rising even more at Powell Frinton's insinuation.

There was a long silence, broken only by the light drumming sound from the chief executive's fingers, tapping on the table. At last, he sniffed. 'So you deny there's been a leak from you, Mr Landon. Ms Stannard . . . do you have anything to add?'

'The report has not left my office,' she said, her face pale, and her lips tight.

'Then we would seem to be in a quandary. Perhaps we should blame the cleaners,' Powell Frinton suggested witheringly. 'All right, we must leave it there for the time being. I have already had three councillors on the phone . . . I imagine there'll be threats of lawsuits flying around — Cossman International, the Adler trustees, and whoever else feels referred to by the comments made on the programme. What disturbs me is the thought that the castigation by this woman on television may well be founded on something that's happened in this department. The matter doesn't end here. We cannot afford to get involved in the kind of lawsuits that are almost certain to be flying around after this. Unless . . . unless what that woman says is true.'

The chief executive rose to his feet. He gave Simon Brent-Ellis a withering glance and left the room. Arnold and Karen Stannard waited for a moment, but Brent-Ellis waved a weary, despairing hand and they left.

'My office,' Karen Stannard said sharply, her eyes hot with anger.

Arnold followed silently in her wake. He closed the door quietly behind them and waited. She stood beside her desk, with her back to him. Her shoulders were rigid with a fury she found difficult to control. He wondered what was coming.

Slowly, she turned to face him. Her eyes were unreadable now as she stared past him, over his left shoulder. He suddenly realized she was finding great difficulty in getting her words out.

'I'm sorry,' she said at last, in a half-strangled tone. He was taken aback. 'About what?'

Her glance slid, her eyes still vague, but with dark shadows of anger staining them once more. She was making a determined effort, but finding it difficult. 'I . . . I had been accused in there by that pompous ass of a director, and then by that cold snake Powell Frinton. I denied leaking the report to Cate Nicholas. That made them home in on you . . .' Her glance fixed on him, bleakly. 'I'm grateful for the . . . for the way you behaved in there.'

'I don't understand.'

She was pale. 'I know it was not you who leaked the report to Cate Nicholas. I'm grateful for your forbearance in not . . . not suggesting it might have been me. Because . . . in spite of my denial to them, it was.' Suddenly, her fury broke, perhaps not least because of her need to show gratitude to Arnold. 'The bitch! I thought she was a friend! After that scene up at Ravenstone we were both mad as hell, both swore we'd get even with Stillwater! That's why I asked you to do a little probing — Cate Nicholas said there was gossip at the university about the Adler deal — and when your report came in I discussed it with her. I didn't lie to Powell Frinton and Brent-Ellis when I said it never left my office . . . but I had discussed it with her. And she used some of it, used it in that bloody broadcast. I never knew she would do that, betraying a confidence, putting my job at risk that way, just to boost her bloody programme and get her revenge on Stillwater for his rudeness!'

She flounced around behind her desk, thumped a frustrated fist on the manila folder, and came out with a surprising string of unladylike obscenities. Then she straightened, expelled her breath in a gust, straining to control the violence of her anger.

'If that bloody woman thinks she can treat me like that, she's got another think coming! Her and that stupid cow Angie Rothwell! Cate Nicholas might feel she's had her revenge on Stillwater, but it's been at my expense. She's used me — and no one gets away with that! She'll find I can scratch as much as any other cat — and more deeply than most!'

She stood there breathing hard for almost a minute, then slowly she raised her head, and stared challengingly at Arnold. The earlier anger and frustration had been overcome. She was now clearly of a determined frame of mind. He also had the impression she was already regretting what she would regard as a sign of weakness — making an apology to a male subordinate.

'This conversation has been confidential,' she warned, her eyes glittering malevolently.

Arnold almost said he wouldn't dream of repeating her obscenities, but allowed discretion to get the upper hand. He didn't think she'd be in the mood for pleasantries. 'Of course,' he said.

There was a degree of uncertainty in the way she looked at him, and then she nodded, abruptly. 'I think that will do for now,' she announced, the old coldness returning to her tones. 'You can go. And you can leave any further action,' she added with a menacing frown, 'to me!'

Arnold had no quarrel with that.

3

Detective Chief Inspector John Culpeper had had a good lunch and was feeling in a mellow mood. He'd been called upon to give a speech to the Rotary Club in Ponteland and having received the necessary permissions — the Chief Constable was a stickler for the regulations — he had enjoyed his lunch and given his talk. He had begun with the old joke against the police — 'There was this man who had trouble. He kept sleeping on the job, so he joined the police' — supplied the local worthies with a string of amusing anecdotes about his experiences in County Durham as a copper on the beat and in Northumberland as a detective, and had sat down to prolonged applause. Moreover, only three of the businessmen present had actually taken their leave early from the gathering. That was a good percentage, he had been informed by the secretary.

'If the speech is boring, they leave in droves,' he'd confided.

Culpeper had therefore been filled with a sense of achievement. It was a pleasant, though cloudy, day, and he hadn't bothered to drive to the village on the outskirts of Newcastle. With a couple of brandies inside him he now enjoyed the walk back to headquarters, which were situated in what had originally been a college of education at the edge of Ponteland. He felt at ease with the world.

As he walked into HQ, he caught a glimpse of Detective Inspector Vic Farnsby, talking to a detective sergeant and a woman, outside one of the interview rooms. He walked on, but there was something about the woman that touched chords in his memory. He had seen her somewhere before. Not in a villain line-up, certainly. She was smartly dressed, not bad-looking, mid-forties maybe, and well-spoken.

Positive in her speech, in fact. Dogmatic, and self-opinionated, — these were the words that came into his head . . . Who the hell was she and where had he come across her?

He walked into the canteen and had a cup of coffee. There were very few people there. The lunchtime rush was over. He sipped the coffee, and mulled over the identity of the woman with the two detectives. She hadn't been looking too pleased; she'd been prodding a finger at Vic Farnsby. Culpeper smiled. He had no objection to people who prodded fingers at Farnsby, in fact, he quite approved of it. The thought warmed him, he hiccupped and, as the taste of brandy rose in his throat, a little light dance tune began to jig in his head.

It had been a good day so far. Then the jingle died. He had a meeting with Farnsby after lunch. He finished his coffee in a mood less light and carefree.

Vic Farnsby was waiting outside John Culpeper's office with a sheaf of files when Culpeper made his way there after dawdling over his coffee. Culpeper nodded and brushed past him. When the detective inspector entered the room behind him, Culpeper waved him to a chair, before ensconcing himself behind his desk with a sigh. These meetings were not something he looked forward to. He disliked being enclosed in a room with the keen ambition of Farnsby, but he was forced to admit that even though the meetings had been Farnsby's idea, they did serve a clear purpose: it meant they were able to get rid of files on a regular basis.

Culpeper did not care for Farnsby. The man was intelligent and sharp-witted, was certainly a favourite of the Chief

Constable's even though he had come through the accelerated graduate scheme, but Culpeper felt there was a weakness, a hollowness about the man that would tend to make him ineffective in the long run. Of course, it could be a matter of prejudice — Culpeper was honest enough to admit that to himself — since Culpeper was stuck in his job and on the way out while Farnsby had a career ahead of him, and was clearly destined to go further, and faster, than John Culpeper ever had or would.

'So, where do we start?' Culpeper asked sourly.

Farnsby stretched his long legs under the desk and leaned back in his chair. He shuffled through the files in his left hand. Culpeper watched him — the man's features were of a saturnine cast, his eyes a pale, washed-out blue. There were occasions when he could make a man shiver. 'Well?' Culpeper barked.

'There's this file first, sir,' Farnsby said, extending the sheet towards Culpeper. 'That series of burglaries out at Darras Hall. Bears all the hallmarks of Tony Weightman, but he got nicked last week and he'll be facing a stretch of three years.'

'Is he going to ask for the Darras Hall jobs to be taken into consideration?'

'Hasn't admitted them yet.'

'No evidence at his house?'

'He'll have fenced all the stuff by now.'

Culpeper grunted in dissatisfaction. 'Put the screws on him, see if he'll help our clear-up rate by coughing on them. Otherwise, even if we're convinced it's him, we'll have to keep the file open. Next?'

'Joe Wiseman. Had a heart attack last week, and there's no way he's ever going to be standing up in court. We've had an open file on him for two years, but intensive care says he won't last the week.' Farnsby shrugged. 'I don't think we'll ever pin the Shields jobs on him now.'

'Close the file.' After a moment, Culpeper added, 'Assuming he doesn't come out of intensive care on his own two legs. I don't trust that villain, heart attack or not.'

'We've then got these three files,' Farnsby said, waving the sheets in front of Culpeper. 'No leads, seven years old, sexual assaults, couple of flashings, but nothing for two years now. I think the files are dead, the guy could have moved out of the area . . . not much point keeping them on hold.'

Culpeper nodded. 'Log them on the computer, but otherwise let's cut down on the paperwork.'

Farnsby nodded. He pulled another sheet and inspected it quietly for a little while. Culpeper leaned back, stared out of the window. He wondered whether he'd better get some new gear for their visit to Greece, him and the missus. It could be hot there and he didn't want to present the image of the typical Brit abroad, white shorts, sandals with socks and a Kiss-Me-Quick hat . . . Farnsby raised his head, clearing his throat, bringing Culpeper back to the present. 'There's this Interpol thing, sir.'

'Interpol? We're holding a file on an Interpol operation?'

'We've held it for almost four years, sir.' Farnsby scratched at his cheek. 'They're advising that the thing can be withdrawn now. It's that Ken Allison case — you remember?'

'I don't. No doubt you do.' Because you've got the bloody file in front of you, Culpeper thought sourly.

'Allison was running a business in the Midlands: computer systems, microchips, that sort of thing. Had an offshoot up here at Newcastle, which ran some Ministry of Defence contracts, another in Edinburgh. Then the Department of Trade and Industry started asking questions. You might remember we opened a file at their request. There was a strong suspicion that Allison had been selling restricted software into Europe — not least into what is now the Czech Republic.'

A vague memory stirred in Culpeper's mind. 'Yes . . . we were asked to keep an eye open for him. But when we tried the company premises they'd closed down—'

'And he'd done a runner. Skipped. Went to earth. The DTI inspectors came up here, sniffed around a while—'

'I remember,' Culpeper growled. 'There was a stuck-up young bastard still wet behind the ears — he more or less implied we'd let Allison slip through our fingers . . . But where the hell were they down south when it mattered?'

Farnsby nodded in sympathy. 'Well, anyway, the last we heard of Allison was that they'd fished him out of the river . . . what was it called?' He consulted the file. 'The Vltava, in Prague. Wherever he'd been hiding himself in the meanwhile, that's where he ended up — in the Vltava. He'd been knifed. Interpol sent us the information that they had a witness to the killing and had a few leads on the killer — gave us a description, suggested that the killing had a connection with the earlier software sales into eastern Europe — though it had been made to look like a mugging, down by the riverside—'

'I remember. You're now suggesting we can close the file?'

'Interpol are suggesting it. It seems they've tracked down the man who did the killing of Allison. A former member of the Stasi, it seems, turned into a hired contract killer for anyone who could put up the money. His name was Havel.'

'Was?'

'He was cornered by the Dutch police in Amsterdam a month ago. Two policemen killed. Havel took a bullet in his throat in the end. They had to fish him and his car out of the canal. Cowboys and Indians stuff. Anyway, as far as Interpol are concerned, that's it.'

'I don't understand,' Culpeper said slowly, his glance fixed on Farnsby's tanned features. They're suggesting we close the file now they're convinced the killer of Ken Allison is himself dead'?'

'That's right.'

'Well, that might suit the information centre we know and love as Interpol, but that can't be the end of the matter, surely. What do the DTI have to say about it?'

'How do you mean? I imagine that now Allison's dead, and his killer has also choked it, that will be that as far as they're concerned.'

Culpeper grunted in irritation. 'The DTI were chasing Allison for these sales of restricted software into eastern

Europe. Allison jumped before they could get their hands on him. He went to earth in Europe. When Allison surfaced, it was from the river. Interpol told us they'd found Allison and were chasing his killer. Now they tell us the Dutch have put a bullet into this . . . Havel character. End of story? I don't see that it is. End of Interpol involvement, maybe. But what about Allison's activities? Are the DTI going to shrug it off, write it off as yesterday's news? In other words, does the trail end with our dead friend Allison?'

'As far as we're concerned—'

'Who the hell paid Havel to kill Allison? And why?'

Farnsby was silent, staring at the file. At last, he said in a nettled tone, 'I was only suggesting we close the file sent to us by Interpol—'

'No. We close the file when we've contacted the DTI for their attitude on the whole thing. What I don't want is another snotty little inspector from a government department running up here to tell us how to operate, or suggesting we've in some way fallen down on the job. I'd be more than happy to close the file on Allison — we've got no bloody leads anyway — but I don't want to do that while there's still a chance that the DTI are going to chase us up. So check with them first, and do nothing with the file until we get a response.'

Farnsby nodded, a dark flush staining his lean cheeks. He proceeded to plough his way through a number of other files that he was recommending they should now close. Culpeper was generous. The brandy was soothingly warm in his stomach and he felt in a better mood now that he had drawn Farnsby's attention to an obvious slip. But then, that was the difference between callowness and experience; between making promotion the hard way, from the beat, through the ranks, instead of being given promotion on a plate, just because there was a degree in the background. He sat back in his chair while Farnsby droned on, flicking through the files. Farnsby had a boring voice, Culpeper concluded.

Some twenty minutes later, Farnsby came to an end. His mouth was tight. He'd been aware of Culpeper's nonchalant waving through of some files. He raised his eyebrows and Culpeper nodded. It had been a fairly painless meeting, for once. There were occasions when Culpeper had to disagree quite severely with Farnsby. He knew the younger man felt that Culpeper kept some of the files open far longer than was necessary, but Culpeper was a hoarder. You never knew when a piece of information in a file might come in handy.

Farnsby, of course, was into computers. He'd never be an old-style copper, not like Culpeper. He was destined for a different kind of job, eventually, that would take him a long way from the realities of the work, and stick him in with the politicians. Wine, dinner-dances, public functions, image . . . not a lot to do with hard-nosed policing.

'That's it, then, sir. Is there anything else?' Farnsby was asking.

Culpeper shook his head. 'No, I don't think so. But don't forget that check with the DTI,' he could not help adding.

Farnsby flushed, rose, and headed for the door. Then a thought struck Culpeper. 'Wait a minute.'

'Sir?'

'When I came in this afternoon you were talking to someone downstairs.'

'Downstairs?' Farnsby raised his eyebrows, pondering for a moment. 'Detective Sergeant Waters, you mean?'

Culpeper nodded. 'Yes, that's right, but there was a woman with you.'

'Hah!' Farnsby's features broke into a malicious grin. 'That's right. Waters was getting an earful from her. I overheard. Thought I'd better help out. Explain the community-policing function, and stress how our manpower was overstretched, that sort of thing.'

'Humph! It's just that her face seemed familiar, but I'm damned if I can recall where I've met her.'

'It might not be that you've met her, sir. She's got a programme on television.'

Culpeper scowled in thought. Television! Of course, that was it. 'Her name . . .'

'Cate Nicholas. She works at the university.'

'Damn it, that's right . . .' It was coming back to Culpeper now. 'She was on last Sunday night — a week ago. She didn't half tear into people. And there was a piece on Monday morning, in the *Journal* — they reckoned she'd be heading for a couple of libel suits, though I have doubts myself. People run scared on those things — especially if there's a bit of truth in it all. And I wouldn't put it past some of these jockeys in the building industry.' He frowned. 'So what was she doing in here, giving young Waters an earful?'

'Said she wanted police protection.'

Culpeper raised his eyebrows. 'She sounds off on the telly and then asks for police protection? What the hell for?'

Farnsby shrugged. 'A stalker. She reckons someone's been following her. Said she found it . . . unnerving.'

'She identify this stalker?'

Farnsby shook his head. 'Not really. He's been in a car, but she didn't get the number. He's been hanging around her flat in Kenton Bar during this last week, she reckons. But she admits it's a feeling, rather than anything else. Senses she's being watched and followed. But when Waters tried to explain that there wasn't a lot we could do in the circumstances, she got really stroppy. Started shouting the odds about how we'd never laid a finger on anyone after the break-in at her cottage on the fells—'

'Hold on, hold on—' Culpeper interrupted. 'You mean this isn't the first time she's been in complaining?'

Farnsby sniffed and clutched his sheaf of papers to his dark-suited chest. 'No, she's been in before — a couple of times. Waters was telling me he's been in the firing line more than once. Phone as well. It looks to me as though she could well be a professional moaner. Surprising, really, because she's no little old lady, nor a shrinking violet.'

'That was apparent from her television programme,' Culpeper grunted. 'But what was the story on her cottage?'

Farnsby shrugged. 'As far as Waters could make out, she'd been left this cottage in a will — somewhere up on the fells. But it hadn't been used for a while . . . I gather there was some problem about the will, or something like that, so the place was empty for quite a while. Anyway, by the time she got the job at the university and tried to move in, it seems vandals had got in there first. The place had been really done over — stuff smashed, furniture thrown around. Must have been a really wild party, there.'

'And she reported this to us.'

Farnsby nodded. 'More than just reported, it seems. Started shouting and throwing accusations around. Said it was deliberate, an attempt to get at her. This was quite apart from all the yelling about police inefficiency, of course.'

A memory stirred in Culpeper's head. 'An attempt to get at her . . . You know, Farnsby, I seem to recall . . . Yes, when I was down in Newcastle the other week, I was told she'd been in to lodge a complaint down there, as well.'

'So we're not the only ones to suffer the rough edge of her tongue.'

'It seems not. They had to fish her car out of the Tyne after she'd been to some concert at the Theatre Royal. You can tell young Waters that he has friends in Newcastle who've been through a similar experience to his.'

'Dumping in the Tyne, eh? At least that's nothing to do with us.'

'That's right — but she started naming names then, apparently.' Culpeper squinted thoughtfully at Farnsby. 'Who did she accuse of wrecking her cottage?'

Farnsby shrugged and shook his head. 'I don't know, I'd have to check — it's Waters who's been dealing with her. It was my first acquaintance with the lady.'

Culpeper scratched at his thinning hair. 'She certainly seems to be an unfortunate woman. Car in the Tyne, wrecked cottage, stalker . . .'

'Maybe there are some who'd say she's been asking for it,' Farnsby suggested. 'The people she knocked on her television programmes, at least. Anyway, I'll check on the name of the guy she's pointing at, if any. The stalker she can't describe. But as far as the wrecking of the cottage is concerned . . .'

'That's right. Check. See if it's the same name she was throwing around after her car got ducked. Pitcher, I think it was . . . can't remember the first name . . .'

4

There were still considerable rumblings of discontent at the Department of Museums and Antiquities. A week had gone by and Karen Stannard's temper had not improved. Simon Brent-Ellis was appearing more often in his office, to his own clear annoyance. He obviously felt under threat after the chief executive's meeting, and there was a rumour that his wife had advised him to put in some steady hours at work to deflect criticism she was picking up on the council benches.

His presence had an unsettling effect on the work of the department; staff were not used to seeing him around so regularly, and morale suffered.

On the Wednesday, Arnold had had enough and decided to pay another visit to see Dr Rena Williams at the Garrigill site. He took a route rather longer than the normal one, by way of Byerhope Bank. There the lead miners of old had supplemented their lead winnings with smallholdings on in-by land where they had grazed the odd horse, a few milch cows, chickens and a scattering of sheep on the fell. It was a place for ghosts, with abandoned stone dwellings, decrepit, crumbling dry stone walls and a high, keening wind on which the hovering kestrels soared. He passed Byerhope Reservoir, built by the Blackett-Beaumonts' globetrotting engineer to create a regular supply for the lead-washing operations at the bottom of the valley, and then Arnold climbed up over the grey-green fells, on the road to Garrigill.

Rena Williams was at the site and pleased to see him. She took him across to the shack where the team laid out the artefacts for checking and noting, and where there was a camp stove and facilities for making coffee.

'How's the dig going?' Arnold asked.

'Should be wrapping up for this season soon,' Rena Williams replied. 'We'll be covering the pit. It's about all cleared out now.'

She glanced at him curiously, clearly wondering whether he had any sleepless nights as a result of his experience in the burial cavity, six months earlier. 'And we've also completed the work on the cave temple under the hill. So thereafter you can write us off.' She brought Arnold a cup of coffee, where he sat at the rickety table. 'Still, we're much honoured today, aren't we?'

'By my visit?'

'You and the deputy director, on the same day!'

'Karen Stannard? Has she been up here today?' Arnold grimaced. 'She didn't tell me she was coming up — but then, there was no reason why she should, I suppose. But I thought she was leaving the reporting to me — you've not had any problems, have you?'

Rena Williams laughed. 'None that I can't handle.' She observed Arnold over the rim of her cup. 'What about you? How are things going in the department?'

'Well enough, I suppose,' Arnold replied. 'We've had a bit of a dust-up. Arising out of that television programme two weeks back. Cate Nicholas.'

'Ah, yes, I heard about the programme.' Rena Williams shook her head ruefully. 'I gather she laid about her some-what. I know Paul Stillwater was furious.'

'You know him?'

Rena Williams smiled. 'The world of archaeology is a small one, Arnold, you should know that. We're all in touch with each other on the digs — there's a sort of bush telegraph. I was curious about the Ravenstone dig, and was talking to Sam Loxton on the phone about it, so he suggested I went over and took a look. I was fascinated by the site — the cemetery is an extensive one and should be a rich source. Very impressive system they're putting in, too — it's clearly going to cost a hell of a lot of money, but if the government is prepared to stump up—'

'Did you meet Thor Cameron?'

She shook her head. 'Just Paul Stillwater — he came storming up, as though he was expecting trouble.'

'Stillwater didn't try to throw *you* off site, did he?' Arnold asked mischievously.

Rena Williams laughed. 'He looked at first as though he was thinking about it — but as Sam explained later, maybe when he saw a woman on site, at a distance, he thought it was Cate Nicholas again. Throw me off site? No . . .' She raised her eyebrows archly. 'Far from it. We had quite a chat. He seemed very friendly, even attentive.'

'Somewhat different from his treatment of Cate Nicholas, then, when she was there with Ms Stannard and me,' Arnold suggested.

'So I hear . . .' Rena Williams was silent for a little while, then she shrugged. 'I wonder why he did that? She has a solid reputation — and some innovative ideas—'

'Feet,' Arnold supplied.

Rena laughed. 'That's right. But it's all serious stuff, and a valuable addition to research, even if easy to parody. However, it was clear to me there's no love lost between Paul Stillwater and Ms Nicholas. He didn't tell me about throwing her off the site, or his reasons for doing so . . . though Sam told me a bit about it later . . . but whatever they were, the situation certainly hasn't been improved by her television appearance. Stillwater was hopping mad about that. I didn't see the programme myself, but I gather she was pretty swingeing in her comments.'

'She certainly was,' Arnold agreed. 'She didn't come right out with straightforward accusations, but there was a good deal of hinting at skulduggery over at Ravenstone. I'm not surprised Stillwater was angry. I won't be surprised, either, if his boss Thor Cameron — doesn't sue.'

'That bad, was it?' Rena Williams shook her head thoughtfully. 'She's a bit of a harridan, really, isn't she, from what I hear. Paul Stillwater was saying to Sam Loxton and me that more than a few people had been hurt by her wild allegations. Have you come across a character called Towers? Stillwater was talking about him.'

With a start, Arnold glanced at her guiltily. He nodded. 'Yes, he's the solicitor who acts as a trustee and legal adviser to the Adler Foundation.'

'The people who sold some land to Cossman International.' Rena Williams nodded. 'That's right. Well, according to Stillwater, she must have had something nasty to say about that poor man, as well.'

'She certainly did. But . . . poor man?' queried Arnold.

She shrugged. 'I didn't quite understand it all, but the gist is that apparently Towers has a sick wife—'

'So I understand.'

'Mrs Towers saw the television broadcast and was very upset about it. Later that night she had a heart attack — she was taken to hospital. Stillwater reckons that Towers was very disturbed about it all — he believed that Cate Nicholas's television broadcast was responsible for his wife's attack.'

'I gather Towers is obsessive about his wife . . . Certainly, Cate Nicholas made a number of accusations,' Arnold agreed, 'suggesting that the legal advice given was unsound . . . or even corrupt. I don't know whether the allegation was serious enough to cause Mrs Towers to have a heart attack . . .'

'It will depend on her constitution, I suppose,' Rena Williams hesitated. 'Talking of constitutions . . . is Karen Stannard all right?'

Arnold thought back to the last time he had seen the deputy director, fired up by rage. 'As far as I know, she's as hale as ever, and even more dangerous!'

Rena Williams laughed. 'I get the impression you and she have a somewhat uneasy relationship. However . . . I just thought she didn't seem too well, when she called here a little while ago. You've only just missed her, in fact, I'm surprised you didn't pass each other on the road.'

'I came by way of Byerhope.'

'Ah, that explains it. Still, I thought she looked a bit . . . peaky. She wasn't herself — I can't quite put my finger on it, but she seemed . . . preoccupied.' She hesitated, glancing at Arnold warily. 'As you know, there was a time when we were friendly . . . though that seems to have died a death.'

Arnold gained the impression she was not displeased that their friendship had cooled somewhat. He could understand that. He had been aware at the time that she had been disturbed by Karen Stannard's attentions.

'I just thought,' Rena continued, 'that she was worried about something. Departmental anxieties, maybe?'

Arnold wondered whether Karen Stannard had been hauled over the coals again by the chief executive — he had heard nothing, not even from Jerry Picton, who would normally have his ear to the ground. On the other hand, when he had last seen Karen Stannard, she had seemed to him to be girding herself for a confrontation with Cate Nicholas. He wondered whether they had yet had their shouting match . . . and whether that was the reason why the deputy director had seemed to Rena Williams to be worried.

'Anyway,' she mused, 'we should be packing up on this site shortly. The pit and the temple cave have been excavated and I think we've found all we're going to. I'm now tempted by Sam Loxton's suggestion, to go and join him at Ravenstone.'

'Really?'

She nodded. 'There's something rather interesting up there. Sam tells me he's uncovered some Celtic iconography with a distinct zoomorphic feel about it.'

Arnold frowned. 'I thought the site was largely Saxon in its dating.'

Rena Williams shrugged. 'That was my understanding. But Sam seems to have uncovered some composite "monster" god forms — you know, human, but with horns, antlers, hooves, animal ears . . .'

'There's always been an intimate link between gods and beasts, as far as the Celts were concerned,' Arnold agreed. 'And anthropomorphic deities are a very old concept—'

'I'm talking *zoomorphic*,' Rena interrupted. 'We know the Celts worshipped animal gods — there was an animistic element in Celtic religion. But what Sam has found would seem to suggest something else. It's a Saxon cemetery, remember — and yet there are elements of Celtic iconography. You ever see those bucket-mounts they found in the river Ribble some years ago?'

Arnold nodded. 'Human torsos — female — with eagle heads.'

'Right. Well, Sam suggests there's something different at Ravenstone. A series of carvings, which he thinks suggest an anthropomorphic being moving to a horse, to a bull, to an eagle.'

'He's *found* these?' Arnold shook his head. 'There's nothing in his reports.'

Rena grimaced. 'They're scattered through three graves, and he's ready for analysis yet. He talked it over with me . . . they're puzzling. An ancient world, Arnold,' she sighed.

And a bloody one, Arnold thought, as he recalled what they had found in the Garrigill pit.

He left the site about four in the afternoon. He had driven up to Garrigill by one slightly roundabout route. Now, on an impulse, he decided to take another diversion on the way back, and drive past Bickley Moorside to see Cate Nicholas's cottage.

He dropped down into the valley and began the ascent the other side, crossed the burn and made his way past straggling cottages until he came to the old quarries. The moor had been first worked by the Romans and brown, thin-soiled mounds of quarry spoil dotted the slopes, like small mesas, while water spilled over the edge of the rock canyon of the quarry face.

When he finally breasted Bickley Moor, he could see Parkstone Bank's ancient oakwood, used now by a trust trying to develop and rediscover lost woodland management techniques. Arnold had walked those woods and seen the flowers that were indicative of old woodlands: bluebells, dog's mercury and wood anemone, wood sorrel and cluster-flowered ransoms.

He was near the remains of the Far Slit mine-workings and he passed the crumbling stone walls of a bousestead — a storage bay for bouse: the mixture of galena and waste rock — and a little further on, the remains of a washing floor where the ore had been processed by the lead miners of old.

He crossed the bridge, passed the old mine shaft itself, and then the road swung left, running along a ridge which fell away steeply to his left. He slowed, pulling in to the edge of the road, and stopped with his wheels on the grassy verge. He got out of the car and walked to the edge, looking down to the steep slopes of the valley and the grey-green scarp of the fell ahead of him.

He could make out the track running downwards, zigzagging in the slope of the fell. It would be the track leading down to the cottage owned by Cate Nicholas — it was the only place he could think of from her description. Bickley Moorside was a bleak, wildly beautiful area, and there were few cottages. As he stood there, he could see its grey roof, half hidden by a small copse of beech, grown as a windbreak against the winter gusts that would come powering down from the fell.

He could see a dark-blue car parked near the cottage. Even as he stood there it moved, reversing to take the bend back up the track to the main road. Arnold hesitated, then moved back to his car. It was probably Cate Nicholas. He disliked the woman and had no desire to meet her up here on the fell. She would no doubt accuse him of snooping on her — with the number of enemies she seemed to have gathered already there was no need for him to be added to the list.

Arnold headed back north, to Morpeth. When he got back to the office, just to check whether there had been any messages left on his desk, he noted that there were no other cars in the car park. Everyone else had left. There were only the caretakers to greet him.

* * *

Arnold worked in the office for the next two days, with no further jaunts out to the fells. He had some catching up to do with back files, and there were several departmental meetings to attend, chaired by Karen Stannard. He observed her with interest. Rena Williams had been right. There was something wrong with the deputy director. She had dark circles under her beautiful eyes. There was a preoccupied, almost nervous air about her and she seemed to find difficulty concentrating on the matters in hand.

He told Jane Wilson about it at the weekend. He had driven down to Durham to see her and take her out to dinner on the Saturday night. He was in Jane's living room talking about it while Jane was busy working her way through some old photograph albums, resetting various prints that had become loose in their mountings.

'I've no idea what it is that's bothering her,' he said, 'but I have a feeling it will be tied up with the Ravenstone business. She's still smouldering, I reckon, about Cate Nicholas — the woman let her down badly by using confidential information Karen Stannard had given her.'

'From your report.'

'That's right,' Arnold hesitated. 'And she's not alone in being bothered about that. I'm not too bright myself. I can't help feeling vaguely guilty.'

'About what, for goodness' sake?' Jane straightened, staring at him.

Arnold shrugged awkwardly. 'Nick Towers. His wife was taken to hospital with a heart attack — as a consequence of watching the Nicholas programme. Clearly, she recognized the allusions Cate Nicholas made, she was shocked to hear her husband being attacked that way, and the anxiety triggered the heart attack. Towers will be beside himself — he's very uxorious, it seems — and I just feel . . . well, guilty about the whole thing. It was I who first raised the question about the legal advice he gave to the Adler Foundation. If I hadn't put that in the file, Karen Stannard wouldn't have been able to pass it on to Nicholas, and she wouldn't have used it in her television programme—'

'Oh, Arnold!' Jane interrupted in exasperation. 'That's just ridiculous. You're implying that none of these other people carry responsibility for their own actions! You can't be serious, blaming yourself for Cate Nicholas's behaviour.'

'Even so . . .' Arnold was unconvinced.

'Oh, get out into the kitchen and make us a cup of tea before I throw something at you,' she snapped impatiently. She rose and switched on the television. 'Perhaps your gloomy mood will disappear when you take me out for an expensive meal tonight.'

Arnold laughed. 'Or become even blacker when I see the size of the bill!' He walked out to the kitchen and filled the kettle. Behind him, from the sitting room, he could hear a newscaster speaking on the television, the sound muffled by the closed door. He switched on the kettle and reached up to the cupboard to take down the cups and saucers. Jane was right, he thought, it was stupid taking on board the responsibility for the illness of Mrs Towers — he might have provided the bullets in the first instance, but it was others who had aimed, and fired the shots. Nevertheless, irritatingly, he was still unable to get rid of the light, nagging guilt in his mind.

He turned, hearing a small sound behind him, the door opening. It was Jane. She was standing in the doorway, her eyes wide and startled, her skin pale.

'Arnold—'

'What's the matter?' He took a step towards her, held out his hand. She took it. Her fingers were cold. 'What's the matter?' he repeated, stupidly.

'The news . . . it was just on the news,' she said. Her voice was subdued, a little shaky. 'What we've just been talking about — Cate Nicholas.'

'Cate Nicholas? What about her?'

Jane hesitated. 'She's been found dead, Arnold — up at her cottage on the moors.' Her fingers tightened against his. 'The police . . . they say they're treating it as murder!'

CHAPTER FOUR

1

Detective Chief Inspector Culpeper heaved a sigh. These things always seemed to happen when he was otherwise engaged. He liked to get to the scene of a crime early, before the big feet trampled everywhere, before mistakes were made on site, before eager young constables started suggesting theories and looking for clues, and before the journalists began to swarm like big fat bluebottles to a rotting piece of meat.

He'd been called away to a murder enquiry in Warwick, which had proved, in his view, to be a waste of time, so it was with a jaundiced outlook on life that Culpeper finally found himself driving over the fells to the cottage at Bickley Moorside. As soon as he had returned to Ponteland he had tried to contact Farnsby, only to be told that the detective inspector was up at the cottage. Culpeper decided to join him to get his own view of the scene of crime, convinced that Farnsby had already spent too much time on the fell, instead of interviewing suspects.

The drive over the fells soothed him to some extent, and when he breasted the fellside and looked down at the zigzagging track that led to Cate Nicholas's cottage, he appreciated that there were few places in the North where it would be more possible to get away from the pressures of a working life.

A good place to spend spare time, not a good place to die.

She would have been heard by no one when she cried out, if she had time to cry out. The isolation of the cottage would make it a good place to kill, and be seen by none. He drove down the track, thinking, and yet aware of the grey stone of the old cottage, the massive stone slabs of the roof, the tiny mediaeval window high below the eaves, and the thick clematis that clung around the doorway, resisting — successfully the rigours of the fell winter, but never succeeding to bloom with great success. The doorway was a Georgian addition, a date — 1718 — cut in the sandstone lintel above the open door. Culpeper parked his car, reversing up to the side of the cottage as Farnsby emerged, standing in the doorway, staring at him, lean, dark-suited, hands on hips.

Awkwardly, Culpeper clambered from the car, any lightness of mood being washed away by the sight of Farnsby. He grumbled his way mentally up to the detective inspector, and eyed him malevolently. 'You solved it yet, then, soldier boy?'

Farnsby flushed slightly, his eyes narrowing, and shook his head. 'I thought I'd better come up here again, when it was quiet. Get the feel of the place.'

'Scene-of-crime unit been and gone, forensic finished, all tidied away?' Culpeper asked.

'Two days ago, sir.'

Culpeper humphed. 'So who found her, then?'

Farnsby gestured up towards the fell. 'There's a small hill farm, just over the brow up there — three miles or so away. They keep a couple of goats, of all things, and it seems that Ms Nicholas was partial to goat's milk.'

'Is this relevant?' Culpeper growled.

Farnsby looked offended. Persistently, he went on. 'When she came up here at weekends, or whenever, she usually called in to collect some goat's milk at the farm. This time, she hadn't done so. But one of the farmworkers had seen her car parked at the back of the cottage, so he came down to see if she wanted any milk.' Farnsby hesitated. 'At least, that's what he says. Really, I think he was also a bit . . . inquisitive. She didn't usually come up during the week, and he'd seen the car parked there the previous two days.'

Culpeper sighed. They say that you can't get away with anything in the countryside. There are more eyes around . . . . 'So, this was on the Saturday?'

'That's right.' Farnsby nodded. 'Anyway, the front door was unlatched, he stepped inside — and what he saw gave him the fright of his life.'

Culpeper was silent for a while. 'Is he in the frame, this farm worker?'

Farnsby shook his head slowly. 'I don't think so. The day she died . . . Wednesday . . . he was at a sheep auction, over at Kirkby Stephen.'

'So that lets him out.' Culpeper nodded. 'Preliminary suggestions?'

Farnsby shrugged doubtfully. 'You'd better come inside, so I can show you what a mess the place is in. We've started sifting, but when I heard you were coming back I called a halt. Thought you'd want to see it.'

He led the way into the cottage, his heels ringing on the stone flags of the entrance hall. The cottage was low-beamed, two small rooms, one either side of the hallway, the back of the property descending steep-roofed to a rear scullery only six feet high. 'Nothing's been done to this place for centuries,' Farnsby complained. The man has no soul, Culpeper considered.

'She was found in here.'

Farnsby was standing in the doorway of the room to the right. It had served as a sitting room. A large stone fireplace was flanked by bookcases — the books were scattered across the floor. Two easy chairs had been overturned; one of them had been slashed along the seat and arms, as though in frustration. A standard lamp had been shattered, and there was a general air of confusion and destruction in the room.

'Whereabouts was she?' Culpeper asked.

Farnsby pointed to the corner of the room, beside the strewn bookcase and an overturned CD player. 'She was slumped down over there. The killer had really worked her over. Early suggestions from forensic are that the blows that killed her were the ones to the temple, and to the back of the head, as she twisted and fell sideways. But he'd had a real go at her apart from that: nose smashed, cheekbones depressed . . . Whoever it was, he really didn't like her one bit. Must have been in a real frenzy to lay into her the way he did.'

'You keep saying "he",' Culpeper remarked. 'That based on forensic?'

'No, sorry.' Farnsby shook his head. 'There's been no suggestion the weight of blows would have had to be from a male hand. It could have been committed by a woman — but we don't have the weapon, so we can't be sure how heavy it was. Forensic reckon it could have been a monkey wrench, or something similar. On the other hand, we don't know what Ms Nicholas kept in her collection here, so it could be something that was snatched up.'

'Collection?'

Farnsby gestured towards the other room. 'There's a case in there — also overturned, with some damage. Collection of bones — from feet, mostly—'

'Feet?' Culpeper said in disbelief.

'It was her line of work.' Farnsby nodded. 'An expert on ancient feet.'

'Now I've heard everything,' Culpeper grumbled. 'You're not going to tell me she was clubbed to death with somebody's big toe.'

Patiently, Farnsby said, 'No, sir, but there are other artefacts in there. Some mediaeval scabbards, an old spur, pottery — most of which is smashed — and other bits and pieces of old iron that I wouldn't know about. But some of the stuff — she's obviously collected them at digs — is pretty heavy. Maybe the killer picked up some old piece of iron to belt her with.'

'Or maybe, in premeditation, he brought it with him.'

Farnsby wrinkled his nose. 'I don't know, sir. It's one reason why I came back up here. I just have the feeling that .

. . well, this was like a rage . . . you know what I mean? The way she was beaten, hammered as she lay in the corner over there. The guy was beside himself with rage—'

'Or *she* was,' Culpeper warned sourly.

'As you say, sir. And that kind of rage, it could have arisen on the instant. Picking one of her implements up, he could have taken a swing at her, chased her into the sitting room—'

'So it started across there, where she keeps her collection?' Culpeper asked.

'That's what we think. The attack started there, she fled across the room, or was thrown into the sitting room, and she tried to cover up in the corner. Her left forearm and right wrist were broken as she tried to protect herself . . . Then the head blows did her in. Somebody really did not like Ms Nicholas.'

Culpeper stepped gingerly around the sitting room, and then went back to pace around the room where Cate Nicholas had kept her collection of artefacts from her archaeological work. For a little while he stared with distaste at the scattered foot bones that had been strewn over the floor. 'Better get a squad up to sift through all this,' he suggested. 'We might find something, but where the hell we start, I don't know.'

Thoughtfully, he walked out to the doorway and surveyed the fellside, staring up at the track winding its way up to the summit of the fell. It was a lonely spot. His attention was drawn to the beech trees, planted long ago to screen the cottage from the wind. 'The killer might have waited for her, forced his way in. You checked through that copse of beech trees?' he asked.

Farnsby nodded. 'Found nothing of any interest. No one has been hiding out there, as far as we can make out — no signs of anyone waiting there for her to arrive.'

'And any approach to the cottage would have been noted easily in this isolation. By Cate Nicholas, if by no one else. The door hadn't been forced?'

'No, sir. She knew the killer, I would guess. Let him in when he called—'

'Or maybe had even been expecting him . . . or her. A friend, possibly . . .' Culpeper hesitated, glancing back into the hallway, thinking about the disorder in the rooms. 'What do you think, young Farnsby? Looking for something, our killer?'

Farnsby didn't care for references to his age. His lips thinned in annoyance. 'I considered that, sir. Have my doubts. I think what we have here is a discussion that got out of hand and turned to a murderous rage. There must have been bad blood between the two of them, and it spilled over—'

'Quite a lot of it spilled over,' Culpeper growled. 'So you're discounting a wandering stranger, and you don't think the killer was after something Cate Nicholas had.'

'Too early to make decisions,' Farnsby replied, but then added stubbornly, 'but the way I see it—'

'Yes. I understand the way you see it.' Culpeper stared up at the sky, considering. 'Not the first time this place has been turned over, though, is it? There was that complaint she made, shortly after she acquired the place. It had been smashed about then, hadn't it?'

Farnsby shrugged. 'The view Detective Sergeant Waters held was that it was just vandals. The place was taken apart, but it looked more like malice than anything else.'

'But you reckon our killer was showing just a little bit of malice,' Culpeper suggested, 'when he allowed his temper to let rip.' He sighed. 'I don't think we should discard any theories just now. Do you?'

'No, sir,' Farnsby replied reluctantly.

'So, I'll have another mooch around for a while, you can go back. Then we'll take a look at the possible names you've got, and start interviewing.' He glanced at Farnsby quizzically. 'I suppose you do have a few names?'

'I do, sir.'

Inevitably, Culpeper thought, given the kind of nasty lady Ms Cate Nicholas had been in life.

* * *

Culpeper parked his car near Eldon Square and locked it, then made his way to the Haymarket, before striking up towards the university buildings. Knowing that university life was such that lecturers might not be on the premises, or might be teaching, or in committee, he had taken the precaution of telephoning in advance.

He'd received the information he wanted from the departmental secretary. Mr Pitcher would be available to see him, in his room at the university. She was a pretty little woman in her thirties — and most helpful. She willingly showed him the departmental diary for the last few weeks, where staff movements were recorded. 'When they bother to tell me at all.' She smiled, deprecatingly. Then she showed him to Joe Pitcher's lair.

It was a work room: cramped, stuffy, with a narrow window that let in little light. The walls of the room were lined with bookshelves, largely on archaeology and mediaeval history. There was a small, cluttered table on which various manuscript sheets were scattered, and two chairs. One was a hard, upright, plastic-moulded chair behind the desk. The other was a badly worn armchair, out of the back of which the stuffing was beginning to emerge. Culpeper was reminded of the damaged armchair at the cottage at Bickley Moorside.

'Mr Pitcher?' Culpeper asked. 'I'm grateful that you were able to find time to see me.'

Joe Pitcher gestured to the armchair. 'Take a seat. I hope this won't take too long. I have a class at three, and a heavy schedule here.' He waved a diffident hand towards the papers on his desk.

Culpeper eyed him carefully. Pitcher was of medium height, slight, narrow-featured with a light, wispy beard that he probably wore to disguise the petulance of his mouth. He had sharp, quick eyes that never seemed to stay still. He was unwilling now to meet Culpeper's glance, but that might have been normal. Culpeper gained the impression that Pitcher was constitutionally edgy, a twitchy man who would always be on the move: feet, fingers, mouth, eyes. As Culpeper sat down, Pitcher took the plastic chair and folded his arms. The muscles in his upper arms flexed and flexed again, and he blinked rapidly. 'What can I do to help you?'

'I would like to talk to you about Ms Cate Nicholas. You knew her.'

'Of course,' Pitcher snapped. 'She was the head of this department.'

'She was no friend of yours, I gather,' Culpeper said aggressively, getting straight to the point.

'That's common gossip,' Pitcher sneered. 'For that matter, she wasn't anyone's friend in the department. Except one or two of the women. You might say she was generally disliked.'

'Why was that?' Culpeper asked gently.

'Because she was an arrogant cow.' Pitcher clearly had no reservations about speaking ill of the dead. 'She walked into this department and lorded it right from the start. She was the only one entitled to hold opinions. She ran roughshod over systems and attitudes. She homed in on budget allocations that had already been agreed and changed them. She made public criticisms of staff in committee meetings. She played favourites. She disliked men. But apart from that, if there was any way to make herself unpopular, she found it.'

'She had a good academic reputation?' Culpeper asked.

'Some would say so,' Pitcher said petulantly.

'You do not.'

Pitcher made no reply.

After a few moments, Culpeper leaned forward in his chair. 'Quite apart from her general unpopularity, I understand you had your own special reasons for disliking her.'

Pitcher's mean eyes slithered a glance at Culpeper, then looked away. He shrugged. 'I suppose I did.'

'I understand it had something to do with the television programme you had been appearing in? I am informed that you got very upset about it. But surely, it wasn't a particularly important matter, was it, for two academics—'

'*Important*!' Culpeper had touched a raw nerve, and Pitcher exploded. 'You've no idea! That bloody woman cost me at least ten thousand quid! The programmes I'd been running were popular, getting good vibes from the public — then she came along and aired her views! She was so bloody persuasive, and that little madam Angie Rothwell — and she's another one, just like Cate Nicholas — she got cold feet after she heard Nicholas whine on about what she called my unsupported theories. And then Rothwell got her knickers all heated up by the thought that if she took on Nicholas, she'd get a controversial programme running — and all this just at the time I was about to be given a new contract which would have . . .'

He frowned, his voice dying away as he realized he was saying too much, getting too excited. His eyes narrowed and he clamped his lips together. Culpeper eyed him. The man was almost obsessive, Culpeper realized: one word, and he was likely to launch into a rerun of his grievances, diatribes against a woman he had hated.

'So she cut you out of a television contract. Nasty.' Culpeper paused, watching the man's thin face from under heavily lidded eyes. 'Is that why you shoved her car into the Tyne?'

Pitcher shuffled in surprise in his chair, and then his body became very still. His eyes flickered up to glance uncertainly at Culpeper, and then an odd half-smile appeared on his lips. 'She deserved all that she got. She'd have received insurance money, anyway. And I got questioned about that by the Newcastle police. Just the once. There was no way they could pin that on me.'

'But you got a warning, I understand.'

'I told you — they couldn't pin that on me.'

His chin had come up defiantly, but Culpeper had noted his choice of words. 'Even if you did do it . . .' Culpeper mumbled, almost to himself. 'Tit for tat . . . you lost your contract; she lost her car. That didn't get you even, though, did it?'

Pitcher's mouth twitched. 'How do you mean?'

144

'Cate Nicholas certainly was infuriated by losing her car — but as you said, insurance would cover that. On the other hand, you lost your contract . . . Is there much chance of getting it reopened?'

Sourly, Pitcher shook his head. 'I doubt it. She killed that one off good and proper.'

'And now *she's* been killed,' Culpeper said softly. 'And what was it you said earlier . . . ? She deserved what she got. Does that include killing, Mr Pitcher?'

The university lecturer was silent for a little while, staring at his folded arms. Then he looked up, a strange angry light in his eyes. 'Just what is it you're trying to say?'

'Nothing yet,' Culpeper replied smoothly. 'But as you'll have heard, Ms Nicholas was murdered up at her cottage. You ever go up there, Mr Pitcher?'

'No.'

'Not even when you started following her around?'

Pitcher stared at him, his mouth stiff with tension. Then he made a visible effort to relax, prevent himself being wound up by Culpeper's questions. He unfolded his arms, tucked his elbows in defensively, and grimaced. 'Why the hell should I follow her around? Saw too much of her here as it was!'

'I thought you might have been seeking other opportunities. To get even with her, to do mischief.' Culpeper smiled grimly. 'I mean, this contract thing rankled. It's been a running sore between you . . . shoving a car into the Tyne helped, but didn't assuage the anger, did it? There could have been other opportunities if you kept an eye on her—'

'I wouldn't waste my time following her,' Pitcher snarled. 'And no one can say it was me who shoved that car into the river. You can't prove anything—'

'And you'll be able to tell us where you were when Cate Nicholas died?' Culpeper interrupted.

Joe Pitcher shivered. Culpeper could not tell whether it was anger, or distress. The man's glance darted about the room as though seeking some means of escape. 'I told you I've never been up to Bickley Moorside.'

145

'So you said . . . But I'm asking you another question. It's about your movements on the day she died. I've already had a look at the departmental diary, kept by the departmental secretary. It seems you were not on the premises, here, all day.'

'It was a weekend,' Pitcher argued. 'I wouldn't be here on a Saturday, when the body was found—'

He stopped abruptly as Culpeper fixed him with a look. Culpeper smiled thinly. 'The body was found on the Saturday, by a farm worker who she used to buy milk from at weekends. But she *died* on the Wednesday, as far as we can make out from forensic evidence, not the day she was found. So I'll ask you again, Mr Pitcher. Where were you on that Wednesday? You weren't here at the university. So where were you? I'd like to know, so we can eliminate you from our enquiries.'

'It's none of your bloody business where I was — and you can't sling responsibility for the murder of that Nicholas cow around my neck! There's no way you're going to pin that one on me!'

2

The following morning Culpeper was at his desk early. Farnsby had placed a number of files out for him, relating to Cate Nicholas. Culpeper pored over them while he drank his first coffee of the day; he had been trying to cut down on his girth after certain aspersions had been cast by his wife. 'You'll never cut a dash on the Greek beaches, bonny lad, with a beer belly like that!' She had always been direct in her comments, had his lass.

Farnsby had done a meticulous job. He had produced information for Culpeper's consumption, relating to Cate Nicholas's earlier life: her home background — an only child, both parents now dead — a first degree from Manchester University and a doctorate from Leeds, her job as a museum curator at Gloucester, and then her work on archaeological digs at various centres around the country. There were cuttings of several articles she had written about the bone structures of mediaeval feet and an investigation she had made into the distinctions to be drawn between Roman feet and Bronze Age feet — even to the differences found between Cotswold and Wiltshire feet from the same, Anglo-Saxon, period. Culpeper found the arguments presented fascinating, but doubted whether they would throw much light on his own investigations.

Just after ten o'clock Farnsby tapped on his door and entered the room. Culpeper waved him to a chair, and gestured to the files. 'I've been going through these. There seems to be a bit of a gap in her career . . . just before she took up the appointment at Newcastle.'

Farnsby nodded. 'That's right. She took a job at Manchester, at the university, but then resigned, and there seems to be a hiatus thereafter . . .'

He paused, as Culpeper rolled his eyes and muttered, 'A hiatus . . . !'

Farnsby's mouth twisted in annoyance, but he went on with deliberation, '. . . a hiatus until she was appointed as head of department at Newcastle. It could be that she was chasing around at archaeological digs, or working on a thesis or something, but I've no concrete information even about where she was living, until she walked into the job up here. And the cottage.'

Where she died. Culpeper sucked at his teeth thoughtfully. 'Well, I guess the university records should be able to tell us what she was up to. She'll have had to tell them all about her previous academic record. You'd better arrange a check there.' He thought about the little departmental secretary and eyed Farnsby, and then mentally dismissed the thought that Farnsby might enjoy interviewing her. He wasn't the type for light-hearted dalliance. 'So, who have we got in the frame now, for us to concentrate on?' he asked.

'You've already seen Pitcher,' Farnsby replied.

Culpeper grunted. 'Not that it did me much good. He's a nasty bit of work in many ways, and slippery. I wouldn't put it past him to have bludgeoned the woman — he certainly hated her guts, and I'm sure he was the character who shoved her car into the Tyne. Whether he's also the stalker that Nicholas came in to complain about, I'm not so sure. He seemed almost indignant at the thought. But he's going to be tricky to pin down: always been slapdash about booking in and out of the department, so it's difficult to trace his movements independently of his say so. And at the moment he's refusing to tell us where he was on the day Nicholas died.'

'Should we pull him in?'

Culpeper shook his head. 'No, let him stew a bit. I came on pretty strong about his lack of cooperation, so maybe he'll change his mind. He's hiding something, of course — he damn well knows where he was but doesn't want to tell us. Maybe it'll incriminate him — or someone else. Who knows? We'll get back to him. But who else have we got?'

Farnsby consulted his notebook with a frown. 'The programme she put out, a couple of weeks before she was killed — she didn't name names in it, but there were some pretty broad hints. There's one we've been able to check on, and who I think should be interviewed: a solicitor called Towers. Cate Nicholas had implied he'd been up to some shenanigans over land sold by the Adler Trust to Cossman International. He's based in Morpeth.'

Culpeper nodded. 'I could get to see him tomorrow. Haven't been to Morpeth in a while. But does he have a motive?'

Farnsby shrugged. 'I would have thought the veiled allegations about bad legal advice might have stirred him up. And I did hear something about his wife being taken ill after the broadcast. He could bear a grudge.'

'Seems a bit thin . . . Anyone else?' Farnsby nodded.

'Paul Stillwater.'

'And who might he be?' Even as he asked the question, something stirred in Culpeper's mind. He stared thoughtfully at Farnsby as the detective inspector consulted his notes again. It was something to do with Farnsby, but it fluttered from Culpeper's reach for the moment.

'He's the PR man for Cossman International. It seems he might have been the link between Towers and Cossman — certainly, that was what Nicholas was hinting at in her broadcast, it seems.'

'And you think that's a motive for murder?' Culpeper asked.

'It's not just that, sir. It would seem there was bad blood between them. There was an altercation of some kind up at

149

the Ravenstone dig, which ended with Cate Nicholas being thrown off site. Words were exchanged between her and Stillwater.'

'Was this before or after the broadcast?'

'Before,' Farnsby replied. 'In fact, it could be it was that disagreement that caused her to have a go at him on the television programme — so university gossip has it. What we don't know is why they had a barney at Ravenstone. But whichever way you look at it, they weren't happy with each other — so I think we should be having a word with Mr Stillwater.'

The name resounded in Culpeper's head. He stared at Farnsby in irritation. He was bothered: the name, a file . . . an image kept twinkling in and out of his mind's eye, a butterfly eluding his grasp . . .

'Dead files,' he said suddenly.

'What's that, sir?' Farnsby asked, startled.

'Dead files. You brought in some files for chucking the other day. I told you to hang on to some.'

'Yes, sir.' There was a note of grievance in Farnsby's voice.

'That's right . . . I told you to hang on . . . but I also told you to do a check on one, with the DTI. Have you contacted them yet?'

Farnsby nodded. 'I have. But no comment so far. They say they'll get back to me. But you know what they're like: civil servants don't shift their arses very quickly for anyone.'

The comment was unlike Farnsby. One of the DTI people must have rattled his cage with uncooperative remarks, Culpeper thought. He shrugged. 'Maybe in this case it's just as well. I have a feeling . . .' He tapped his fingers on the desktop in front of him. 'That DTI file — I want you to pull it for me. I want to take another look at it. Now.'

Farnsby scowled. He clearly felt this was an irrelevance in the context of their present discussion. He rose to his feet and headed for the door. As he did so, the phone on Culpeper's desk rang. He picked it up. Farnsby hesitated in the doorway, uncertainly.

'Mr Culpeper?' The officer on reception was Irish, and had a soft brogue, borrowed from his mother. 'There's someone here downstairs who says he would like to see you.'

'Who is it?'

'He calls himself Cameron. He says he's the chairman of Cossman International — you'll know them, sir, the people doing that leisure complex.'

Culpeper frowned. 'What's it about . . . did he say?'

'He did, at that.' There was a short pause. 'He wants to talk to you about the death of Cate Nicholas.'

'Send him up,' Culpeper said, and gestured to Farnsby to stay in the room.

* * *

There was no doubt Thor Cameron had a presence. He was a big, broad-shouldered man of over six feet in height. He made Culpeper think of old prints he had seen of the men who had swept into Lindisfarne to destroy the abbey and loot it of its ancient treasures. 'From the fury of the Northmen, the good Lord deliver us . . .' Cameron's red-gold hair was cut short and his skin suggested he spent a good deal of time in the open air. His features were well-defined, his mouth friendly, but there was a firmness and strength about his jawline that suggested to Culpeper the man could be a fighter in a corner. A successful businessman, it seemed, but one who could make a powerful enemy. Easy of manner, confident, but right now something was bothering him, for his sharp blue eyes were troubled and there was a general air of unease about him as he sat hunched in the chair in front of Culpeper, while Farnsby hovered in the background.

'So, what is it I can do for you, Mr Cameron? They tell me you want to talk about Cate Nicholas.'

Cameron's eyes clouded and he nodded. 'That's right. I . . . I thought I'd better come in and talk to you before you . . . heard things from other sources.'

'Things? What things? To do with the Nicholas murder?' Culpeper glanced at Farnsby, who was leaning against the wall near the doorway, with his hands tucked behind him. 'And what do you mean, other sources?'

'Gossip has a habit of travelling around rapidly,' Cameron muttered, 'and it usually gets garbled. So I thought . . .'

His voice died away in reflection. Culpeper stared at him. The man was ill at ease, and yet controlled — it was as though he was projecting his personality onto a screen, observing his own performance. Or maybe just looking back, digging deep into the past. 'This gossip . . . would it be about you and Ms Nicholas? You maybe had a . . . relationship?'

Cameron snorted in quick contempt. His sharp eyes flashed at Culpeper and he shook his head. 'Relationship? Not in the way you mean. Didn't you *know* about her?'

'Know what about her?'

'Her damned homosexuality,' Cameron retorted. 'She was a lesbian. Hadn't you heard?'

Culpeper glanced at Farnsby, who was now standing away from the wall. 'There had been . . . rumours, I suppose.'

'Exactly. Well, they were rumours based on fact!' Cameron snapped. 'Take my word for it! I've scars to prove it!'

Culpeper contemplated the top of his desk for a little while and the silence grew around them. Almost casually, he asked, 'I'm afraid you're losing me, Mr Cameron. If Ms Nicholas was a lesbian, what has that got to do with you?'

The silence gathered around them again. Cameron did not meet Culpeper's glance. He was staring down at his hands. At last he said quietly, 'This isn't an easy story to tell; you must appreciate that. I've tried to put it all behind me, but it isn't easy . . . it can still . . . enrage me, from time to time, if I let it get to me.'

'What is it that gets to you, Mr Cameron?' Culpeper asked in a persuasive tone.

'Cate Nicholas broke up my marriage,' Thor Cameron said bluntly, and there was a deep, savage hurt in his eyes.

Culpeper frowned. He picked up a pencil and played with it nervously between his fingers. 'Perhaps you'd like to tell us just how she managed to do that,' he suggested.

Cameron nodded. 'That's why I came in. When I heard that she'd been killed . . . murdered at that damn cottage, I wasn't sure what to do. There's been bad blood between us for years, but it's not a story that's well-known around here, and I . . . I wasn't keen to be the butt of gossip. But that's the problem, isn't it? Things get out, people get facts wrong, stories get garbled . . .' He raised his head defiantly. 'So I thought I'd better get in first, tell you how it was, before you get the wrong idea . . .'

'I'm listening,' Culpeper said, injecting a note of sympathy into his voice.

'I was married in Gloucester,' Cameron said abruptly. 'I had a small property business in those days. She . . . Joanna . . . she was about twelve years younger than me, and I suppose she never really appreciated what she was letting herself in for. I was doing well. The business was growing satisfactorily . . . but then there was the recession and I suddenly found I had to spend more time at work than she had expected.' He paused, then shrugged his broad shoulders. 'Oh, I have to admit there was more to it than that. I've always been compulsive about work. A workaholic. And she, well, she was a bit unsophisticated, easily impressed . . . and neglected, as she saw it. Anyway, after a few years we began to drift apart, I suppose. I tried to pull her in, get her interested in the business — she worked with me on a new venture for a while . . . but it didn't pan out. We became . . . we began to lead separate lives. That's when Cate Nicholas came along.'

'Where was this?'

'In Manchester. I'd moved. I was busy building Cossman from scratch . . . anyway, Joanna got it into her head that her life was unfulfilled.' He made a brief, angry gesture of impatience with his left hand. 'She started spouting all sorts of psychobabble about the purpose of life . . . and I knew most of it came from the people she was meeting at university

153

— she'd gone there to fill her time, do some short courses on archaeology. That's where she met Cate Nicholas. They became friendly . . . they went on digs. And at some stage, when things changed from intellectual matters to emotional ones, that bitch must have made an approach . . .'

'They became lovers?' Culpeper asked.

'I never went into the details,' Cameron replied harshly. 'I didn't even know about it, suspected nothing, until one day Joanna just packed and left. There had been a few rows before that, over trivial things, but I thought nothing about it really — woman's temperament, you know, feeling left out of things, neglected . . . but I was building a business, damn it! Anyway, she left me . . .' He fell silent, a brooding look on his face as he contemplated the past, perhaps considering how things could have been, allocating fault, seeking reasons . . .

'What happened then?' Culpeper asked.

'Can't you guess?' Cameron snapped. 'I went after her, didn't I, and there was a hell of a row, my pride had been hurt, I couldn't really understand or accept what was going on, and I swore I'd cut her off without a penny of what I'd put into the marriage. She didn't care, it seems, she and Nicholas were shacking up together — but it was Nicholas who pushed her, I know, pushed her into demanding a share of family assets. She — Joanna — was even persuaded by Nicholas to raid my offices on one occasion to check on company assets . . .' He stopped suddenly, frowning, as though he felt he was saying too much. 'Anyway, it all got very nasty.'

'You divorced?' Culpeper queried, shifting uneasily in his chair.

Cameron shook his head. 'No. It never became necessary. She died.'

There was a short silence. Farnsby's head was cocked on one side, and he was tensed, as though waiting to leap on some admission from the man they were interviewing. 'How did it happen?' he asked.

Cameron glanced back over his shoulder, almost wearily. 'A car crash. She'd been living with Cate Nicholas for almost a year. She was driving up to Leeds to see her. It was a wet night, she skidded, and she went straight into a telegraph pole. It seems she had been drinking somewhat . . . life apparently was getting to her.' He grimaced, in self-disgust. 'Maybe I was responsible in part for that . . . I couldn't handle her desertion. I kept pestering her, making things difficult for her . . .' He stopped, stared at his hands. 'There's no doubt I have to take some of the responsibility.'

Culpeper watched him silently. The man had ghosts to contend with; shadows that still affected him when he had time to reflect. He cleared his throat self-consciously. 'How did Cate Nicholas react to the death of your wife?'

There was a short silence. Cameron raised his head slowly, his eyes regretful. 'She took it badly. So did I. We . . . we fell out even more violently than before. I blamed her for Joanna's death. If she hadn't left me, she wouldn't have been driving to Leeds . . . that sort of thing. Cate Nicholas, on the other hand, blamed me, saying I'd been unsupportive of Joanna, had driven her away, and then caused her anxiety and distress by my persecution after she'd gone. It wasn't really like that, you know . . . but Cate Nicholas could have a bad mouth. Anyway, that's when things got really nasty . . . I mean, petulant, trivial nastiness . . .'

'What happened?'

Cameron shrugged. 'I suppose, looking back, I overreacted. But it was like a slap in the face — Joanna had made a will. She had money of her own, and she had a cottage up on the fells. The cottage at Bickley Moorside. It had been left to her by an aunt, years before, and it was in Joanna's name. Well, Cate Nicholas came up with a copy of a will written in Joanna's own hand — a holograph will, they call it — by which she'd left a number of personal items to Cate Nicholas — jewellery, safe deposit, that sort of thing — and I was unhappy about that. No, not unhappy — mad as hell, maybe unreasonably so. But you see, it sort of . . . emphasized things, the breakdown of our relationship — you know what I mean? And so when I heard she'd left her the cottage as well, something snapped. I disputed probate.'

'You tried to overturn the will?' Culpeper asked, surprised. 'But were you short of money—?'

'Oh, I didn't *need* the damned place. But Joanna and I had spent time there in the old days. Good times. I was angry . . . and the longer it went on between me and Cate Nicholas, the more bitter it became. It was almost two years of bickering and unpleasantness — and I regretted ever starting it. But it was too late to go back, too late to back down.' He shook his head miserably. 'The thing was a disaster, from start to finish.'

'You failed to overturn the will,' Culpeper said.

Cameron nodded. 'She was allowed to keep the cottage, and the rest of the personal things.'

'Is that why you went in there and trashed the place?'

The room was suddenly still. Cameron stared at Culpeper dumbly, taken aback. His eyes were blank, unreadable, but his mouth had tightened with a sudden tension. 'I don't know what you're talking about.'

'Oh, surely you do,' Culpeper said easily. 'It's understandable in a way. I mean, you'd lost your wife to this woman. She'd bested you in a probate battle, she'd moved north to a job at the university and was able to use the cottage now she'd won probate — it would be only natural to go in there and cause damage, in a fit of anger and resentment.'

'Not natural for me,' Cameron replied coldly.

'So you didn't take the place apart, when she finally got hold of it?' Farnsby pressed.

Cameron didn't turn his head. 'No,' he said shortly. Culpeper waited for a little while, toying with the pencil thoughtfully. 'So what happened then?'

Cameron raised his eyebrows in puzzlement. 'Happened? Nothing. What I'm telling you is all old history. I found the whole thing a hassle — this probate business — but Joanna's been dead almost two years, my life's moved on, the business is going well — and that's about it.'

'So you've had no contact with Cate Nicholas since she moved into the area?'

Cameron shook his head. 'I'd not even spoken to her.'

'But she's spoken about you,' Culpeper suggested.

'I'm not aware of it.'

'The television broadcast, surely!' Culpeper leaned forward. 'She made allegations, suggesting some sort of skulduggery was going on up at the Ravenstone operation. She was aiming a barb at Cossman International — your company. Didn't that have any effect on you? Didn't that make you angry — the way she was intruding into your life again?'

Cameron smiled contemptuously, and shook his head. 'I saw a tape of that broadcast. I wouldn't even give it the accolade of responding to it. She was talking a lot of rubbish. Unsubstantiated rubbish. If I had dignified it by entering into an argument with her, I would have been playing into her hands. She was just out to niggle at me, pay me back for the hassle over the cottage. Childish, stupid, irrelevant. Just an attempt to make her programme controversial and seemingly hard-hitting. I've got other things on my mind, Mr Culpeper. There was no way I was going to even respond to her vague allegations.'

'So it didn't upset you?'

'It caused me a moment's irritation, no more.' Cameron shook his head and smiled confidently. 'I've got a business to run and no time to mess about any longer with Cate Nicholas. She'd already taken a chunk out of my life. I'd already made a bad two-year investment with her affairs.'

'So the television programme didn't make you want to go out and brain her?' Culpeper asked tastelessly, but smiling, as though to take the sting from his words.

'She wasn't worth the time or effort,' Cameron replied calmly.

'And you've no information you can give us about her death?' Thor Cameron grimaced. 'None whatsoever. I . . . I came in here today to make things clear to you. I hated that woman's guts. She destroyed my marriage. She caused me two years of hassle I could have done without . . .' He held up a hand. 'All right, maybe it was largely my own doing, the

157

probate case . . . but that's as far as my resentment and anger went. I've had no contact with her since — and didn't want any. That was it. I was getting on with my life. The broadcast was a minor irritation, a pin prick. But when I heard she'd been murdered . . .' He hesitated, stared frankly at Culpeper across the desk. 'I knew when you made enquiries there would always be the chance, when you looked into her background, that something about all this would come out. I thought it better to tell you myself . . . before someone else did.'

'So you can tell us nothing more about the circumstances surrounding her death?' Culpeper persisted doubtfully.

'Nothing.' Cameron's tone was firm and precise.

Culpeper nodded. He glanced towards Farnsby, to see if the detective inspector had anything to ask. Farnsby shook his head slightly. Culpeper smiled. 'Well, I'll just thank you for coming in, Mr Cameron. You're right — telling us yourself is the better way. We probably would have heard something . . . but you've helped clear the air somewhat. Meanwhile, if there is anything else that occurs to you that might be relevant . . .'

Culpeper stood up. Cameron rose also and extended his hand. His grip was firm. 'If there is anything I can do to help . . .' he mumbled. 'I hated the woman, but . . .'

Culpeper smiled benignly. 'Well, that's all water under the bridge, isn't it? We'll be in touch if there is anything . . . Although . . .' he paused, eyeing Cameron in a calculating manner. 'There is one thing you might be able to help us on.'

'What's that?'

'I understand you have a man working for you called Paul Stillwater.'

Thor Cameron blinked. His chin came up, and he nodded slowly. 'That's right. He's my PR man — deals with the press, and generally makes himself responsible for company image — that sort of thing.'

'How long has he been with you?'

Cameron shrugged. 'Paul joined us about eighteen months ago, when we started planning the Ravenstone tender. He's got excellent contacts and he's proved to be a useful member of staff.' Cameron hesitated, his eyes wary. 'Why are you interested in Stillwater?'

Culpeper frowned thoughtfully, and shrugged. 'Well, it seems there was bad blood between him and Cate Nicholas.'

'Not that I was aware of,' Cameron said quickly, in surprise 'I don't believe they even knew each other.'

Culpeper regarded him steadily. 'We have information to the effect that there was an altercation between Cate Nicholas and Paul Stillwater up at the Ravenstone site. Words were exchanged, thereafter, Nicholas was advised to leave the site. Indeed, we are reliably informed' — from the corner of his eye he saw Farnsby wince at Culpeper's description of university gossip — 'that she was barred from the site by Paul Stillwater.'

Culpeper paused. 'It's one of the reasons, we believe, why she had a go at you all, on her broadcast. There was bad blood between her and Stillwater — so she tried to get her revenge by veiled hints of illegal practices—'

Thor Cameron chuckled mirthlessly. 'You've got it wrong, Mr Culpeper. There was no cause for argument between Cate Nicholas and Paul Stillwater. As far as I'm aware Paul didn't know her. You're following a false trail there. The fact of the matter is that when Cate Nicholas walked into that room at Ravenstone, I was on the platform party. I saw her come in. When the presentation was over, I made it clear to Paul in no uncertain terms, that I didn't want that woman on the premises. He knew — could see — I was annoyed, but I didn't explain my reasons. I simply told him to get her off site, and to ban her from any further visits. It was a . . . an immediate reaction on my part to seeing her there. But as I said, I've never even spoken to her since she arrived up here. Paul did the speaking for me that day. He doesn't know why I wanted her off site. So I wouldn't even bother talking to him about it. He's had no relationship with her. There was no quarrel between them. The quarrel was mine.'

He hesitated, and his eyes became steely. 'In fact, I'd be grateful if you didn't bother him at all with this. He's got a lot on his plate right now — negotiations with the Treasury, having to persuade people to put money where their political mouths are — I don't want him . . . side-tracked. He'll have nothing to tell you about Nicholas. You'd be wasting your time. And his.'

'I see.' Culpeper chewed at his lip. He was left with the impression that Cameron felt strongly on the subject of Stillwater's time being wasted in murder interviews. Noncommittally, he said, 'Well, that gets one little problem out of the way for us, I suppose. Once again, thanks for coming in. Farnsby, will you see Mr Cameron off the premises? Then perhaps you'll call back with that file I requested earlier . . .'

Farnsby returned some ten minutes later with the DTI file tucked under his arm. He expelled his breath in a low whistle as he came in, and shook his head. 'Well, that was a funny old tale, wasn't it, sir?'

'What did you make of it?'

Farnsby shrugged. 'Sounded straight enough to me. Except in one respect. My bet would be that it was Cameron who trashed that cottage. Or had it trashed. In his position, I think I would have done it. He certainly disliked Nicholas enough — and it would have been natural to want to get his own back when she won the probate case.'

'You may be right. But trashing the cottage out of resentment is one thing, it's quite another, bashing her head in later. Just out of pique. What did you think about the television-broadcast issue?'

Farnsby pursed his lips. 'He sounded confident — even casual about it. I don't think it worried him. He hasn't taken it seriously.'

'Well, he wouldn't, would he? Not now the woman's dead. Still, I tend to agree . . . he took it in his stride when I challenged him. He sounded confident, brushing it aside as irrelevant and not worth pursuing.'

Farnsby nodded, and handed the DTI file to Culpeper. 'So maybe we can leave it. I was happy he cleared things up with regard to the Stillwater-Nicholas feud, too. There wasn't one, it seems, it was just Stillwater carrying out his boss's orders. So I suppose we can forget about him as far as interviewing is concerned.'

Smugly, Culpeper opened the file Farnsby had handed to him. 'Ah, well, I'm not so sure about that, young man. One of the advantages of age and experience is that one develops sensitive nostrils. When a smell emanates, even a very old one, the nostril hairs get excited.'

Farnsby stared at him, uncomprehending.

Culpeper tapped the file with a predatory finger. 'You remember I told you to hang on to this file? Well, it's always a good thing, hanging on to old files. Until you're sure they're really dead, I mean.' He leered in self-satisfaction. 'I think you should take a look again at this folder, Farnsby. Because it's been on my mind for some time, ever since Paul Stillwater's name was mentioned in connection with this murder enquiry. I kept thinking . . . I've come across the name before.'

Farnsby creased his brow. 'In these papers?'

'Exactly. It may well be that Stillwater had no quarrel with Cate Nicholas, but he does have an interesting sort of background. If you look at that file you'll see his name. He was once employed by none other than our friend Ken Allison — the man who was wanted for questioning about the illegal sale of sensitive software into eastern Europe. The file says he was cleared, was Stillwater . . . and presumably that was when he came north and joined Cossman International — but I don't like loose ends. Allison is dead, the man who knifed him and shoved him into the river in Prague is dead. And Stillwater's name is on that file.'

'Coincidence. Could mean nothing.'

'Or might mean something.' Culpeper smiled cheerily. 'Let's find out, anyway — keep an eye on our friend Stillwater. We'll interview him in any case, put some pressure on, see what emerges.'

161

And in any event, Culpeper had the satisfaction of knowing that he had been proved right, keeping the DTI file open. Moreover, from the irritation in Farnsby's eyes he could see that Farnsby knew it also — which was a source for even greater satisfaction as far as Detective Chief Inspector Culpeper was concerned.

3

Culpeper's appointment with Nick Towers was for three o'clock so he had time to spare. He drove across country from Ponteland to Morpeth and the roads were quiet. He took a leisurely lunch at the George Hotel, and finished it off with a brandy — he had no doubt Towers would appreciate the rather more mellow tones he would probably adopt now he had that inside him. Not that it would damage John Culpeper's perceptiveness, of course, he considered, though his missus might have other views.

After lunch he took the luxury of an amble through the town, glancing in various windows as he made his way towards the address Towers's secretary had given him over the phone. He was still in the main street when he caught sight of a familiar face.

'Mr Landon! And how are you?'

Arnold Landon stopped, surprise mingled with a certain vague guiltiness. He was carrying a plastic bag with a supermarket symbol. 'Been shopping in work time?' Culpeper greeted him.

'I had a little shopping to do, yes. And I took a late lunch break.' Landon appeared slightly flustered about something as he looked at the chief inspector. 'What brings you to Morpeth, Mr Culpeper?'

'A policeman's lot, you know,' Culpeper replied cheerfully. 'In fact, the Nicholas enquiry.'

'I see.'

Culpeper observed Landon, squinting at him in the weak afternoon sunshine. He scratched his cheek. 'Of course, you knew the woman, didn't you?'

'Cate Nicholas? We'd met, yes,' Landon replied shortly.

'That's right. I hear you were with her when she made that complaint down in Newcastle — about her car being shoved into the Tyne.'

Landon nodded. 'I gave her a lift up to the station, from the Quayside. Did they ever find out who did it?'

'Oh, we've a pretty good idea about the culprit. But there just wasn't enough to go on to make an arrest. Though there may be other charges pending, in due course . . .' Culpeper paused. 'So you didn't know her well, then?'

'Not really,' Landon said, a shade too quickly for Culpeper's liking. 'I met her through . . . through Karen Stannard.'

'Ah yes, the deputy director . . .' Culpeper frowned, thinking about rumours he had heard concerning the elegantly beautiful Ms Stannard. And she had been a friend of the dead woman. It was something to think about, he considered — Karen Stannard and Cate Nicholas. 'So Ms Stannard . . . it was she who introduced you.'

'That evening . . . after the concert in the Theatre Royal.'

'You came across Ms Nicholas again though, didn't you?' There was a short silence.

Arnold Landon shuffled uneasily, and nodded. 'I did. I was up at Ravenstone — at the presentation when she and Ms Stannard had an argument with . . .'

'Paul Stillwater?'

Landon hesitated. 'That's right. Stillwater as good as threw her off the site. It was more than a little embarrassing.'

'Hmmm.' Culpeper watched Arnold Landon for a few moments. There was something nervy about him; he was on edge about something. It took a great deal to upset Landon — that was Culpeper's view. He had depths to him that Culpeper would never understand — his passion for wood and stone was well-known but Culpeper had also seen evidence of the man's mental toughness. But something was bothering him now. Culpeper felt he'd like to find out what it was. 'You going back to the office?'

'I'm on my way now.'

'I have an appointment in a moment — should be a little while. But I ought to be finished before you knock off work. I wonder whether I might be able to call in to see you at the office. Perhaps you could lay on a cup of tea for me. Earl Grey, if you can manage it.' Culpeper grinned guilelessly. 'And then maybe we could have a little chat, bonny lad — about you, Karen Stannard, and the Nicholas woman.'

He could see that Landon was not enamoured of the prospect. But he nodded, and began to move on.

'I'll be at my desk, Mr Culpeper. You know where to find me.'

'I do indeed, bonny lad,' Culpeper said happily and brushed on past him to make his way towards Nick Towers's office at the far end of town.

It was dingy, in a dingy street, in a dingy part of the town. Culpeper was used to seeing solicitors in rather grander premises, even when they made their living by representing villains from Newcastle, Shields, and all points north of the Tyne. Towers clearly was not of that merry band. His practice could not be up to much and if he expected to encourage clients to beat their way to his door, he had selected the wrong part of town. Maybe it was all he could afford.

As for Nick Towers himself, he was equally unimpressive. He looked inexperienced. His youth would have something to do with that, but it was also emphasized by his thin, unhappy features, and lugubrious, downtrodden air, as though he had the cares of the world on his narrow shoulders. He had a hangdog look about him, and the hint of a perpetual, subdued panic at the back of his eyes. He was a man who did not face life with confidence and Culpeper began to appreciate why he came to have an office in a backwater like this. Maybe he was even hiding from possible clients, Culpeper thought sourly. Perhaps he couldn't face them bringing problems he couldn't solve.

'So, what is it I can do for you, Chief Inspector?' Towers asked, struggling to raise a smile, but managing only an ineffectual grimace.

'I'm investigating the death of a woman called Cate Nicholas. I've no doubt you've read about it in the newspapers. There have been more than a few headlines — and screwball theories.'

Towers licked thin, nervous lips. 'The gentlemen of the press are known to be somewhat . . . erratic on occasions.'

'That's right.' Culpeper smiled generously. 'Solicitors, now, they're a different breed. Upholders of the law — careful, cautious, precise — all that sort of thing.'

'Yes . . . So . . . ?'

Towers was not enjoying Culpeper's presence. That interested Culpeper. He leaned back in his chair in the dingy office, at ease and confident. 'How well did you know Ms Nicholas?'

Towers blinked. 'Know her? I didn't . . . not at all. I just read about her and—'

'You didn't know her? But she seemed to know things about you, Mr Towers,' Culpeper said in mock-surprise.

Towers didn't want to say it, but he did. 'I don't understand. What things?'

Culpeper smiled a bland smile. 'As I understand it, she must have carried out some investigation or other, which would seem to have involved you, because she took part in a television programme which suggested that the legal advice received by the Adler Foundation had been . . . not entirely to its advantage.'

There was silence in the room. Towers stared at Culpeper and his face was pale; a nerve twitched in his cheek, but there was something behind the inevitable sadness in his eyes. Culpeper could have sworn it was a growing anger. 'The comments she made . . . on that programme, could not be substantiated. It was a farrago of innuendo, and in other circumstances I would have sued—'

'The other circumstances being . . . if she was still alive?' Culpeper asked.

Towers was silent, his mouth taut as a bowstring. But the anger was still in his eyes. 'I'm not sure what you're getting at, Mr Culpeper. Are you insinuating—?'

'Now hold on, Mr Towers,' Culpeper interrupted. 'Let's not talk about insinuations. I'm here to investigate a murder. Now, I've no idea whether what Cate Nicholas claimed on that broadcast had a basis in fact or not. That'll be for others to find out, maybe — though we've had no formal request to open an investigation into what went on over deals between the Adler Foundation and Cossman International. Not so far, anyway. I'm just interested in—'

'Wait a minute, Mr Culpeper,' the solicitor almost gasped. 'You might be inclined to dismiss the statements she made on that occasion, but I cannot — and will not! What she said was defamatory. I cannot do much about it now other than take it up with the producers — which means the matter is left hanging over me, a slur on my reputation. As for your suggestion that the matter will be looked into by others, I would welcome that. When I advised the trustees of the foundation, my advice was made in good faith. It was time to end a long-standing feud, and it was to the advantage of the foundation that the land should be sold. When Mr Stillwater came to me in the first instance—'

'Stillwater?' Culpeper interrupted. 'It was he who conducted the negotiations? But I thought he was just a PR man.'

Towers licked his lips. 'I wouldn't know about that. All I can say is that he came to me as a representative of Cossman International and discussed the matter with me. He explained that the programme could be badly affected — they had discovered that access would not be possible to take fullest advantage of Farston land without the areas owned by the Adler Foundation. He made a good offer. I put that offer to the trustees and they accepted it.' His tone had become excited, his words tumbling out almost frantically. 'I then went to the Charity Commissioners. It was agreed by them. Everything was done properly. It was all above board—'

'So why did she query the whole thing?' Culpeper interrupted deliberately, stoking up the fires of the solicitor's anger.

'How should I know? Malice. Hatred—'

'She disliked Stillwater? Or you?' Culpeper pounced.

'I didn't *know* her!' Towers insisted. 'As for Stillwater . . . look, I really didn't know what their relationship was. All I can say is that her allegations caused me great distress, and my wife . . .'

His voice died away and he bit his lip. Culpeper leaned forward sympathetically. 'Ah, yes. I gather your wife was taken ill . . .'

Towers nodded bitterly. 'She's still in hospital. My wife . . . Marjorie . . . she's not been well for years. She's . . . delicate. Asthma. A heart condition. She'd been watching that damned programme. She knew what that Nicholas woman was getting at. She was upset. She tried to ring me. She got overexcited and it brought on an attack. They had to rush her to hospital. I was beside myself . . .'

He was sweating. A line of perspiration ran along his upper lip and he was gripped by a fierce tension as though he were reliving the painful experiences of the last few weeks. He would normally be a man of relatively mild disposition, Culpeper guessed, but under stress a fierce anger could break out. And a threat to his wife . . .

'You're very fond of your wife,' Culpeper said slowly. 'You looked after her . . .'

'Of course,' Towers snapped.

Culpeper was silent for a little while as Towers sat there and sweated. He tried to imagine Towers getting into a real rage, picking up something heavy . . . Towers had got very excited at the discussion of the allegations made against him on television, and he had got even more heated at explaining what had happened to his wife as a consequence. But there was something else too. Culpeper wondered what it was.

'This isn't a very big practice,' he suggested quietly.

The sad, angry eyes suddenly grew careful. 'It's big enough.'

'One-man show?'

'I like working alone.'

'But not too many clients.'

'There are enough.'

'Yes, but I suppose in a small office like this, with not too many clients, your turnover wouldn't be all that large. I was just wondering . . . do you have any corporate clients?'

'What do you mean?' Towers asked edgily.

'Well, a country solicitor like you, you'll have shopkeepers, farmers . . . but what about corporate clients? Big companies. Not many on the doorstep, of course. Except maybe . . . Cossman International.'

Towers was silent. He waited, knowing what was coming; perhaps he'd been expecting it for some time.

'Do you have Cossman as a client, Mr Towers?'

The answer had been well rehearsed, even though his mouth was dry. 'I'm not at liberty to discuss with you who my clients are, Mr Culpeper. It's a matter of confidentiality.'

'Of course.' Culpeper smiled. He had already guessed the answer. If there had been an approach from Stillwater for the Adler Foundation land it was quite on the cards that Stillwater could have made another proposal — veiled or otherwise — to Towers. With a practice like this, Towers would have found it hard to refuse. Not that it would have affected his advice to the foundation trustees, of course, Culpeper said to himself, cynically.

'Still,' Culpeper continued, 'I suppose a small practice like this has other advantages. I mean, you can spend more time with your wife, especially if she's ill. Or you can go fishing when the mood takes you. Do you fish, Mr Towers?'

'No.'

'Walking, then.'

Towers was silent. Culpeper smiled thinly. 'Yes, this practice would give you time to get out and about. Your secretary . . . is she full time?'

'One full day, three half-days a week,' Towers replied reluctantly.

'So she wouldn't be able to tell me exactly when you were in the office . . . and when you weren't.'

There was a short silence. Finally, Towers screwed up enough courage to ask, 'Why would you want to know?'

Culpeper shrugged. 'It's just a thought I have. You see, after Cate Nicholas made that broadcast — which upset more than a few people, it seems — she made a complaint to the police. She claimed she was being followed . . . she said she had a stalker. She wanted police protection. She didn't get it, because her story was a bit . . . hazy. She hadn't seen the man in question . . . and a lot of it was a sort of . . . creepy feeling of being watched.'

'Why are you telling me this?' Towers asked stiffly.

'Well, I was just thinking, if you go out for walks when there's not much on in the office, and your secretary isn't here, I was just wondering where exactly you might choose to go on such walks. Newcastle? Quiet university precincts? The fells?'

Towers seemed to be having difficulty breathing. 'I didn't say I took walks.'

'That's right. You didn't.' Culpeper's tone took on a steelier note. 'But you were upset about the attack on your legal integrity. You were even more upset when your wife suffered from that broadcast. And you had time on your hands, to brood while she was in hospital and there were no clients at your door. Are you telling me you didn't do anything about it? You didn't take out a writ, did you? So what did you do? Did you go for a few walks, Mr Towers? Were you stalking Cate Nicholas . . . wondering how to get your own back on her? Or maybe wondering how to shut her up for good?'

He'd blown it — gone too far. Towers was standing up, indignation, forced or otherwise, boiling over. 'I don't have to respond to such insinuations, Culpeper! I agreed to this interview to be of any assistance that I could. But this is outrageous! You're implying there's truth in these rumours spread by that woman. You're even suggesting I had something to do with her death!' He was spluttering with a hollow, forced fury now. 'I think this meeting is at an end.'

Obscenities rolled around in Culpeper's mind as he cursed himself. Stupid. Overreaching. And yet there was something more than mere righteous anger in Nick Towers's demeanour. Culpeper detected panic, in addition. Fear was sweating from every pore in the man's face.

Time to go for a cup of Earl Grey, Culpeper thought sourly. There was no more to be gained from the solicitor now.

* * *

When Arnold heard the door to his office open, he expected to see Detective Chief Inspector Culpeper, but it turned out to be the bane of office life, the gossiping Jerry Picton.

'So, what's new, Arnold?'

'Nothing as far as I'm concerned, though doubtless you've picked up something riveting as usual.'

Picton bared sharp, yellow teeth. 'Well, you know how it is, Arnold. Can I help it if people tell me things? It's not for me to say they shouldn't!'

'I can't imagine what possesses them to talk to you. What do you want, anyway? I'm expecting a visitor.'

Jerry Picton shrugged diffidently. 'Just calling in for a chat. Quiet moment, end of the day.' He watched Arnold for a few moments, his mean eyes narrowed in contemplation. 'You found out what's got into our amazingly beautiful and talented deputy director yet?'

'I don't know what you're talking about.'

'Of course you do, Arnold,' Jerry Picton said testily. 'She's been walking around with a face like thunder and a temper like a bear with a sore backside! I mean, she's bad enough at normal times, but the last couple of weeks or so she's been putting the knife into everybody! I mean, the story was it was that broadcast by Cate Nicholas; it may well have upset her, and I hear she got carpeted by the chief executive and our pink-shirted director for letting some cats out of the bag or other . . . you wouldn't know anything about that, would you?'

'No.'

Jerry Picton leered. 'Lying bastard! You were involved, bonny lad — I know it for a fact. But I don't hold it against you, keeping your mouth shut. An admirable trait.'

Arnold glanced at him cynically. 'Pity you don't observe it in practice.'

'Ah, well, not in me constitution, you know!' Picton grinned wolfishly. 'Anyway, I didn't put too much store in that story myself. I reckon there was something else in the wind. You want to hear my theory?'

'No.'

'Well, I'm in a generous mood today so I'll tell you anyway.'

Picton announced, leaning casually against the door jamb. 'Fact is, I hear our delectable Ms Stannard was more than a bit sweet on that Cate Nicholas — they'd got right chummy these last couple of months. Going to the theatre, private dinners and all that — but you'd know that anyway, wouldn't you, Arnold?'

When Arnold made no reply, Picton leered again, confidentially. 'Well, no matter. What I hear is that the affair was a bit short-lived, like. Karen Stannard fell out with her bosom pal not so much because of that broadcast — it was more like because Cate Nicholas started chumming up with someone else. Want to know who? Why, man, that Angie Rothwell — the presenter of her programme on television. Ravin' lesbian, man. And our Karen got her nose put out of joint — getting the heave-ho wasn't her idea of fun at all.' He prodded a triumphant finger in Arnold's direction. 'So that's why she's got the hump these days. It's because Cate Nicholas dumped her.'

Arnold leaned back in his chair, his mouth thin with contempt. 'You're talking about someone who's just been murdered, Picton. Why don't you just leave things alone?'

Jerry Picton spread innocent hands wide. 'Hey, bonny lad, I'm just an observer of life, like! Can I help it if I'm surrounded by swirling cesspools of humanity? I—'

He stopped abruptly, turned his head as he became aware someone was standing behind him in the corridor. 'Hey, sorry, man! You wantin' to come in?'

'That's the general idea,' Culpeper said, and stepped past him. 'Not interrupting anything, am I?'

'Mr Picton was just leaving,' Arnold replied shortly.

'That's right.' Picton grinned, oblivious to the contemptuous looks he was getting. 'Not business really, just chewin' the fat, like.' He kept the grin as he stared at Culpeper, but his eyes were sharp. 'Don't I know you?'

'I don't know you,' Culpeper replied. Arnold got the impression from the coldness of his glance that Culpeper wouldn't have minded coming across Picton, in other circumstances.

'It's Chief Inspector Culpeper, isn't it?' Picton said, snapping his fingers excitedly. 'Seen you on the regional news a couple of tunes. So what you doin' here, then?' He flashed a glance in Arnold's direction. 'Been up to somethin', has he?'

'Social call,' Culpeper announced easily. 'Come in for a cup of tea.'

'I'll just get it,' Arnold said and rose to leave the room. Disappointed, Picton went on his way.

When Arnold returned a few minutes later, with a cup of tea for Culpeper and a coffee for himself, Culpeper was leaning against the window, looking out into the car park. He turned as Arnold came in, holding out the cup. 'Thanks . . . Who was that mean-faced little bugger?'

'Office gossip.'

'I wouldn't mind feeling his collar some day,' Culpeper remarked. 'Can you give me an excuse?'

Arnold smiled. 'Only if gossip is a criminal offence.'

Culpeper grunted, and sipped his tea. It wasn't Earl Grey, but Arnold guessed he wouldn't complain. Culpeper was no fool. He was here for a reason. He had seen something in Arnold when they had met in the High Street, detected some of the unease Arnold had been feeling for some days.

'So, how is life treating you, Mr Landon?' Culpeper asked affably.

Arnold shrugged. 'We have enough problems to contend with.' He hesitated. 'And you . . . how is the investigation going?'

Culpeper gave him a wintry smile. 'Let's say we are pursuing various lines of enquiry. One of them affects you, really. I gather you were up at the Ravenstone site when there was a quarrel involving the deceased lady. Is that right?'

Arnold nodded. 'Yes. She was refused lunch . . . turned away from the site.'

'Barred, I understand . . . Whose doing was that?'

Arnold hesitated. 'Paul Stillwater. I don't know why he behaved so . . . rudely, or what motivated him. But I have to say he was pretty hard-faced about it.' Arnold stopped. He had the feeling from something in Culpeper's face that there was more to it than that. He did not pursue the matter.

'Maybe he had reasons . . .' Culpeper mused. 'Did you come across Thor Cameron also?'

'Yes. I'd met him earlier. We didn't speak at the presentation.'

'Did Cate Nicholas meet him?' Culpeper asked, elaborately casual.

'Not that I'm aware.'

Culpeper shrugged and was silent for a little while, sipping his tea thoughtfully. At last, he said quietly, 'I get the impression something's bothering you, Mr Landon. When we met in the High Street you were . . . preoccupied, nervous about something. I didn't know I made you nervous . . .'

Arnold stared at him. Slowly, he nodded. 'It's not exactly nervousness, Mr Culpeper. It's . . . indecision.'

'Now what would you be being indecisive about, bonny lad?' Culpeper asked smiling encouragingly.

Arnold hesitated. 'It's just that . . . maybe I should have come to you before. It's been on mind and I don't want to start hares—'

'What's been on your mind?'

Culpeper's tone was harder, steel-edged. Arnold held his glance firmly 'It's just that . . . well, I understand Cate Nicholas was killed sometime on Wednesday last.'

'That's what forensic tell us. Discovered Saturday but killed on Wednesday,' Culpeper agreed, his one eyebrow raised questioningly. 'Do you have a problem with that.'

Arnold shook his head. 'No. It's just that . . . well I was up there on Wednesday afternoon, late on.'

'You were up there? At Bickley Moorside?' Culpeper put down his cup carefully. 'What were you doing there?'

'I'd been to the Garrigill site. I took the back road back over Bickley—'

'That's some distance out of your way.'

Arnold held his quick glance. 'It was on impulse — I was curious to see the cottage . . . just inquisitive really.'

'And did you go down to the cottage?' Culpeper asked sharply.

Arnold shook his head. 'No. I didn't . . . You see, although I was curious to see the cottage, I didn't get on well with Ms Nicholas. I didn't like her, she probably reciprocated. So I parked on the ridge and just looked down at the cottage . . . it was about five, or thereabouts . . .'

'Go on.'

Arnold shrugged. 'That's about it really.' He hesitated, frowning. 'I just thought you should know. She'd have been dead by then, wouldn't she? Do you know exactly what time she did die?'

Culpeper ignored the question. His eyes were unrelenting.

'You haven't told me everything. What else happened? What else did you see there?'

Reluctantly, Arnold said, 'I was some distance away, on the ridge. I couldn't see much. I didn't want to meet Cate Nicholas. So when I saw a car turning around in front of the cottage—'

'You saw someone there?'

'Not really . . . I mean, I saw the car, turning to come back up the fellside. I assumed at the time it was Cate Nicholas, leaving. I didn't want to see her. So I went back to my own car, and left.'

There was a short silence. Culpeper stared at him, expectantly.

At last he said, 'You should have come forward with this information before now.'

Uneasily, Arnold nodded. 'I know.'

'So why didn't you?' When Arnold made no reply, Culpeper glared at him in the lengthening silence. 'There's something else, isn't there? You saw something else.'

Behind him, in the car park, there was the sound of an engine starting. Arnold rose, and walked across to the window, stood looking out.

'Well? What is it you saw, Landon?'

'Nothing really. I mean, I didn't see the driver. But . . .'

Culpeper joined him at the window, puzzled. 'But what . . . ?'

'It was a blue car. It was turning up the fellside. It was only later that I realized it couldn't have been Cate Nicholas. And then, I thought . . .'

He fell silent, concerned that he might be saying too much, getting things wrong. The policeman was standing beside him. Culpeper dragged his glance away from Landon's face, turning to see what he was staring at down in the car park. A blue Montego was just pulling away, through the gateway to the car park. Culpeper watched it go, as a slow excitement began to stir in his veins.

'You say you saw a blue car coming up from the cottage last Wednesday. Whose car is that down there?' he asked.

Arnold's tone was flat, and reluctant. 'Karen Stannard's,' he said.

CHAPTER FIVE

1

'Mr Cameron didn't want us to talk to you,' Culpeper said cheerfully to the big, craggy-featured man sitting across the desk from him in his office. 'I suppose he thought there was nothing you could say to help. I'm grateful, anyway, for your finding the time to come in to see us.'

'I was in the area,' Paul Stillwater replied. 'It was no great problem for me — and I'm happy to do anything I can to help.' Culpeper observed the big, broad-shouldered man with the greying, short-cropped hair, and nodded. 'Mr Cameron told us you didn't really know Ms Nicholas at all.'

'That's right. I guess that's why he would have said you'd be wasting your time, talking to me. I didn't know her — only spoke to her the one time.'

'That would be when you . . . ah . . . turned her away from the Ravenstone site.' Culpeper paused. He eyed Stillwater carefully, noting the man's firm jaw and heavy, ridged eyebrows. A strong character, he suspected, one who wouldn't bend too easily. 'As far as I understand, the discussion you had with her was somewhat . . . harsh.'

'I wouldn't say that,' Stillwater disagreed. 'I merely told her she wasn't welcome at the site.'

'Why was that?'

'Why she wasn't welcome? I've no idea,' Stillwater replied blandly. 'I was just obeying my instructions.'

'From Mr Cameron.'

'That's right.'

'And he didn't explain the reasons? He didn't tell you why she was to be sent packing?'

Stillwater shrugged. 'He didn't have to. He's the boss.'

'But weren't you curious?'

'It was obvious that there had been some . . . disagreement between them, at some time or another.' He paused, eyeing Culpeper carefully, a slight frown on his brow. 'You see, Thor Cameron saw her enter the presentation room when he was still on the platform. Once the presentation was over and people were about to go in for lunch, he grabbed me. He told me in no uncertain terms that she hadn't been invited, he didn't want her there and she was to be told to leave the site — it is private property, after all — and that was that, because, like I said — he's the boss.'

'I see. So as far as you and Cate Nicholas were concerned there was no personal . . .' He appealed to Farnsby, seated across the room. 'What's the word?'

'Animus,' Farnsby supplied.

'Yes. No personal feelings,' Culpeper said drily, staring at Farnsby mockingly. Farnsby flushed, as Culpeper turned back to Stillwater. The big man raised his heavily ridged eyebrows. 'No, why should there be, on my part? I didn't know her at all. That was the first — and only — time we met.'

'So you say.' Culpeper nodded thoughtfully. 'Mind you, I suppose things changed later.'

'How do you mean?'

'Well, I suppose you were more than a little displeased about her television broadcast. That would have caused you to have . . . personal feelings.'

'I didn't see the broadcast,' Stillwater replied abruptly.

'But you must have heard about it — I mean, surely it was discussed at Ravenstone!'

Irritably, Stillwater nodded. 'Of course it was discussed. Thor Cameron spoke to me about it. But it was no big deal. Certainly, Thor intended doing nothing about it — it was a pin prick, a flea bite. We all had much more important things to worry about. It wasn't worth bothering with.'

Culpeper widened his eyes in mock amazement. 'Is that right? Not worth bothering about? The company's financial state had been called into question. Veiled comments had been made about the relationship between the Adler Foundation and the company, hints of skulduggery were thrown around, and you yourself—'

'Look here,' Stillwater interrupted, the edge of irritation now clear in his tone. 'I've told you it wasn't important. There was nothing in those wild statements that could have been substantiated. She was just talking hot air. It didn't bother Thor Cameron and it didn't bother me. There was no way she could have proved any of the allegations she made.'

'*Proved?*' Culpeper grimaced. He noted that Stillwater was not saying the allegations were untrue — merely that Cate Nicholas couldn't have proved them. 'Well, we don't know about that, do we? It may well be that in due course we'll have to take a look at these . . . allegations.'

'Without the person who made them being around to stand up and justify them?' Stillwater scoffed. 'I can hardly believe that.'

'So her death was a convenience then, as far as you and others are concerned.'

'No, you don't catch me out on that one! All I can tell you — repeat — is that we weren't going to proceed against her,' Stillwater growled. 'There was going to be no defamation writ. It wasn't worth the trouble. She was just trying to make a noise, boost her programme. We were going to take no action.'

'And now you don't need to take action anyway, because the cause of the problem is dead.' Culpeper paused, and a mocking tone entered his voice. 'And you didn't really know her anyway. And you weren't upset by the allegations she made against you.'

Stillwater's features were composed, though his jaw was set hard and his mouth tight. He made no reply.

After a short interval of silence, Culpeper said, 'This Adler Foundation thing — it was you, I understand, who did the negotiating with the trustees?'

'That's right.'

'How did that come about?'

Stillwater shrugged. 'It was when we were doing the feasibility study for Ravenstone. We realized that there would be problems regarding access, so we approached the Adler Foundation. I met their solicitor, we had several discussions, and we were in general agreement about the stupidity of the continuance of an ancient quarrel — that did no one any good. At his suggestion I met the trustees and at the end of the day they sold us some of their holdings.' He paused, his dark eyes holding Culpeper's glance squarely. 'It made a big difference to our costings — made the whole thing feasible.'

'So striking a deal with the Adler Foundation was pretty important to Cossman?'

Stillwater shifted easily in the chair. He nodded, with confidence. 'We've never made any secret of that.'

'If it was so important to the company, why did they use you to negotiate? You'll forgive me, but you're just a PR man. How come you were chosen to do the talking with Towers?'

Stillwater's eyes were cool. 'I guess I was the one available at the time. There was no particular reason, otherwise — it was a matter for common sense in business, not for strictly legal consultations. And I think Thor himself was away in London, politicking, at the time.'

'So you and Mr Towers got together.' Culpeper smiled gently. 'I suppose he'll have done quite well out of it, himself, for a country solicitor.'

'How do you mean?'

'Oh, come on, Mr Stillwater,' Culpeper said heartily. 'We're all men of the world here. You must have given him some incentive to give the trustees the advice he did!'

Paul Stillwater was silent for a little while, his eyes fixed on Culpeper. At last, carefully, he said, 'I'm not quite sure what you're driving at.'

'No quid pro quo? No, you scratch my back, I'll scratch yours? No little legal consultancy for Towers out of the deal?'

Stillwater frowned, his dark eyes clouding below his heavy eyebrows. He glanced briefly at Farnsby, silent behind him, and then turned back to Culpeper. 'What's this all about? I came in here at your suggestion, ready to help in any way I can over the Nicholas murder but . . . why are you questioning me about other matters?'

'General background, bonny lad — general background, that's all. It just helps us get the whole picture, if you know what I mean . . . but if it bothers you, we can leave all that.'

'It doesn't bother me,' Stillwater growled irritably. 'There's nothing in what that damned woman said, and you're wasting your own time as well as mine by pursuing it.'

'As you say, as you say,' Culpeper soothed. 'So you didn't know her, knew nothing about her death . . . How long have you been working for Cossman International, Mr Stillwater?' Stillwater grimaced at the abrupt change in tack. 'About eighteen months or so.'

'What were you doing before that?'

'Various things. I joined Cossman from a job further south.'

'But not in PR, was it?'

'No.'

'So what exactly were you doing?' Culpeper asked.

'I was in electronics. I don't know what this has to do with—'

'Electronics? Would that include, say, software engineering?' There was a short silence. Stillwater's body seemed to have stiffened, as though he could guess what was coming.

'Yes, that's right. I was on the sales side. Systems design, computers . . .'

'And what was the name of the company?' Culpeper's fingers strayed to the manila folder on the desk in front of

184

him. Slowly he opened it and glanced briefly at the sheet inside. 'Ah, yes, Allison Products.'

'If you knew that, why did you ask me about it?' Stillwater said harshly.

'Just checking, bonny lad, like I said. General background.' Culpeper smiled, and closed the file. 'So you worked for Ken Allison, hey? Knew him well, did you?'

An angry wariness was now apparent in Stillwater's eyes. He cleared his throat nervously. 'Of course I knew Allison. And to save time, let's get things out in the open, on the table. I knew Allison, worked for him, but knew nothing about what he was up to in eastern Europe. I didn't know the Customs people were investigating him. I knew nothing about the Defence people getting on to him. I just got on with my job there, and it was a complete surprise to me when he suddenly disappeared. I learned later he was supposed to have gone on the run in Europe, but I had my own fill of questions about it all in the West Midlands. I knew nothing then, and I know nothing about it all now.'

'But I expect you know Allison is dead, don't you?' Culpeper suggested.

Stillwater made no reply.

'They fished him out of the river in Prague. Didn't you spend some time in Prague yourself at one time, Mr Stillwater?'

'You seem to have done your homework,' Stillwater said sourly. 'Yes, I worked there for a while, before I was with Allison Products. But there was no connection between the two activities. I was representing a firm involved in textile imports—'

'Did you know that the Dutch police finally tracked down the man who killed Allison?'

Stillwater was silent for a little while. 'No,' he said at last, heavily, 'I didn't know that. I haven't kept myself up to date with the Allison business. I've no great interest in it. The whole thing is in the past, I wasn't involved, and—'

'So, you didn't know what Allison was up to, and you know nothing about his death, and you didn't know Cate Nicholas really, and you know nothing about any fiddle over

185

the Adler Foundation, and you've nothing to tell us about the death up at Bickley Moorside . . . This interview really hasn't been very productive, has it, Mr Stillwater?'

The man's jaw was like granite. He glared at Culpeper. 'It was your idea to get me in here, not mine. Perhaps you should have taken Mr Cameron's advice in the first place.'

Culpeper smiled, leaned forward. 'And yet, you know, I have this odd feeling . . . experienced coppers get feelings like this, bonny lad . . . I just get the vague kind of impression that there's some things you're not telling me. Now why would that be?'

'You're wrong,' Stillwater replied calmly. 'I'm holding nothing back because there's nothing to hold back. I can't help you over the Nicholas killing. I've no idea why you've also dragged up the Allison business, but once again, I've nothing to say that can be any help to you there. This has just been a waste of time. And I've got work to do.'

Culpeper rose, scraping back his chair. 'Then we won't detain you any longer, Mr Stillwater.'

* * *

After Stillwater had gone, Culpeper looked at Farnsby. 'He's lying.'

'About what?'

'I don't know. But he's lying. I can feel it in my bones. He knows more about the Nicholas thing than he's letting on.'

'But he claims to have barely known her!'

'The hell with that! He needles me . . . and he's too damn innocent about the Allison business as well! I want a close watch kept on Mr Stillwater. Dig out what you can on him, in relation to Allison — and his time in Prague. The file is thin. Have a word with the DTI, and the Customs people. See if there's anything else.' He snorted angrily at the look on Farnsby's face. 'I have a *feeling* about this man, damn it!'

'Well, all right,' Farnsby said reluctantly. 'Meanwhile, I've been talking to university staff. There's been a bit of gossip about Joe Pitcher and the wife of the Dean of Humanities.'

'You mean he's been having it off with a colleague's wife?' Culpeper snorted disbelievingly. 'I wouldn't have thought any woman would fancy him. You think that's where Pitcher was on the Wednesday — with her?'

'It could be the reason why he's refused to tell us his whereabouts.'

'Then you'd better check it out.'

'What about Nick Towers?' Farnsby asked.

'You've run a check on his movements?'

Farnsby nodded. 'You were right about his secretary — she couldn't help over his diary. So he could well have been the one who was stalking Cate Nicholas. He's obsessive about his wife, and he was very shaken at her admission to hospital. It could have been enough to push him into a confrontation with Nicholas.'

'But as yet we can't place him at the scene of the crime.' Culpeper paused, and then added grimly, 'Whereas that's something we can certainly do as far as Karen Stannard's concerned, if Arnold Landon is right.'

'You interviewed her yesterday.'

Culpeper nodded. 'She's scared, rattled, but sticking to her guns. She denies ever having been up there, to the cottage. She admits a . . . close friendship, you might say, but told me it had cooled, ever since Cate Nicholas started palling up with that TV presenter Angie Rothwell. Have you run a check on *her*, by the way?'

'I have. She was out of town on the Wednesday — London. It's been verified.'

'Well, Ms Stannard is a tough lady and she's toughing it out. She says she was not angry with Cate Nicholas over the break-up of their friendship. And she was not at the cottage on Wednesday. But she can't really explain where she was for a period of time. She went to Garrigill and Evison Church, but she's vague about timings. I'm going to have to put some more pressure on her — maybe bring her in here.'

'You think she's lying?'

'I'm damn sure she is!'

2

Arnold had been dreading the thought of meeting Karen
Stannard. He had seen her at a distance on several occasions
in the building, but there had been neither the opportunity
nor need to speak to her. She had been hurrying off somewhere or other in her usual positive manner, papers clutched
under her arm, striding determinedly to her meetings. He
was certain that Culpeper would have interviewed her by
now, but surprisingly enough, not even Jerry Picton had
picked that up as a piece of gossip, so the interview must
have been carried out at police headquarters at Ponteland.

On the other hand, staff had clearly noticed her preoccu-
pation and the sharpness of her temper. She could be aggressive and cutting at the best of times, but of recent weeks she
had seemed completely out of sorts, impatiently vicious with
everyone whose path she crossed. Picton put it down to the
fact that she had been cut out with Cate Nicholas by Angie
Rothwell, and was taking out her anger at being discarded on
people around her. His retailing of the rumour gained him
an even greater degree of vituperation than usual. However,
most people had not met Cate Nicholas and disliked Picton's
sneering remarks about someone who had recently been
murdered.

Arnold had, of course, talked the matter over with Jane. After he had realized the car he had seen could have been Karen Stannard's, he had discussed with Jane what he should do. 'Talk to the police,' Jane had said firmly.

'But I can't be certain it was her,' Arnold had argued. 'All I saw was a blue car . . . I don't *know* it was hers. It was just that when I got to thinking . . . realizing she was up on the moor that day, and she was a friend of Cate Nicholas, the thought began to worry me.'

'You tell the police — let them worry about it.'

But he hadn't, for days. Perhaps he might never have done, if it hadn't been for the chance meeting with Culpeper in the street, when maybe the anxiety expressed in his demeanour had awakened Culpeper's interest. Because Arnold had been anxious. He had a gut feeling it had been Karen Stannard up at Bickley Moorside, but in suggesting this to Culpeper he had felt guilty. He could not be certain it was her. And he was betraying a colleague. Even if it was a colleague with whom he did not get on very well.

And in a sense, now that it was done and he had told Culpeper of his suspicion, he felt even worse. Culpeper hadn't told Arnold what he was going to do about it, but clearly he would have interviewed her. As the days went by, Arnold expected her to approach him, say something, demonstrate the bitterness of her anger, but nothing happened. He began to think that maybe Culpeper hadn't told her who had seen the car up at the cottage. He began to hope the whole thing had blown over, been satisfactorily explained.

So it was with a sinking heart that he saw her pause in the corridor a few days later, look back at him and then turn to walk deliberately towards him. She looked magnificent: her eyes a tawny colour, he thought, her lips compressed in decision, her bearing positive and determined. She stopped in front of him, riveted him with the coldness of her glance.

'Mr Landon — are you in the office all day today?'

Arnold nodded. 'I have a short meeting at two in the Planning Department, but apart from that—'

'Good,' she interrupted brusquely. 'I want to have a word with you at five thirty. I'll call on you at your office.'

She turned, and walked away. His throat remained curiously dry all day.

She was punctual. She appeared in the doorway of his room at five thirty exactly. Most of the other staff in the department had either left, or were on the way out. She stood there staring at him for several seconds, and he wondered what she was going to say.

'You wish to come in and sit down?' he asked, at last.

She shook her head. 'No. I want you to take me out for a drink.'

He was astonished. There had been little love lost between them during the period since she had taken over as Simon Brent-Ellis's deputy. She had taken every opportunity to put him in his place. Certainly, there had been very little between them that could be described as social intercourse. The suggestion she now made took him aback. She saw it in his eyes, and she smiled coldly.

'I would suggest the King's Arms. You have your car?' He nodded.

'Then I think you should go now. I'll meet you at the pub, in the lounge, in fifteen minutes.'

She turned on her heel and left. After a few moments, a little dazed, Arnold rose and began to collect his papers together.

He walked to the window. In a little while he saw her making her way to the blue Montego in the car park. Hastily, he grabbed his briefcase and clattered down the stairs, out of the building.

It was a warm evening. The sky was a pale blue, darkening towards the hills, and the streets were busy with home-going workers. Arnold edged his car out into the main road and headed across town, towards the King's Arms, on the edge of Morpeth, running north. He found a space easily enough in the pub car park, but saw no sign of Karen Stannard's car, and she was not in the lounge when he entered. He waited for a few minutes, then ordered himself a half of lager. He took a seat in the lower part of the lounge, tucked away from the door, half hidden from the bar.

A little while later he saw heads turn at the bar, and he guessed she had come in. She took the two steps down into the sunken area and saw him. She glanced around, apparently approving of his choice of location. 'Snug,' she said.

'What'll you have to drink?'

She looked at him steadily for a moment, calculation in her eyes, and then she shrugged. Her tone was edgy. 'I'll have a gin and tonic. Make it a large one.'

She sat down while he went up to the bar. When he came back with her drink she was sitting still, hands folded in her lap, looking almost demure. She did not thank him for the drink. She took a hefty gulp at it, and remained silent.

'You know this pub well?' he ventured uneasily, after a short silence.

'I've not been in here before.' She turned her eyes on him, large, brilliant, and diamond-hard. 'You shopped me, didn't you, Mr Landon?'

Arnold hesitated, holding her gaze, but his hesitation made her impatient. Irritably, she fluttered a hand at him. 'Don't bother denying it — Culpeper's had me in for questioning. He didn't name names, but he told me it was a colleague who saw me up on the moor, and I know you were the only one in the area that afternoon.'

Arnold took a deep breath, glad in a way that it was out in the open. 'I didn't say it *was* you. I just said—'

'I denied I'd been up there,' she interrupted sharply. 'Denied everything . . .' Her eyes held his. 'But I was lying.'

Arnold did not know what response to make, so he remained silent.

'So, before we go any further,' she said menacingly, 'let's get a few things straight. Cate Nicholas was a friend. We fell out . . . but that was largely because I felt she betrayed my trust over the report you made for me. I know there are rumours in the department about her and Angie Rothwell . .

. that weasel Jerry Picton . . . but it was the betrayal that upset me. That's why I was so angry . . . so mad I couldn't deal with it immediately. I brooded over it, and at last I decided to have it out with her. That's why I went up to the cottage.'

'You'd been up there before?'

'Yes. Several times.' Her eyes seemed to him now to be grey as flint. They had an infinite capacity for change, or maybe it was his own imagination, his own inability to determine their colour. 'I rang the university — they told me she was not in the department, so I guessed she was up at Bickley Moorside. So, after I'd been to Garrigill and Evison Church, I drove across to her cottage. I got there late afternoon. Then I walked in—'

'How did you get in? Did you have a key?'

'Cate gave me one weeks ago . . . suggested I might like to use the cottage sometime, even if she wasn't there, to work in. We had been planning to produce an article together . . . for the *Archaeological Magazine*.' She picked up her drink and sipped it, her hand was shaking slightly. 'Anyway, when I got inside the first thing I saw was the absolute shambles . . .'

Arnold was silent. He could not understand why she was telling him things she clearly had not told Culpeper. He was not accustomed to acting as a confidant of the deputy director.

'Then I found her in the corner,' Karen Stannard's face displayed no emotion. She had had time to wash the external appearances of distress from her features over the last two weeks, controlling her reactions. But Arnold knew she was still hurting at what she had found. The memory would still be churning at her, deep inside. 'She'd been beaten to death — and I was on the scene of the crime.' Her glance flickered up, holding Arnold's levelly, with a hint of sardonic humour. Coolly, she added, 'You'll be surprised to know that I panicked.'

'Not surprised. I think that it's understandable,' Arnold sympathized. 'To find your friend—'

She didn't want sympathy. Her tone hardened. 'I panicked, and I got out of there. I thought I saw a car on the fellside ahead of me, but didn't know it was you. And on the way back, thinking no one had seen me up there, I decided not to tell the police. Two days later the news broke anyway. She'd been found by a farmworker. Over the next week, when I wasn't approached, I thought I was safe from investigation — so Culpeper's call was a shock. And by then, I'd made up my mind anyway.'

'How do you mean?'

'If it was known I'd been at the cottage, I'd be treated as a suspect,' she said flatly. 'I had motive — the way she betrayed me — there were rumours like Picton's floating around — and although I didn't kill Cate there would be gossip, suspicion, talking in dark corners, maybe disbelief in the end. I had a lot at stake: my reputation, my job, my future prospects — the publicity would harm me. I'd already had a run-in with that slimy bastard Powell Frinton, over the leaking of your report — which was Cate's doing. This would be further ammunition for Powell Frinton — the scandal — maybe enough to get rid of me. I didn't want that. I knew what it could do to my career.'

She had always been fixated on her career. 'So, you didn't tell Culpeper the truth,' Arnold said quietly.

'I denied ever having been there.'

'In my view — well, I think that was a mistake on your part.'

'I don't give a damn what you think. You shopped me. And your interference has pushed me into action I'd been thinking about. Now it's become necessary.' She finished her drink abruptly. 'You *owe* me, Mr Landon.'

'Look, I'm sorry, but—'

'Give me your car keys.' She tapped the bench on which she sat. 'Put them here. Then finish your drink. Within ten minutes I want you to go to your car. I'll be waiting for you there.'

He stared at her in astonishment, then glanced around the room. There was no one else there. 'Now look, I don't know what you have in mind. Cloak-and-dagger stuff of that kind—'

'Do as you're told!' There was a tension in her that brooked no disobedience. Reluctant, but also curious, wondering what she intended doing, Arnold placed his car keys on the bench. She picked them up immediately and walked out in the direction of the side door, where the washrooms were located. Arnold stared at her empty glass, puzzled. He was vaguely aware of someone else coming down the steps to the sunken section, and walking out towards the washrooms, but he didn't look up.

Slowly, he finished his drink, dawdling over the last of it, frowning, attempting to puzzle out what she was up to. He was certain she had made a bad mistake not telling Culpeper the truth, but there was something driving Karen Stannard, something more than the anger she felt at having been exposed to suspicion by Arnold's remarks to Culpeper. There was a coiled determination, the tension of a spring that was eager to explode into action. He stood up and walked into the car park.

She was already seated, hunched down in the passenger seat of his car.

'Drive,' she commanded.

They left Morpeth on the road north, then at her suggestion swung west until they picked up a lonely secondary road that curved around the outskirts of Morpeth and which finally took them south. Several times she looked back behind them, as though to check whether they were being followed.

'Where are we going?' Arnold asked uneasily.

'Where the hell do you think?' she snapped.

He glanced at her and frowned. 'Just what is this all about?'

'I'll tell you what this is about,' she said fiercely. 'I've been saddled by you — now you're coming along for the ride. We're going back to Bickley Moorside, and you're going to help me sort this out!'

He braked, slowing in the narrow road and stared at her in exasperation. 'That's crazy! There's no way I'm taking you up there—'

She slammed her hand hard on the top of the dash-board. 'Do as you're damned well told! You put me in this fix! Anything I say to Culpeper now will be regarded as trying to wriggle out of the spot you've put me in — so I've got to do something about it, not just sit back and let things happen! I've got to get into that damned cottage, because I know there's something there that will point the finger right at the man who killed Cate!'

'You're not serious! You're not telling me you know who killed her — and you haven't told the police?'

'I know who it is, but I can't prove it yet!' she responded, almost hissing in her anger and resentment. 'Cate was all set to nail him, all set to expose him, but she made the mistake of letting him know she had the evidence to do it. That's why he killed her.'

'But—'

'That's why he trashed the cottage the first time! That's why he beat her to death, trying to make her tell him where she held the evidence. That's why he tore the furniture apart while she was dying! And you owe me, Landon — you've got me into this mess and you've got to help me find that evidence. It's at the cottage — she told me she kept it there. I've got to find it — the evidence that'll point the finger straight at her killer!'

* * *

At Ponteland, the telephone jangled in Detective Chief Inspector John Culpeper's office. He hesitated, on the way out through the door. Reluctantly, he walked back to his desk and picked up the receiver. It was Farnsby. His voice was tense.

'You ordered tails on Karen Stannard and Paul Stillwater.'

'Well?'

'We've lost them both.'

Culpeper swore.

3

As they rose from the valley floor and drove across the edge of the fell, they could see the height to which the cultivated fields — the 'intake' fields brought in from the surrounding moorland — reached up to the south-facing side of the dale. It was hill-farming country, the pattern of the land shaped and dictated by the breeding habits of the sheep, and Arnold usually enjoyed the beauty of the place.

But not this evening. 'You haven't explained that performance in the King's Arms,' he muttered to Karen Stannard.

'Since my interview with Culpeper,' she replied, 'I'm sure I've been followed, whenever I've left the office. It was the same this evening. So I parked up in the town, dodged through a few alleyways to get to the pub — and then got you to use your car. I think we're clear now,' she added, glancing back again to the road behind them.

'The police have been following you?' Arnold frowned. 'That must mean they think your story was not acceptable.'

'Police . . . or someone else.'

He looked at her, startled. 'What do you mean?'

'Oh, come on, this isn't a game we're playing here. The man who killed Cate knows I was her friend. Maybe *he's* keeping an eye on me, I don't know. Remember, Cate was being bothered by a stalker before she was killed.'

Arnold gritted his teeth in silent frustration. He felt adrift, not knowing what he was doing, not understanding why he was driving this woman up on to the fells. 'I think you'd better explain things to me. I'm not happy about this.'

She was silent for a little while, as they wound their way through narrow lanes, climbing all the while. Then she nodded. 'I don't know the full story myself . . . Cate was a close person — she kept things to herself, but she liked to tease, drop hints . . . that sort of thing. But it became clear to me, after the meeting at Ravenstone that day, that there was considerable animosity between her and Paul Stillwater.'

Arnold shook his head. 'I think you're wrong there. You told me yourself they barely knew each other.'

'Don't you believe it,' Karen Stannard snapped. 'Their relationship predated Ravenstone, even if they both chose to say otherwise. I'm convinced of it. And from what Cate told me from time to time, she hated him — she never mentioned him by name, typical of Cate, mysterious, careful . . . but she had something on Stillwater.'

'How do you mean?'

'I don't know what it is,' Karen Stannard replied. 'It's something she learned about him previously — before she came to Northumberland. And I think it was exacerbated by what she told me regarding his involvement in the Adler Foundation business. She saw that as a way of getting at him . . . Anyway, the real reason why Stillwater was so cold towards her at Ravenstone is that he knew she had something on him. And he suspected it was kept at the cottage.'

'How can you be sure of that?'

Karen Stannard turned her head to look at him. 'She as good as told me so. She said she had evidence there that would sort out her enemy — that's what she called him — and she was only waiting for the best time to expose it. She intended doing it on her programme — a follow-up to that last exposé.'

'What does this . . . evidence . . . comprise?'

Karen Stannard shook her head. 'I don't know. But it's hidden at the cottage. That's why the place was turned over. Stillwater was looking for it.'

Arnold shook his head slowly. 'I don't know what you hope to achieve by this. It's best left to the police. You should tell them about Cate Nicholas and Paul Stillwater—'

'No!' she said fiercely. 'Cate was my friend. That bastard killed her because she was going to expose him. Now it's up to me.' She paused. 'The police would never believe me anyway.'

Arnold had more than a few doubts himself. Once again, he wondered what the hell he was doing, driving this determined, wrong-headed woman to the cottage on Bickley Moorside. And yet his own interest was now aroused, and a stab of excitement coursed through his veins, as some of her passion and determination came across to him.

The feeling remained with him as they twisted and turned along the back road that wound its way up to the moorland above. At the top they passed the old mine shafts, and then they were looking down towards the cottage where Cate Nicholas had died.

* * *

The sun had dropped over the rim of the fell as they parked behind the cottage, near the beech trees and screened from the road. Karen Stannard suggested he bring a torch with them as they entered the cottage. 'This could take some time,' she warned, 'and we don't want to turn any lights on that can be seen from the top road. We don't want an inquisitive farmer calling in while we're breaking and entering.'

At least she was acknowledging that what they were doing was illegal, Arnold thought, still regretting the part he was playing in this venture. Then, when they entered the cottage Arnold could see that some attempt had been made to tidy the devastation that had been caused in the struggle between Cate Nicholas and her killer. As the police had searched for evidence, they had gradually replaced items into some semblance of order. Even so, it was clear that considerable damage had been caused, with ripped furniture, smashed glass and damaged bookcases.

'Where the hell do you start?' Arnold asked. 'You don't even know what you're looking for!'

'There's something here,' she insisted, 'and I'll know it when I see it. I'm damned sure *he* didn't find it. She was confident, was Cate, when she told me she had incriminating information cached here at the cottage she gave me the distinct impression she felt it was quite safe — and no one would find it.'

'So what makes you think we'll lay our hands on it?' Arnold queried.

'We've got to look!' Karen Stannard said desperately.

They looked. As the light slowly faded in the cottage they worked through the debris of the rooms, Arnold feeling vaguely foolish, searching for something when he had no idea what he was looking for, his deputy director impatient, frustration breaking out at regular intervals with explosions of anger.

The cottage itself was interesting: low-beamed, probably seventeenth-century in the main, but with features clearly robbed from older buildings. There was a square fireplace with four stone panels, one slightly damaged and different from the others but each panel containing a carved fluted shield set in a cusped quatrefoil — clearly robbed from some grander house in the neighbourhood, reused in a humbler setting. There were two small windows on the end wall of the room, set in rectangular casements which had been secured by iron bolts — of which the holes remained — and originally protected by an iron grille at a time when glass was regarded as a luxury. He had already noted, when they entered, that the doorway had been chamfered, and there had been signs of a porch entrance, which would probably have had an outer chamfered order. The cottage would not have been a place where peasants had lived. There were signs that it might possibly have been used as a small hunting lodge, maybe, or as the home of a well-heeled yeoman farmer at some stage, if some of the features, robbed from other buildings, were anything to go by.

'Are you concentrating?' Karen Stannard hissed.

'Sorry,' Arnold apologized and turned back to survey the devastation of the sitting room. 'Is this where she died?'

Karen Stannard nodded. He could not see her face in the fading light, but her voice was steady, and controlled. 'She was over there, I believe, in the corner. He must have battered her, trying to make her tell him where the information was. She held out; she must have done. I knew her. She was determined, and she wouldn't have given in — not to violence. And she hated Stillwater. She . . . she was a strong-minded woman.'

Arnold turned away. This was all a waste of time. He picked up a cupped object on top of the damaged bookshelf, puzzled over it for a moment and then put it down, shook his head in frustration. He didn't know what he was looking for. But he would play along with her for a little while, it was the least he could do, since she was so furious about the predicament she felt he had placed her in. 'It's getting dark,' he said.

'We can use your torch,' she snapped in frustration. 'That's why you brought the bloody thing.'

Arnold was silent for a little while, standing in the centre of the room. Something fluttered in his mind, a thought, an image . . . Slowly, he asked, 'What was it you said earlier . . . about this evidence Cate Nicholas was holding?'

'Said?' Karen Stannard turned to him. 'What do you mean? She was hiding it here in the cottage—'

'No.' Arnold frowned, thinking back. 'That's not what you said. You said she had *cached* it here.'

'So?' she asked impatiently. 'You're going to criticize my use of English?'

'No. I want to know if that's the actual word *she* used.'

Karen Stannard was silent for a little while. He could hear her breathing hard. 'I suppose it was, but so what?'

'Don't you think it's an odd word to use . . . or a precise one?' Arnold suggested.

'What the hell are you getting at?'

Arnold shrugged. 'My impression of Cate Nicholas is of someone who was controlled, clear-minded and determined. She was a trained archaeologist, who'd built up her own specialism and was making a name for herself. She wasn't given to looseness of phrase. She was a precise woman. To me, a cache implies a hiding place—'

'For God's sake, what do you think we're doing here if not looking for a hiding place?'

'But maybe looking in the wrong places,' Arnold said quietly. 'At the moment, we're just ploughing through things — but a cache, if she meant what she said . . .'

There was a short silence. At last, Karen Stannard said, 'Tell me.'

'This is a late-mediaeval building, originally,' Arnold replied slowly. 'It's been added to, features brought in from outside, changes made over the centuries — but essentially it's still an old building. And in old buildings there was often a tendency — because there weren't banks available — to keep valuable items in specially constructed caches.'

'You think there might be a mediaeval safe or something here, then?' she asked breathlessly.

Arnold shook his head. 'Probably not in the mediaeval parts of the house — it would have been insufficiently wealthy farmers using it then. But later . . .' He began to prowl from room to room, exploring. After a little while he switched on the torch and began examining the walls carefully. Karen Stannard stood just behind him, watching, as the beam flickered around the old walls, searching. The evening light was gone, darkness was gathering in the corners of the rooms, unfamiliar shapes were leaping up and dancing against the ceiling, strange and menacing, hovering around them and above their heads.

They returned to the room where Cate Nicholas had died. Arnold was irresolute, thinking, trying to pin down something he had seen earlier, something slightly puzzling. There was a distant sound, a car driving past on the top road, but it faded, and they ignored it, Arnold concentrating, Karen Stannard watching him silently.

He stood there for a long time, playing the torchlight around the room, uncertain, but finally settling on the two windows, and the fireplace. 'These features aren't original, you know. At some stage, maybe in the eighteenth century, a manor house or a large farmhouse would have been pulled down in the area. Bits and pieces of it would have been sold off — or just taken by locals — and then installed elsewhere. The windows, and the fireplace . . . they're examples.'

The windows. He grimaced . . . he swung the torchlight slowly to the top of the bookshelf. He walked over and picked up the cupped object he had noticed there earlier. He frowned. He recognized it now. 'Do you know what this is?'

She peered over his shoulder, and shook her head. 'I've no idea. What is it?'

'You've never seen glaziers, carrying a large sheet of glass? They use this kind of cup, lock it into place with this device here — it forms a vacuum . . .' He glanced at the old windows. 'Why would Cate Nicholas want it? Was she a do-it-yourself person? Did she fix windows?'

Karen Stannard snorted contemptuously at the thought. 'Shall we get on?'

Arnold barely heard her. He stood lost in thought for a long while, swinging the torch beam around contemplatively, until it flickered at last over the old fireplace. 'Interesting . . .'

'What?'

'The fireplace. Its irregularity. You see,' Arnold explained, pointing, 'it has the four square panels running along the top . . . you see the fluted shields'? They're from someone's coat of arms. Then there's the cusped quatrefoils . . . but you see these square labels with the out-turned ends? There's a monogram at each end. I wonder whose it was? I wonder where it came from . . .'

'Does it really matter?' Karen Stannard asked impatiently. She shook her head angrily. 'This whole thing is a waste of time. I know that now. How the hell I should have expected—'

'No, look more closely.' Arnold leaned forward, playing the light on the monograms. 'I agree — it's unimportant whose monograms they were. But look — you see the irregularity here? The monogrammed section doesn't sit exactly right, in relation to the lower edge of the quatrefoil above. And there's a small crack running up into the quatrefoil as though the stone has been broken at some time.'

'Maybe when it was brought here and installed,' she suggested. 'Bad workmanship—'

'No. I don't think so. But it might have been damaged when part of it was taken out, cut away and replaced later, for some reason.' Arnold paused, thinking. 'Take another look at the cementing, as well.'

'What about it?'

'It doesn't exactly match the cementing that runs below the other quatrefoils. It's slightly discoloured . . . as though a different mix was used.' He turned to Karen Stannard. 'Hold the torch.'

Arnold took a small penknife out of his pocket and began to scratch away at the cementing below the right-hand quatrefoil, directly above the monogram. The grouting flaked away easily. Karen Stannard came closer, leaning over him as he worked, her breath warm on his cheek. He found her closeness distracting, and he dug deeper at the grouting. The cement flaked away and he grunted.

'What?' she asked impatiently.

'I'm not certain,' he said, scraping away at the cement until suddenly his knife point slid into the cavity. The cement was surface only. It did not extend to the depth of the stone block on which the monogram had been carved. Quickly he slid the knife point down the side of the monogrammed block and the cement flaked away easily. He worked his way right around the square of the stone and Karen Stannard swore under her breath in excitement.

Arnold straightened. He closed his pocketknife and used his fingers to clear away some cement debris. There was a narrow cleft now running around the monogrammed block where he had cleared the grouting. He glanced at Karen Stannard. She was breathing hard. She pushed past him, eagerly.

She gripped the edge of the small block with her fingers, tried to move it and then swore, biting at her fingernail. Arnold eased her aside and tried to pull at the stone himself. He had little more than fingertip purchase on its edges. He pulled and dragged at it, but the stone did not move.

His fingertips became sore as he struggled with the sandstone edge, and then Karen Stannard tried again. She swore viciously as the stone remained secure. There was insufficient purchase for their fingers.

'Of course . . .' Arnold expelled his breath slowly and moved away. He picked up the glazier's cup and came back to the fireplace. Karen Stannard watched him as he pressed the cup to the stone block, locked the handle. Gently, he pulled at it and the stone moved slowly out of its setting. It was only a small block, two inches deep, whereas the rest of the fireplace would be at least eighteen inches deep to the back wall. He peered into the narrow opening; behind it a larger aperture was revealed. Karen Stannard shone the beam of the torch inside . . . and they realized the aperture went back to the stone of the wall behind.

'There's your cache,' Arnold said, and Karen Stannard plunged in her hand.

'There's something in here!' she gasped, and then a beam of bright light flashed over them. They both swung around in surprise, and the man in the doorway said, 'What the hell are you doing here?'

* * *

They stood there for several shocked seconds, frozen in the beam of the torch, and then Karen Stannard swung up her own torch. The beam flickered in the man's face. He put up a hand to shield his eyes but they had recognized him immediately.

'*Stillwater*!' Karen Stannard said, and the man started, then came forward across the room, lowering his torch. Arnold moved to one side, uncertain what to do, and Paul Stillwater half turned towards him, began to say something. Before the words came out Karen Stannard had stepped sideways across from them both, and then with a wild, vicious swing she struck Stillwater across the temple with the heavy torch she carried.

He grunted, staggered, and, with his shoulder crashing into the wall, he slid sideways, striking his head again on the edge of the stone fireplace. He lay sprawled across the hearth, his breathing was stertorous, but ragged. Arnold seized the torch from Karen and knelt beside the man on the floor.

'What the hell did you do that for?' By the torchlight, he could see an ugly wound on the side of the man's head, blood oozed darkly from the wound. 'Hell's flames, you almost killed him,' Arnold muttered.

'He got what he deserved,' Karen Stannard replied, half panicked, half excited. 'He was after this!' She turned away, plunged her hand back into the recess in the fireplace and after a short struggle she pulled out what looked like a tightly bound, waterproof package. 'I've got it!'

Arnold glanced at her, hardly aware of the package. 'We'll have to get help for Stillwater. I don't like the sound of his breathing.'

She was standing beside him, staring down at the stricken man and her own breathing was quick. 'But this was what he was after! He must have guessed we'd come here. He must have followed us after all — maybe it wasn't the police who've been following me. It must have been him—'

'It hardly matters now,' Arnold interrupted. 'He needs attention badly. And I don't think we should try to move him. Is there a telephone here?'

'No. Cate wanted the isolation — she didn't want to be interrupted at work up here. She had it disconnected. That's why I had to come up here that day rather than—'

'Never mind that now,' Arnold interrupted impatiently. 'I'll stay here with him. You get back to the car. There's a farm about two or three miles from here, over the rim of the fell. You can get help from there. Hurry!'

She still hesitated for a moment, clutching the waterproof package in her hand, and then she nodded, turned away and hurried towards the door, the torchlight playing on the walls ahead of her. Moments later he saw the flash of the torchlight through the window and then he was left in darkness with the injured man.

Paul Stillwater moaned lightly and stirred, but then his breathing grew heavy again, a snoring sound issuing from his open mouth. Arnold was reluctant to move him, but decided he should turn him on his side, place him in the recovery position. He achieved it only with difficulty. The man was heavy. But when Stillwater was turned his breathing seemed to ease somewhat. It was still ragged but the snoring had stopped.

It was then that Arnold realized he had not heard Karen Stannard start the car.

Puzzled, he waited for a little while, and then rose from his kneeling position beside Paul Stillwater. He cocked his head, listening, but could pick up no sounds from outside the doorway beyond the small hall. He eased his way forward, edging towards the door, careful not to stumble over anything in the darkness, and then he heard a light, quick scraping sound on the flagstones outside. He stopped, his heart thudding, at the surreptitious nature of the sound and then he moved forward quickly, stepping into the hallway and across into the room beyond. He waited, his muscles tensed as he became aware of a dark shadowy figure appearing in the doorway.

The man stepped lightly but he seemed enormous, his shape indistinct in the faint light that entered the cottage. He stood silently in the hallway for several seconds, half crouching on the balls of his feet, listening. From the room across the hallway the breathing of the injured man rattled, and

Arnold tensed as the shadowed man half turned towards the sitting room.

Arnold had no idea who had entered the cottage, but there was no sound or sight of Karen Stannard, and the way this man moved was enough to convince Arnold he spelled danger. If he only turned his back fully, Arnold might be able to take him by surprise . . . the way he must have taken Karen Stannard. He tensed, ready to leap across the intervening space and then suddenly the man was straightening, swinging around, and the harsh light of the torch stabbed across the hallway, directly into Arnold's eyes, half blinding him.

'Landon!'

Arnold did not recognize the voice immediately, but beyond the beam of the torch, extended to one side, he saw the muzzle of the heavy revolver. It was pointed straight at Arnold's chest.

4

'Outside.'

The gun and the torch pushed him. Arnold turned, and stumbled out into the night air. He could make out the rim of the fell, a faint luminescence edging it against the darkness of the night sky. He stood there irresolute, until the gun muzzle prodded him in the back. 'Around to the car.'

Arnold walked carefully around to the back of the cottage, near the beech trees. The car gleamed faintly in the dimness. The driver's door was open and the courtesy light gave a little illumination, enough for Arnold to see the untidy heap, bundled on the ground near the door. It was Karen Stannard.

Arnold walked quickly towards her, dropped to one knee and reached out for her. In the faint light he could see that she was still alive; a livid mark ran along her jawline, she was unconscious, but she was still breathing.

He turned his head. 'What the hell's going on here?'

The man behind him chuckled warmly. 'Nothing that need concern you,' he said, and waved the gun. 'Now pick her up I want her brought inside.'

It was then that Arnold, with a start of shock, recognized the man's voice. He half turned, to stare at the gun; it was rock steady, aimed directly at his head. 'No foolish ideas . . . Bring her inside,' the gunman repeated.

Arnold stooped, cradled his arm under Karen Stannard's back and lifted her into a position where he could ease her across his shoulders. It was difficult: she was inert, a dead weight, and she was heavier than he would have guessed. But he managed to lift her and straighten. The gunman stood to one side to allow Arnold to pass, and he headed back into the cottage.

'Take her where you've left Stillwater.'

They entered the room, the flashlight causing a grotesque shadow to dance ahead of them, Karen Stannard draped across Arnold's shoulder. The easy chair with the ripped arm was in front of him. Arnold stopped and slid Karen Stannard into the chair. She lolled sideways, moaning slightly. He realized she was stunned only, and was gradually recovering consciousness. He stood up, stepped away from her.

'Do nothing foolish, Landon.'

Arnold faced the man with the gun. 'What's this all about?' There was a short silence.

'The package, of course.'

The man was stepping to one side, the torchlight wavering as he drew closer to where Stillwater was lying on the ground. 'My God, you really belted him one. Or was it that vixen?' He laughed shortly, and then fixed the beam on Arnold. 'Where did you find the package?'

'The fireplace.'

The gunman turned his head slightly. He could see the gaping hole. 'So that's where the bitch hid it . . .'

'What's in the package that made you kill Cate Nicholas?' Arnold asked.

The torchlight danced back to him, and the man grunted. 'Nothing very much. A few papers, that's all. But nothing that'll concern you — nothing to bother your head about.' Arnold sensed he had turned again, to look down at Stillwater. Silence grew between them as the man stood there, thinking.

'So where do we go from here?' Arnold asked at last. 'Whatever you think you can—'

'*Know*, not think,' the man interrupted decisively. 'The police have already been questioning Stillwater. He told me they've been looking into a little mess he was in some years ago. This wouldn't have been necessary if he hadn't started to panic, argue . . . Anyway, what will the police think when they find him, and you up here? I'll slide the stone back in the hole . . . Two people dead with bullets in them . . . Stillwater, dead from a head wound, but the gun in his hand . . . It'll puzzle them, but they'll probably conclude that it has something to do with the Allison business, that Nicholas and Stannard found out something about it, and you . . . unhappily, you just happened to be along for the ride . . .'

'Allison? Who the hell is Allison?' Arnold asked.

'It's of no account to you, my friend.' The torch was trained full in Arnold's face now. 'Time to say your goodbyes.'

There was one long, dragging moment when Arnold waited for the thunder of the gun in the enclosed space of the cottage, and then a bubbling groan came from Paul Stillwater, lying across the hearth to Arnold's right. It was an unexpected, distracting sound, and the torch wavered just slightly, but enough for Arnold to know that the gunman had turned his head, startled. In that split second Arnold launched himself at the torch.

The gun exploded and a hot searing pain swept along the side of Arnold's neck. Next moment he was colliding with the big man who staggered backwards, crashing into the wall, and the torch went out, falling to the floor behind them. Arnold was aware of the gun hand, pulling towards him, and he grabbed for the man's wrist, found it, and they were locked for one long moment before both lost their balance and crashed down to the ground, smashing a small coffee table to one side as they went.

Fingers clawed at Arnold's jawline, and he realized the gun was lost. The realization gave him a surge of adrenaline; strength powered through him and he locked his arm against the man's right wrist while he tried to hammer at his head with his free hand. He took a blow on the temple and the room swam. Another came, misdirected and wild, and it struck him on the throat so that he gagged and the breath whistled out of his chest. It was then that he knew his assailant was too strong for him. He was swung sideways, rolling against the wall and his antagonist was on top of him, knees locked against his ribs, predatory, hooked fingers groping for his throat. Stars seemed to be exploding in Arnold's head. He tried to raise his arms to fight off his assailant, but his blows were weak, partly parried by the man's upper arms, and the fingers dug deep into his throat, cutting into his windpipe, sapping his strength as the agony grew in his chest, became a fire that roared through him, until he knew the roaring was in his ears and he was slipping away.

The roaring was suddenly edged with a high, screaming sound. Through waves of nausea and thunder Arnold thought he could hear an obscenity, echoing through the cottage, and then the weight on his throat and chest was released, the heaviness above him was rolling sideways and he was gasping for air, retching, seeking to drag life back into his chest.

He lay there for what seemed an age, until his senses began to return and he could hear heavy, racked breathing that was not his own, became aware of the vast weight half straddling him, and then he pushed it aside, began to struggle to his feet. He heard the sounds of someone else moving. He was on his knees when the cottage lights came on, slashing across his eyes painfully. He blinked, slowly adjusting to the pain. He looked around.

Karen Stannard, white-faced, was standing beside the light switch, all strength seemingly drained from her, but still clutching in her right hand the glazier's cup fixed to the monogrammed stone from the fireplace. It was dark-stained. Arnold looked at the man lying beside him.

The back of Thor Cameron's head was matted with oozing blood. Arnold looked up at the woman who had saved his life.

'I got the bastard, didn't I?' she whispered, then straightened, staggered across to him and sank down to her knees beside him. 'In fact, I got *both* the bastards!' She began to laugh, the sound edged with hysteria. The mark along the jawline was livid but the blow hadn't been enough to put her under for long. She had come round, become aware of the struggling men and in a burst of fury had clubbed Cameron with the first thing that came to hand. Nevertheless, reaction was setting in. She was beginning to shake.

'What a team, hey?' she asked, grinning insanely, half concussed still. She leaned forward, her shoulder touching his and her face close. She was disorientated and her eyes were vague and stained with a strange panic as she stared at him. Tension grew around them. She was shaking violently. Her lips parted, her breathing was ragged and then to his surprise she reached for him, took him by the shoulders and kissed him. In any other circumstances it would have been a pleasurable experience. Now he knelt there rigidly, taken aback, aware of the softness of her mouth on his, the exploration of her tongue, the shuddering confusion of her slim body, quivering in shock. Then she broke away, leaned back to stare at him as though she had never seen him before.

He was clear about the colour of her eyes now. They were a deep, dark green. He was sure of it, at last. But then they clouded, she looked down, and burst into a flood of tears. 'Look at my bloody nails!' she raged.

5

When he told Jane about the struggle at the cottage a few days later she was able to explain the violence of Karen Stannard's reactions, of course. Delayed shock. Karen Stannard had come around from the blow Thor Cameron had given her at the car. She had heard the sounds of the struggle between Cameron and Arnold and had found enough strength — fuelled by fury — to crawl across and pound at Cameron's head with the first weapon that came to hand — the monogrammed stone where it lay on the floor in the darkness. But when her incoherent attack on Cameron was over the delayed reaction had taken over: shuddering, a losing grasp of reality, an inability to cope with unimportant matters.

But it was Culpeper who had provided Arnold with the background to the attacks in the cottage.

'You don't need to know the details of the Allison business, bonny lad, but both Stillwater and Cameron had been involved. Paul Stillwater had worked as a front man for Thor Cameron years before when Allison Products was set up. Cameron stayed in the background of the illegal software business, but he had financed it. He was behind the trade in eastern Europe. Cameron's name never appeared in the company records — but he was the main mover, using

Allison as a nominee director. We think that when the DTI investigation of the company began, he persuaded Allison to run. But Allison wanted money. Cameron lost a great deal in the collapse of Allison Products and Allison was a danger, pressing him with exposure. We think it was Cameron who hired a contract killer to get rid of Allison when he became too much of a liability — and Cameron was busy building a new, and legitimate, business.'

'So what was Cameron after in the cottage?'

'Just some papers, documents, letters . . . but they incriminated him, showed that he was involved in the Allison business. They'd been held over his head for three years or more.'

'By Allison?'

'No. By Joanna Cameron. You see,' Culpeper explained, 'when Cameron's wife left him, she went to live with Cate Nicholas — but she was scared of Cameron's reactions. He was a violent man, so she took some "insurance" with her. She knew about Cameron's involvement with Allison. She raided his office — took some incriminating documents. The papers gave her protection — she just wanted to be left alone, with Cate Nicholas. She knew he'd react violently to her leaving with Cate, so she warned him — she'd expose him if he caused trouble for her. She hid the papers in the cottage — papers which showed his involvement with Allison . . . But then she died. Cameron thought he would be safe but was infuriated — and worried when he couldn't find the papers and he learned his wife had left the cottage to Cate in her will. Cameron tried to upset the will, failed, and then went on the rampage, seeking the documents that he guessed his wife had hidden there. He didn't find them.'

'Then Cate Nicholas finally took possession.'

'That's right. Joanna Cameron must have told her about her "insurance" — she knew there was something there in the cottage which incriminated Cameron, but it took her a while to find it. When she did, she decided to use the material. She hated Cameron — for his treatment of her over the will and the damage he'd done to the cottage. She probably didn't know the full significance of the documents, but it was a great chance to get at him, put some pressure on him. He was poised to take on a big contract, with government assistance. If his shady deals with Allison came out, government funding would disappear and he'd be ruined. She made the mistake of hinting at it in her television broadcast.'

Culpeper had been thoughtful. 'She clearly didn't know enough about him — how ruthless he really was. She let him know she had something on him. He went up there to the cottage, and when she refused to give him the documents, he beat her to death.'

'But how did he come to be there when Karen Stannard and I went up to Bickley?'

'That was due to Stillwater. He had begun to panic. We'd questioned him about the Allison business — he was afraid it would lead to his being involved in Cate Nicholas's death. He didn't know, but he'd guessed Cameron had got Allison killed, and it worried him. He's been telling us the whole story since we've interviewed him last week — singing like a panic-stricken parrot. He knew about the affair between Nicholas and Joanna Cameron. Then Nicholas was murdered, and he couldn't blind himself to that — he felt things were getting out of control. He thought Cameron had gone too far. He remonstrated with him and he began to keep an eye on Karen Stannard — worrying that Cate Nicholas might have said something to her and that she might find out about Allison Products.'

'Cate Nicholas had, of course. But only hinted.'

'Albeit in vague terms.' Culpeper nodded. 'Anyway, he must have seen the pair of you head out of town — my own men lost both him and Stannard — and guessed where you were going. He told Cameron, because he was scared of being tied in with the Allison business, but insisted on going with Cameron — he didn't want the man to overreact again. They drove up to the fell, leaving their car on the road at the top. I think Stillwater was there to try to prevent violence between

Cameron and you two — that's why he went in to investigate and get you out of there. He persuaded Cameron to stay outside, waiting . . . But when Stillwater got clobbered, and Karen Stannard came out with the package, Cameron must have thought it was Christmas. He felt he could no longer rely on Stillwater. He didn't know how much you and Stannard knew, or would be able to guess, so it seemed a neat way to get rid of his problems.' Culpeper grimaced. 'He was a charming man . . . but he was used to killing. It seemed the easy way . . .'

* * *

'So was it Stillwater who'd been stalking Cate Nicholas, earlier?' Jane asked Arnold as they drove together across the fells towards the Ravenstone burial site.

Arnold shook his head. 'No. That was Towers, according to Culpeper. He's in trouble, too . . . not for the stalking, of course — that was just his reaction to the hospitalization of his wife. I doubt he'd have raised the courage to attack Cate Nicholas over that. But the police are starting an enquiry into the Adler Foundation deal now, as well . . . and whether he benefited from the sale of the Adler Foundation land.'

'How is that affecting the Ravenstone development?' Jane asked.

'Badly, as you'll see in a little while. Work has stopped. Our revered MP Rawson's got cold politician feet, government aid has been withdrawn, the whole Ravenstone development idea has ground to a halt without funding,' Arnold grunted. 'Oddly enough, it will give Sam Loxton's archaeologists more time to work on the dig now, since Northern Heritage are still funding that — but they won't have the advantage of all that technology, and working under slab . . .'

'Although more of the burial site will presumably be available to the team.'

'That's right. With the construction work stopped, the cemetery will be less disturbed.'

They drove into the car park and left the car to climb across the deserted building site. The concrete piles that had been erected stood as gaunt reminders of a ruined dream. Arnold thought briefly of Thor Cameron, still held at Durham, awaiting trial, and of Paul Stillwater, singing his heart out to the police.

Sam Loxton was at the dig office. He welcomed them and took them to see what Arnold had come to inspect. Rena Williams was working there as she told Arnold she might: she eyed Jane warily as she took them across to the bench where the artefacts were laid out.

'What are they?' Jane asked, after a short silence. 'Celtic icons,' Rena Williams replied. 'But found in Saxon graves. It's a puzzle. You'll see there, a woman carved in sandstone, with a horse . . . of the many domesticated animals with a sacred significance for the Celts three stand out — the horse, dog and bull. The horse and dog are distinctive. They are anthropomorphic god forms which are dependent upon the animal for their identity and never appear without them. But it's this series which is puzzling us . . .'

Rena Williams gestured towards the group of small stone figurines laid out on the bench top. A torso with a boar superimposed; galloping horses with human heads; deities with horns, hooves, animal ears . . . Arnold watched as Jane handled one of the figurines. He saw her shudder. He moved beside her and picked up a female torso with a bull's head. It was cold in his fingers. He glanced at Sam Loxton. The man was staring at him oddly and for a few seconds the hairs began to prickle at the back of Arnold's neck.

There was a long silence. Rena Williams was staring at the figurines. Jane had replaced the figure she had been holding. She seemed pale. She glanced at Arnold. 'There's a feeling of something almost . . . evil here,' she said in a tense voice.

The others said nothing. Arnold frowned. He was aware of Rena Williams staring at him as he thought, trying to fix the image dancing in his brain and his memory. At last the haze swirled and he seemed to hear harsh breathing, the rumble of powerful hooves, the death-cry of a powerful animal, the thin chanting of shamans and the high cold whistling of the wind across the fells . . .

'The great Bull of Cooley,' he said. 'It had the power to reason and understand, as a human being.'

Rena Williams expelled her breath slowly. She nodded. 'I know . . . the thoughts are in my mind, as well. It's fantastic. I don't understand it, but I feel it, too. Sam, you know what we have here?'

Loxton said nothing. There were shadows in his eyes, a deep doubt that held a hint of panic. Arnold had the odd feeling that Loxton did not want to hear what they had to say.

'The divine bulls of the Ulster Cycle reached their final form after a series of metamorphoses,' Rena Williams explained. 'Originally they were divine swineherds . . . but the phenomenon of metamorphosis always played a prominent role in Celtic vernacular tradition.' She swung suddenly to Arnold. 'But to find evidence here, at Ravenstone . . . You'll join us, won't you? There's fascinating work to be done here.'

Arnold nodded. He knew he wouldn't be able to stay away.

The air about them seemed cold and sharp, and there was a light singing in his ears: ancient voices, unknown languages, the keening of a lost culture, and lost gods waiting for resurrection in the minds of men. Jane touched his arm lightly. 'Arnold? What's this all about?'

'It's about a puzzle. How a Celtic cult with its origins in ancient Ireland could find its way to the high moors in Saxon graves. I will have to come back here . . . join the team. There's no telling what else we might find . . .'

'But what cult is it?' Jane asked.

Arnold was aware of the coldness about him and the strange manner in which both Rena Williams and Sam Loxton stared at him, obviously affected by the figurines.

'The Mórrigan,' he said shortly. 'The Shape-Shifter.'

Driving away from the site, in the clear air of the fell, some of the coldness finally fell away from Arnold. He and Jane had said nothing as they left Ravenstone. She had seemed subdued, equally affected by an atmosphere that none of them could explain. But Arnold knew that he would have to return to Ravenstone, to investigate the ancient burial site further, and reach out to touch the cult of the Shape-Shifter.

At last, stirring herself in the seat beside him, Jane spoke, almost in an attempt to bring them back from the coldness of the little understood past and the dreams that had disturbed men's minds.

'That lecturer . . . what's going to happen to him?'

Dragged back to the present, it was several seconds before Arnold was able to understand what she was talking about. His mind was still with the Mórrigan.

'Joe Pitcher?' Arnold shrugged. 'Culpeper thinks it was Pitcher who shoved Cate Nicholas's car into the Tyne, but that's a charge they won't be pursuing . . .' He sighed thoughtfully. 'She was a much unloved woman, Cate Nicholas.'

'Except maybe by Karen Stannard. How has *she* come out of it?' Jane asked. 'Is she back at work?'

'No. Sick leave. I think Powell Frinton wants an enquiry into her conduct.' He was silent for a moment, as they drove over the hill and the valley opened out below them, distant hills crowned with purple cloud, a copper sheen edging the dying sun. 'She got it *completely* wrong over Stillwater — he hadn't known Cate Nicholas earlier, although he had known of her relationship with Joanna Cameron. Karen had been misled — Cate Nicholas had been hinting about her "enemy", but she'd been talking about Cameron, not Stillwater, when she told Karen about incriminating evidence.' He paused. 'But . . . I owe her my life.'

'So I can be grateful to her for that, at least,' Jane replied, a little tartly. 'If I can also be angry with her for dragging you up there in the first place.' She glanced at him, uncertainly. 'However, I have to say, I admire her for the manner in which she was able to crawl across that room and hammer at Thor Cameron . . . A blow for the courage of women . . .'

Arnold smiled. 'It was also she who belted Paul Stillwater and laid him out. She's been known to have a sharp tongue, but I think people in the office will be looking at her in an even more wary light now.' He hesitated, smiling slightly at the thought. 'I'm not sure whether I'm flattered at what she said to me afterwards, though . . . about us making a good team.'

'*That* was concussion,' Jane said briskly, and leaned against him affectionately as he drove. 'I wouldn't pay too much attention to it.'

Arnold nodded, but the thought crossed his mind again, as it had several times recently — he wondered whether it was only concussion that had put the warmth and passion into Karen Stannard's kiss, when she had knelt beside him, shaking, in the devastation of the cottage.

But he didn't raise the thought with Jane. As a matter of fact, he hadn't actually told her about that moment. He didn't think he was going to do so, either . . .

And in a little while, as the clouds moved, changed shape and colour in the evening sky until they formed a long, menacing, blood-red barrier across the near horizon, his thoughts turned back to Ravenstone and what they might one day find in the ancient graves on the fell.

THE END

ALSO BY ROY LEWIS

ERIC WARD MYSTERIES
Book 1: THE SEDLEIGH HALL MURDER
Book 2: THE FARMING MURDER
Book 3: THE QUAYSIDE MURDER
Book 4: THE DIAMOND MURDER
Book 5: THE GEORDIE MURDER
Book 6: THE SHIPPING MURDER
Book 7: THE CITY OF LONDON MURDER
Book 8: THE APARTMENT MURDER
Book 9: THE SPANISH VILLA MURDER
Book 10: THE MARRIAGE MURDER
Book 11: THE WASTEFUL MURDER
Book 12: THE PHANTOM MURDER
Book 13: THE SLAUGHTERHOUSE MURDER
Book 14: THE TATTOO MURDER
Book 15: THE FOOTBALL MURDER
Book 16: THE TUTANKHAMUN MURDER
Book 17: THE ZODIAC MURDER

INSPECTOR JOHN CROW
Book 1: A LOVER TOO MANY
Book 2: ERROR OF JUDGMENT
Book 3: THE WOODS MURDER
Book 4: MURDER FOR MONEY
Book 5: MURDER IN THE MINE
Book 6: A COTSWOLDS MURDER
Book 7: A FOX HUNTING MURDER
Book 8: A DARTMOOR MURDER

ARNOLD LANDON MYSTERIES
Book 1: MURDER IN THE BARN
Book 2: MURDER IN THE MANOR
Book 3: MURDER IN THE FARMHOUSE

Made in the USA
Columbia, SC
04 February 2022

55368509R00138